ONE FOGGY CHRISTMAS

KORTNEY KEISEL

First edition November 2024

Cover design by Melody Jeffries Design

www.kortneykeisel.com

To my lifelong friends

Aisha
Chelsea
Erin
Erin
Jen
Kenz
Laura
Megan
Mel
Michelle

You ladies sure know how to supportkort!
Thanks for always laughing at my stories, being there through the
hard times, and making me pee my pants.

I can't wait for another thirty plus years of friendship

TRIGGER WARNING

Brief mention of substance abuse and death of a sibling

PROLOGUE

NASH

"Sadie, do you know where you're at?" Dr. Hatchet's voice is calm—something that would soothe a crying baby.

Sadie's brown eyes shift nervously to her mother, not me. I ignore my disappointment, silently watching from the foot of the bed with my hands in my pockets.

"It's okay, sweetie." Lynette Bradley squeezes her daughter's hand, gently nudging her to answer. Behind her, Sadie's dad smiles despite the worry in his eyes.

The reassurance is enough. Her gaze darts back to the doctor, and she answers. "The hospital."

"That's right." Dr. Hatchet smiles. "You were in a bad skiing accident."

The way she gasps breaks my heart.

"You're okay, but you suffered severe head trauma, were on life support for a few days and in a coma for several weeks." Dr. Hatchet hesitates, giving her a second to process.

Traces of panic build behind Sadie's eyes, causing her mom to jump in.

"You're okay," Lynette consoles, pushing her daughter's matted brown hair back from her face. "Everything's okay."

Sadie's eyes travel over her body, taking in the hospital gown, the IV in her arm, and the pulse monitor until she focuses back on her mom as if she were her only lifeline.

Another beat of disappointment.

I'm Sadie's lifeline.

It should be me sitting beside her, brushing her hair back, keeping her calm.

I fight the negative thoughts, knowing this moment isn't about me or us. I'm glad the Bradleys are here for their daughter—something good that came from this accident. Sadie is alive and awake. That's all that matters. Everything else will sort itself out in time.

"I'm okay?" Her words are coarse and feeble.

"Yes, you're very fortunate," Dr. Hatchet answers. "Besides a few lacerations, the doctors have mostly been treating your brain trauma and swelling."

Sadie's brows cinch together in the most adorable way, and I can't help but smile as my eyes fill with moisture.

"Is my head okay?" Her fingers move along her forehead, checking for injuries, stopping on the bandage that covers stitches from one of her deeper cuts.

"It's much better." Dr. Hatchet smiles through her words. "But we still need to check some things out. Is it okay if I ask you a few more questions?"

Her hand drops into her lap. "I guess."

"Do you remember your name?"

Confidence flicks through her eyes. "Sadie Marie Bradley."

Technically, her name is Sadie Carter now, but seeing how she woke up from a coma thirty minutes ago, and she's been confused up until this point, I'm not holding it against her.

"Do you know who these people are?" Dr. Hatchet looks at the Bradleys.

"My parents."

"Do you know their names?"

"Jay and Lynette Bradley." Her lips slightly lift as she stares at them.

She smiled.

It was barely there, but I'm counting it.

"Good. Good." Dr. Hatchet pats her arm before diving into her next question. "Do you know who your husband is?"

My breath halts like I can't be bothered with breathing right now. All that matters is Sadie's answer.

Her brows drop, and a frown pushes her lips downward. "No..." She shakes her head. "I don't... I'm not married."

Her confusion collapses my heart, and now I can't breathe because of the pain.

She looks at her mom for confirmation, for her to tell Dr. Hatchet that she's wrong, but Lynette Bradley is visibly crying. Sadie's eyes drift from her parents to me with a vacancy in her expression I'm not used to. A soft smile holds across my lips, waiting for the same flicker of recognition she'd given her parents moments ago, but her eyes are void. The vacancy should've been my first clue, but it doesn't sink in until she speaks again.

Her forehead lines deepen. "Where's Stetson?"

Stetson Roeshine—Sadie's fiancé before she fell in love with me.

The room tenses, like we're inside a giant balloon, but instead of blowing air in, it's getting sucked out, pulling things tighter.

I feel every eye on me. Not just gazes but *sad* stares. *Pity* stares.

"Stetson?" Dr. Hatchet questions.

"My husband?" It's the most confident thing Sadie has

said, but her confidence wavers as she reads the mood in the room. "Did he get hurt in the accident too? Is that why he's not here?"

Nothing in life can prepare you for this kind of hurt.

It stuns and crushes.

I step forward, wanting to tell her myself, *needing* her to remember.

"Sadie"—I gently place my hand on her ankle, the best I can do from the foot of the bed—"*I'm* your husband. You married me." A hesitant smile forms as I await her response.

She stares blankly back at me, the blankness terrifying me as the milliseconds creep on. Then she retreats into herself, pulling her leg from my grasp.

"No." She shakes her head as her eyes plead with her mom. "He's not my husband. I love Stetson."

My heart pounds in my chest as my life unravels before me.

"Sweetie," Lynette's voice quivers despite her resolve to be strong. "It's okay. We'll figure this all out."

I slowly backpedal to the door, looking for an exit from this Hell.

My wife doesn't remember me.

Doesn't remember falling in love.

Doesn't remember the magic that is *us*.

Three and a half years of life just erased in an instant.

PART ONE

Falling

CHAPTER ONE

Three and a Half Years Ago

SADIE

"FOR IT'S ONE, two, three strikes you're out at the old ball game!" I finish the seventh-inning stretch with one arm slung over Tate's shoulder and the other outstretched in front of me like an opera singer as I hit that last note.

The crowd claps and cheers, proud of themselves for participating in the most iconic baseball game tradition.

Tate sits, but I need to stretch my legs.

"I'm going to get a drink. Want anything?"

"Get me a Coke," he says as I scoot by him.

I take the stairs two at a time and head for the nearest concession stand, finding my place in the back of the line.

"Hi!"

The greeting is so eager it startles me.

I turn over my shoulder. A guy in a backward Cubs hat smiles big at me. What in the name of handsome men is happening right now? Sandy-blond hair curls out from the side and back of his hat, complementing his rogue-ish stubble. His gray t-shirt fits like plastic wrap over broad shoulders, snuggly accentuating every muscle. And are those green eyes? Like, for real?

"Hello." I politely nod then turn forward again, brushing him off as an over-friendly Cubs fan.

"I've been watching you all game in a totally non-threatening and non-creepy way."

I puff out a laugh, glancing back. "Is there such a thing as a non-threatening and non-creepy way to watch somebody?"

"Oh, totally. I think I mastered it here today." The corner of his mouth lifts flirtatiously. "When I saw you get up from your seat, I knew I had to come and talk to you."

"You're not helping your non-threatening argument."

He laughs a little. "I know, but just hear me out. I've been watching you from four rows back, and I don't think the guy you're with is that into you."

"Really?" My brows hike up in amusement.

"The only time I saw you two touch was just now during the seventh-inning stretch, and that's typical baseball stuff. Everyone sways together during 'Take Me Out to the Ballgame.'"

I can't help my growing smile. "Is this some kind of relationship intervention?"

"You could call it that." His green eyes glow with more cute confidence. "I mean, you're not even my date, but you have *all* my attention."

"Wow. Have you been practicing that line the whole game?"

He chuckles good-naturedly, and there's something about his boyish embarrassment that's really endearing. "It's not a line. I honestly can't tell you the score of the game because I've only been focused on you."

"The Cubs are losing."

"See, I didn't know that."

I'm flattered, but I don't believe a word he says. I turn fully to him. "And just what about me has you so mesmerized?" This is usually where guys crash and burn and say something stupid like, 'You have a nice rack.' I stare at him expectantly, waiting for something of that caliber to come out of his mouth.

"You caught my eye, and I haven't been able to look away since." *Okay, I'm listening.* "You seem happy and full of positive energy. That's how I like to live my life, so I'm typically attracted to people with that same vibe." He lifts his fingers, pointing to my face. "And I love your freckles. They're almost unnoticeable, but when you do see them, they add so much character to your face. And then there's your smile." He says it like an afterthought. "You're just really beautiful. How do you describe that instant spark?"

He passed my little test with flying colors.

Now, it's my turn to feel an unexpected spark.

"I hate to break it to you"—I straighten, putting up a clear boundary—"but I'm in a relationship already."

"Yeah, I know. But how serious is it?" He nods back to the seats where Tate sits. "You know, with the guy out there?"

My mouth pulls into a grimace. "Pretty serious."

"But there's wiggle room, right? Tell me there's room for somebody else to maneuver in?"

"I'm afraid not. Me and the guy out there...we're so serious we're like life-long-commitment serious."

"I don't get that vibe with you two at all." He tilts his head with so much confidence it's an unfair advantage over every other guy in existence. "There's absolutely no romantic connection between the two of you."

I roll my eyes, giving in to his game. "He's my brother."

"Brother." His mouth pulls into the most charming smile yet. "That's the best news I've heard all day."

"He may be my brother, but I'm still not interested." I step forward with the line.

"Aw, come on." A small frown appears. "I'm not that bad. You'd go out with me, right?"

I glance up and down his frame like I'm taking inventory. Everything about him passes the physical appearance test, but I still answer, "Nope."

"Why not?" He backs up, throwing his arms out to the side. "My nose might be a little crooked from when my brother broke it in sixth grade, but other than that, I'm a pretty good catch."

I study his lifted brows and raised chin. There's an energy about him too, something more than just cockiness or confidence. Just by his posture and our short conversation, I can tell that he's laid-back and fun—the type of guy who breathes life into a party. He could probably have any woman he wanted, and the fact that he wants me will put an extra spring in my step for the next week, which is perfect timing since I start my new job on Monday. I need all the confidence boosts I can get.

But that's where my relationship with this guy stops.

"You're attractive. I'm sure plenty of women love you, but—"

"You think I'm attractive?"

"I didn't say that."

"Actually, you did."

"I said plenty of women probably love you. Just not me. I'm already in a relationship with someone else."

"Don't lie just to get rid of me."

"I'm not lying." I laugh. "I really do have a boyfriend."

"Give me some credit. It's the classic excuse to let me down gently."

"It's not an excuse. His name is Stetson Roeshine—"

"Sounds made up."

I laugh again. "He's not made up. We've been together since third grade."

"I bet he has a really punchable face." He says it with a smile, letting me know it's just a joke.

"As long as we've known each other, nobody's ever punched him. So I think you're wrong about that."

"I'm available to do the job. I have an excellent right hook." His expression is so fun-loving I realize I can't take anything he says seriously.

"Save your right hook for another guy."

"Alright." He places his hands on his hips. "Your fake boyfriend was the final blow. I'll take the hint and leave you alone."

His head subtly drops in defeat, and I feel bad, but I'm first in line at the counter.

"I can help who's next," the woman yells at me.

"I hope you can at least watch the game now," I say to him before stepping up to order.

"I'll try my best." He smiles, and *wow!* I'm reminded again just how charming it is. I'm madly in love with Stetson, but I tell the truth, and the truth is, this guy has quite a smile. The kind that lights up a room...just not mine.

I order a water and Coke and walk back to Tate.

"Here you go." I hand him his drink, debating whether or not to tell him about the guy four rows above. I decide not to because he'd probably tell me to go for the Cubs fan. Tate's a protective older brother, and with all the recent drama between me and Stetson, he's over that relationship.

The woman behind us taps Tate on the shoulder. "The guy a couple rows up wants you to have this hot dog."

Tate's face morphs into confusion as he looks over his shoulder.

Four rows up, the man from the line points at the dog Tate is holding. "There's a note on it!" he calls over the crowd.

Tate looks down and starts reading the scribbled message written on the wrapper. "Bro, I'd love to take out your sister. If she's lying about having a boyfriend and you don't think I'm crazy, please give her my number." Ten digits follow his note.

Tate turns to me, and my entire face colors.

"You're blushing!"

"No, I'm not." I look straight ahead, ignoring him.

"And what's with that smile?"

I roll my lips together, hiding all the evidence.

"You like him, don't you?"

"Like him? I don't even know him." I give my brother a pointed look. "Plus, I'm with Stetson. I *love* Stetson."

"I hate to break it to you, but you're not *with* Stetson. He broke up with you last week because you moved to Chicago."

"We all know that wasn't a real breakup, just a desperate plea for me to stay."

"Maybe it should be a real breakup, especially now that love-at-first-sight guy is in the picture." He turns in his seat, waving back at him.

I peek back too, feeling my face heat.

I grab Tate's shoulders, forcing him forward again. "Do not encourage him!"

"All I'm saying is maybe you should date somebody new while you're in Chicago. You've never been with anyone else besides Stetson, and on your first day away, you get hit on.

It's a sign that there are more fish in the sea besides your lifelong boyfriend who loves you so much he just dumped you."

"He didn't *dump* me. It was a posture move. Besides, Stetson is...great. I'm one thousand percent confident in my choice to stay with him."

"What an endorsement," Tate says under his breath. "Someday, I hope my girlfriend describes me as great. Maybe she'll add *really neat* to the list."

I roll my eyes. "You know what I meant."

He holds up the hot dog. "Do you want me to save this just in case you change your mind about the Cubs guy?"

"No need. I'm with Stetson."

Kind of.

Technically, he did break up with me, but he was mad about Chicago. I know he loves me, and I love him. By the end of my internship, we'll be back together.

"Well, I've never seen you blush over Stetson or smile the way you did for that guy."

That's because Stetson and I have foundational love. This is just flirting—something we rarely do anymore.

One of the Cubs players swings and launches a ball to right center. The crowd explodes as the ball goes over the wall.

I stand and clap, grateful for the distraction.

Stetson is top-tier. Despite what Tate says, I don't fall over myself or get flustered by other men.

But as I clap, I peek over my shoulder one last time.

Cubs guy is already looking at me. He tips his head, giving me another one of his winning smiles. My heart throbs in the pitter-patter way that has only ever happened with Stetson.

But it's been a *long* time since my heart has had the opportunity to beat like that.

CHAPTER TWO

NASH

"TALK TO ME, REGGIE," I call as I round the corner of one of the cubicles in the office. Harper is at the end of this aisle, scooting along. She's never been great on the Wiggle Cars. I can't say I fault her. They are meant for kids.

"I'm by Eli's desk," Reggie says across the office. "The coast is clear here."

"Where are you hiding, Victor?" I hate losing our office version of tag, but Victor may have us beat.

When I told my assistant, Grace, that I wanted to buy twenty Wiggle Cars for the office—you know, to build team unity—I thought she would quit right then and there. But she bought the carts and even cleared out one of the storage closets to store them in. However, she's never joined in on the games.

Grace is old school, and by that, I mean old.

She styles her graying hair in a bun and wears pencil skirts even though I've told her repeatedly that Superior Health is a casual work environment.

"Nash!" I hear Grace's voice above the commotion, but I don't stop my wiggles.

"Yeah?"

"Nash!" she scolds, and I know I'm in trouble.

My erratic hip motions stop so I can hear her better. "Yes, Grace?"

"Your new intern is here."

"Oh, I forgot about that." I glance at my watch. It's noon —right when I told her to show up. "What's her name again?"

"Sadie Bradley," a new voice says, obviously the intern herself.

Three months ago, Grace and Eli narrowed down the internship applicants to the top ten candidates. I spent the next two weeks interviewing everyone, but Sadie Bradley was finishing her last semester at Syracuse University and couldn't fly in to meet face to face. We decided on a Zoom interview. She apologized over and over again about her camera not working, but it was fine just to do it over the phone. I was immediately impressed by her energy. I'm curious to see if my gut reaction was right.

"Okay, guys. Game over. Green team back to work."

Multiple people groan.

"We'll play again on Friday." I hop to my feet, hidden between the maze of cubicles. "Victor, where are you?"

Victor's dark hair is the first thing I see as he slowly comes to a stand. He's at the other end of the office, almost to the water cooler, which, if you make it to the water cooler before you get tagged, you're the winner.

"Dude, how did you get over there so fast?"

"I like Shakira, so I know how to shake my hips."

That's actually a solid reason.

I spin around, ready to greet the new intern, and that's when my mouth falls open like an idiot. "It's you."

The girl from the Cubs game stands in the middle of my

office. Instead of shorts and a t-shirt, she's wearing a fitted white blouse tucked into black flowy pants. It's a different look than the one over the weekend, but she's still a complete knockout.

Bewildered is the best way to describe her expression. "You're Nash Carter?"

I run my fingers through my hair, suddenly feeling the urge to make myself look presentable after my time on the Wiggle Cars. "Yeah."

"The Nash Carter who owns Superior Health?"

"Guilty."

We stare at each other, neither of us knowing what to say. There's a weird expression written across her face, but unlike a book, I can't read what it's about.

I place my hands on my hips. "Well, don't I feel stupid?"

"I'm lost," Harper says, joining us. "Why do you feel stupid? Do you guys know each other?"

"No way!" Reggie pops up from his spot across the office. "You're the girl from the Cubs game."

"Uh..." I scratch my face, debating how much I want to admit to.

"Nash saw her at the Cubs game and pretty much fell in love and—"

"I did not *fall* in love," I say to Reggie then turn to defend myself to Sadie. "I wasn't in love. I was interested."

Her smile is a good sign she's not completely freaked out right now.

"After he fell in love," Reggie continues, "Nash made a fool out of himself by hitting on her in front of everyone, but she completely shut him down."

"Thanks for that, Reggie." I shoot my employee, who's really more of a friend, a tight smile.

25

"Anytime, boss." Reggie looks at Sadie. "She only shut him down because she already has a boyfriend, right?"

"I *kind of* have a boyfriend."

"Oh, now you just *kind of* have a boyfriend?" I give her a wry smile. "Sounds like you made him up, and now you're trying to come clean with the truth."

Laughter puffs over her pretty lips. "That is the truth. It's complicated."

It *is* complicated.

She's my intern, and I'm her boss. Forget about her *kind of* boyfriend.

This is worst-case scenario.

I can't pursue her now. Superior Health isn't that kind of workplace, and I'm not that kind of boss.

Victor rests both his arms on the top of the nearest cubicle. "How did Nash hit on you?"

"Okay, that's enough of this. Why don't we go talk somewhere more private?" I gesture toward my office and hear the snickers behind me as I lead the way. It's times like these when I wish I'd been more of a serious boss whose employees are so scared of him that they'd never dream of giggling behind his back.

Who am I kidding? I'll never be that guy.

I hold the door open for Sadie to pass and force myself not to smell her perfume as she walks by—mouth breathing for the win. The last thing I need is to be pining over my intern.

"Take a seat." I shut the door and make my way behind my desk. I don't immediately sit. I feel like I need to clear the air first. "Hey, I'm super embarrassed about Saturday."

"Don't be." Sadie swipes her hand in front of her, wisping it all away. "It's not a big deal."

"Obviously, if I had known who you were, I never would've hit on you...especially so aggressively."

She laughs that same adorable laugh that killed me just two days ago. "It's a funny story."

Maybe for her. Not so much for me.

I told her I loved her freckles.

Gosh, this is brutal.

"Right." I nod. "It's a funny story."

"I respect that you shot your shot."

"It was a complete airball, but I did shoot it."

She laughs again, and I do my best to ignore the beautiful sound.

"Let's just move on." I pull my chair out and take a seat. "And I promise to never hit on you again at work. From here on out, I'll be the epitome of professionalism. The most professional boss you've ever had."

She points over her shoulder with a teasing smile. "Was that a Wiggle Car you were just riding?"

"Okay, not the *most* professional boss you've ever had, just *a* semi-professional boss. And those cars are something fun we do to build team unity and a positive work environment. I promise there's a method to my madness."

"I'm not giving you a hard time. I think it looks fun. I can't wait to play too."

She would say that.

Actually, I don't know her at all. My opinions are based on the four hours I watched her Saturday afternoon.

Oh, man. I was in love with this woman for *four* hours.

Reggie wasn't exaggerating.

I was planning the wedding.

The honeymoon.

The three kids.

It was beautiful until it wasn't.

"So work!" I clap, scooting my chair in. "We're excited to have you here for the next six months. As you know, you'll primarily be working with me. I'll teach you the ins and outs of running a healthcare staffing business and how to scale a company and manage a team."

Her eyes beam with excitement. "That's exactly what I'm looking for."

"In addition, something that's different with my interns is that, before your time here is up, I ask you to find a weakness within my company or an area where there's room to grow and develop a plan to elevate it. Oftentimes, I find that the best ideas come from young and eager interns with nothing to lose. It's like a fresh pair of eyes or an outside perspective."

"Sheesh." She tugs at her ear like a nervous tic. "That's a lot of pressure."

"Don't think of it as pressure. Think of it as an opportunity. I'll never put you or your ideas in a box. So don't put yourself in one. The sky is the limit."

She nods as if my words really resonate with her.

"Besides, I wouldn't have hired you if I didn't think you have a ton of potential. You just need to be pushed toward it. That's what I'm here to do during the six months you spend with me. I want to see more of the woman from the interview—the one who believed there was no one better for this internship than her."

"There isn't anyone better." The cockiness behind her smile is wildly attractive.

That's why I look down, fiddling with a few papers. "Grace will set you up with a desk and some of the accounts we're dealing with right now." Feeling more composed, I glance back up at her. "There are a few long-term care facilities that we have our eye on. All of this should be easy stuff for someone who graduated in healthcare administration with a business minor."

Her mouth stretches into an adorable smile. "You remembered."

"You had a really impressive resume."

"Thank you. I'm trying to build my portfolio to take over my dad's home health and hospice business back in Skaneateles."

"Is that how you say it? Ski-nee-at-luhs?"

"Yeah, it's easy if you just think of a skinny atlas."

"I've never been to Central New York or the Finger Lakes."

"It's a beautiful area. My parents have a house right on the water."

"Your family must be proud you were selected for the internship."

"Not really. Everyone was against me moving to Chicago —except for my brother. He thought it seemed like a fun adventure."

"It's only for six months. You'll be home before Christmas."

"I know, but to them, it's a waste of time when I already have a secure job at my father's company."

"And what about your *kind of* boyfriend? Was he against you moving here?" She said his name the other day. "Stayton or Satan or something like that."

"Stetson." She smiles at my poor efforts to remember.

"Much better than Satan."

"Yes, I think so."

Her lips press together, fighting a smile, and a touch of satisfaction washes over me from her amusement.

She smooths her pants and goes back to answering my earlier question. "Stetson didn't want me to move to Chicago either. He actually broke up with me last week before I moved out here."

My brows lift in interest.

"But it's not a *real* breakup," she explains.

"It's not?"

"No, Stetson doesn't really want to end things. He was just trying to get me to stay. Long distance is difficult on a relationship, especially since we've never been apart before."

"Yeah, didn't you say you'd been together since third grade? I thought you were lying, but is that really true?"

"We grew up next door to each other, and our families are best friends. We naturally became friends when we were kids and then more than friends."

"Until he broke up with you." He's an idiot. If Sadie were mine, I'd never let her go, especially not over something as insignificant as a few hundred miles.

She gives me a pointed look. "It's a pause. When the internship is over and I move back home, Stetson and I both know we'll be together."

"Sounds like you gave up a lot for this internship."

"I did." Her chin lifts confidently. "For me, this opportunity is about proving to everyone back home that I can run my dad's company. I don't want to be handed his successful healthcare business just because I'm his only interested child. I deserve it. I've studied and graduated in this field. I beat out hundreds of applicants for this internship, and after these six months, I'll return to Skaneateles with even more knowledge about the healthcare industry than before. I want no doubt in anyone's mind that I'm qualified to take over when my dad retires. That's the goal."

"Unless you discover that you love working here and want to come on board full-time."

"That won't happen. I already have everything planned out."

"Fair enough." My gaze casts over her face and the smattering of light freckles on her cheeks and nose so perfectly distributed they almost look painted on. "Come on. I'll show you around the office." I quickly stand, deciding there's no world where studying Sadie Bradley's freckles is appropriate —at least not for me as her boss.

CHAPTER THREE

SADIE

BEING a city girl is harder than I anticipated.

I've been in Chicago for two weeks and still haven't figured out how to shop for groceries. Apparently, I'm supposed to go to the store several times a week to get a few items instead of one giant grocery run that I try to muscle home. Four blocks don't seem like a lot until you're faced with carrying your load back to your apartment, and then suddenly, it becomes the workout of a lifetime.

I had some extra time this morning, so I stopped at the corner market to grab a few essentials and dry goods. I made sure it was a small amount that I'd be able to carry home from work. Just slowly stockpiling.

And then there's the food delivery. Harper told me that whenever I order food from DoorDash, I need to put a man's name on the ticket in case a sketchy delivery boy drops it off —I don't want anyone thinking a single woman lives alone in my apartment.

It's all very different from the small town I grew up in.

I wear comfortable shoes to walk to work in and then change into my cute ones once I get here—so many things

I've never thought about before. However, there's no dress code at Superior Health, so my cute work shoes are a *me* thing, not a *work* thing.

Without permission, my gaze travels across the office to Nash Carter. He's standing behind Eli, arms folded, looking at something on the computer. Nash has perfected his casual but well-dressed style. His fitted navy t-shirt hugs his arm muscles and chest, ending just past the waist of his jeans, where a stylish belt buckle peeks out. He doesn't give off cowboy vibes, but he definitely looks like he'd be best friends with John Wayne and fit in on a ranch somewhere in Texas—not what I expected when moving to the city. Nash's jeans-in-the-workplace policy took me by surprise. I mean, Stetson wears dress shirts to law school every day, so I expected fancier attire from a major business in downtown Chicago. But Nash's rugged style suits his laid-back personality.

He straightens, and as if he can sense me watching him, his eyes shoot to me. I don't immediately turn away, and I'm rewarded with a small but attractive smile that creates flutters in my stomach.

What the heck was that?

I swallow hard and scoot my chair into my desk like I intend to work my way out of being attracted to my boss.

But it's too late.

He's on his way to me.

When I arrived at work two weeks ago and saw the charming guy from the Cubs game, I about died. My heart exploded in my chest from shock. There's no other acceptable reason for the burst.

Nash has been all business since I got here, just like he promised he would be. I should be grateful. The last thing I want is to be favored in this internship because a man wants a relationship with me. But I'd be lying if I said I didn't miss his shameful flirting from the Cubs game.

It was nice to be pursued.

I haven't had that in years—maybe never. Unless you count the note Stetson gave me in third grade that said, "Be my girlfriend. Circle yes or no." I circled yes, and from that moment on, I've always been his. So much so that he's never had to work hard again to get me to fall for him. My love was just assumed and expected—like a lot of things in my life. Where I'd live. Where I'd work. Who I'd marry. When every decision for my future has already been made, it takes away the excitement of the journey.

That's the problem with Nash. He brings excitement to my otherwise pre-determined life, and I like it.

He stops just outside my cubicle, resting his elbow on the wall. He looks massive in my small space, and the flutters from moments ago swirl to life again, as if his presence gave them their second wind.

"Have you looked at the Green Acres long-term care facility yet?"

Work. Yes, let's focus on work.

"I have." I search around my desk for the file to jog my memory on which facility we're talking about. When I don't immediately find it, I stand and start moving my grocery bags around, looking under each one.

"Did you go shopping?" Nash leans over, peeking inside one of my bags.

"I went before work." I don't want him to think I grocery-shopped during business hours.

"Is that a can of Spaghetti-Os?" He reaches inside, pulling it out. His smile teeters between amused and teasing as he holds the can up for me to see as if I wasn't the one who purchased it.

"I've never actually had Spaghetti-Os." I shift my weight, feeling nervous. "My best friend used to eat them whenever I visited her at college, so I just thought I'd give it a try."

"An American delicacy. I'm sure you'll love it." The playfulness in his eyes makes me think he knows something about Spaghetti-Os that I don't. "What else do you have in here?" He reaches into the bag and pulls out Goldfish crackers, fruit snacks, and Top Ramen. His smile grows more prominent with each item.

My food choices make me look like a freaking six-year-old.

"Your palette reminds me of a toddler," he jokes, noticing what I hoped he wouldn't. He's not wrong. I get everything plain. I don't eat vegetables. Heck, I'd eat cheese pizza if it was acceptable for a grown adult.

"I've never lived on my own. So Spaghetti-Os and Top Ramen seemed like a rite of passage I needed to experience."

"You've never lived on your own?" His brows jump in surprise. "Not even in college?"

"I commuted from my parents' house to Syracuse University. My dad thought it would be best to live at home so I could still be involved with his business."

He nods as if he understands.

I find the Green Acres folder and hold it up. "Here it is." I open the file, looking at the pictures. "Oh, yeah. I wasn't impressed with this facility. It seems dirty, and the bed-to-staff ratio is way off. Plus, every time I called to speak with the director, I was on hold for over ten minutes." I hand the folder to Nash. "I don't recommend we staff it."

He leans back against my desk, crossing his ankles as he reads over my notes. "Yeah, I actually agree with you."

"You do?" I match his position, accidentally brushing my

shoulder against his arm. The way that shoulder brush speeds up my heart is downright illegal.

"Why are you so surprised?" He eyes me from the side.

"I just thought you'd want every account possible. You know, to make more money."

"First rule of business:"—he turns to face me, and I'm keenly aware of how little the seven inches between us are— "you're only as good as the clients you represent. I don't want to staff a facility that's not a great place to work." He hands the folder back to me. "So let's pass on this one. We'll find something better, and when we do, we'll celebrate over a can of Spaghetti-Os." The playfulness in his smile revs up my heartbeats even more.

"They're gross, right? That's why you keep bringing it up."

"I'm not going to ruin your Spaghetti-Os coming-out party by giving you my opinion just to pre-determine yours. It takes the fun out of trying something new. I'm all about the journey."

Trying something new. All about the journey.

This is exactly the kind of shake-up I've been looking for in my life. I just didn't expect it to come from my cute boss.

We're staring at each other, smiling, and it's like the walls of my cubicle close in on us. Suddenly, everything feels *too* intimate. I step back to drop the Green Acres folder on the credenza.

"Is this your family?" He plants his hands on my desk and leans down, looking at the picture pinned up on the fabric wall by my computer. It's of us in front of Skaneateles Lake.

"Yeah, that's my parents; my brother, Tate; and my little sister, Annie."

"Annie looks like a younger version of you."

"I know." I make my way to his side, wanting to look at

the picture with him as if I've never seen it. "If we were closer in age, I think people would mistake us as twins."

"How old is she?"

"Seventeen. She's just starting her senior year in high school."

"And Tate? Is he a big Cubs fan?"

"No, that was his first game. He drove me out here. We decided to catch the game last minute before he flew home."

"That was nice of your brother to help you move to Chicago when he didn't think you should take the internship."

"Oh, Tate was the only one who was all for it. He's Team Sadie." I smile, thinking about the unconditional love my big brother always gives me. "Whatever I want, he wants. No questions asked."

"And is this Stetson?" His focus moves to a picture of us in front of the tree last Christmas. We're both wearing ugly sweaters and giant smiles.

"Uh, yeah." I rub the back of my neck, feeling twisty about Nash staring at a picture of Stetson and me.

"The *kind of* boyfriend you're still loyal to even though he broke up with you." He shoots me a sideways glance.

"If it makes you feel any better, Tate wanted me to keep your number."

His head inclines toward me. "Tate's not pro-Stetson?"

"He was until Stetson gave me an ultimatum about Chicago. Now Tate is pro me experiencing new things, including the charming stranger at the Cubs game."

"I knew I liked your brother." His smile stretches wider. "And did you just admit that I'm charming?"

"You don't need me to admit that. You already know you're charming and happily lean into it."

"But it's more fun hearing you say it."

I should probably check my pulse after that smile Nash gave me—just to make sure I'm still alive and well.

He glances back at Stetson's picture. "You know, I take back what I said about him having a punchable face."

"Is that so?"

"Yeah, he actually looks like a broke Henry Cavill."

A burst of laughter spits out, and I immediately cover my mouth, partly to hide the noise and partly because I shouldn't be laughing at a joke about Stetson's looks.

Nash laughs too but, thankfully, moves on. "You come from the perfect family."

"Oh, don't let the picture fool you. We're all kinds of dysfunctional. My dad rags on my brother for not having a suitable life plan. My mom shoves all our problems under the rug and pretends like there's nothing wrong. Tate seems depressed and lost, and I can't figure out why. Annie is self-centered and oblivious to it all."

"And you?" His green eyes stare deep into mine.

I smile, masking the frustration with my family that's built over the last few months. "I'm living my best life in Chicago."

"Until you leave to take over the family business. Then you'll really be living your best life."

"Actually"—my heart thuds as I say words I haven't admitted to anyone before—"I don't know if my dad will ever let me take over his business. Not really. I can totally see him pretending to retire and then coming into work every day just to micromanage me or tell me how I'm doing everything all wrong."

"I can't imagine a world where your dad doesn't know how capable and incredible you are. I'm sure he knows it but doesn't say it out loud."

"Maybe." I shrug, blowing out a heavy breath. "But until

he does say it out loud, I'm going to work my butt off to prove that I have what it takes. His blatant rejection of this internship made me realize, for the first time, that his love is contingent upon me doing what he wants me to do. I should've realized it sooner with my brother. Tate broke the mold my parents had set up for him, and their relationship hasn't been the same since. By coming out here, now I'm the one that's ruining my life."

"I'm sorry that things are so complicated with your family right now." The softness behind his eyes is enough to melt me.

I've allowed Nash to see parts of me that I usually keep hidden away. I want to ask about his family and learn the struggles that make up the backbone of his life.

My mouth opens to ask about him, but Grace beats me to it, popping her head into my cubicle.

"Nash, Donovan Garcia is on the phone for you."

"I better take that." He follows Grace but pauses to say, "I hope, in the end, your dad sees what I see."

And then he's gone.

I drop into my chair, leaning back to stare at the ceiling tiles.

Opening up to Nash Carter was way too easy. I told him things that I've never even told Stetson.

I'll spend the rest of the day thinking about why I did that.

CHAPTER FOUR

SADIE

"THE MIC DROP." I read the name on the neon sign outside the bar, just confirming that I'm at the right place. I should've been here a half hour ago, but Tate called to see how another week of work went. He seemed slightly off, so I didn't want to rush our conversation.

"Sadie?" Harper appears out of nowhere, linking her arm in mine. "Are you coming inside for karaoke night?"

"Yeah." I smile at my new workplace friend. "I just wasn't sure I was in the right place."

"You definitely are." She tugs me forward, opening the door with her free hand.

The excitement around the office this week over karaoke night was palpable. I guess it's a tradition they do once a quarter—another team unity thing that Nash put in place.

"There's everyone." Harper points straight ahead to several tables in the front. She swings her smile to me as we walk to our group. "What are you singing tonight?"

"How seriously does everyone take this? I'm a horrible singer."

"No worries. We're all terrible. Nash is by far the worst."

"He sings too?" I don't know why I'm surprised by that.

"Oh, he *loves* singing the cheesiest songs. Last time, it was 'Making Love Out of Nothing at All.' You know, the old song by Air Supply?"

My lips curl up, just envisioning it.

"Hey, guys!" Harper unlinks our arms, bouncing over to an empty seat next to Victor.

The group greets us with hellos and raised drinks.

I glance around. The only open chair is next to Nash, who has his own table. Either no one wants to party with their boss, or he was saving it just for me.

The thought thrills me a little.

I've worked every day with him for the past month, and he's been nothing but professional. My rogue heart may speed up when he walks by, but that's a separate issue I'll deal with personally.

I'm just in a weird place right now with Stetson. We've barely talked since I've been in Chicago. He broke up with *me*. I shouldn't have to be the one to reach out. He needs to get over his stubbornness and call me. And he'd be wise to do it soon, because the more days I go without talking to Stetson, the better Nash looks.

I walk to where he's at. It's one of those high-top tables, so I climb into the chair, feeling the weight of Nash's stare on me.

"Hi." A massive smile covers his mouth.

"Hi."

His green eyes flicker over my outfit in an appraising way.

I wasn't sure what to wear tonight. It's Friday night in Chicago, and we're at a bar. And if I'm being honest, I wanted my cute boss to take notice. I know I shouldn't care, but Nash's face crossed my mind every time I stood in front of the mirror in a new outfit until I decided on a black spaghetti strap midi dress with a billowy tiered ruffle skirt. I paired the dress with platform jute wedges. It's flirty and fun but still has that summery vibe, matching the August temps outside.

"You look exceptional."

"Thanks."

Nash doesn't glance away. He just keeps eyeing me with a smile that says he enjoys my choice of dress. *Mission accomplished.* I turn my face, hoping he doesn't see the slight blush creeping up my cheeks.

I forgot how fun it is to be checked out—confidence boost for days.

"I'm glad you came," he says over the music, and I can already tell by the tone of his voice that something's different tonight.

"I thought it was mandatory," I answer dryly, noticing that he's not actually sitting. Instead, the side of his body is propped against the high-top table, arm resting on the top, fingers clasped together, legs crossed. It's the ultimate casual-confident position. And let's not forget about his lopsided smile that could bring crowds of women to their knees.

"Karaoke night is not mandatory. Grace doesn't come." He tilts his head, thinking. "She came once but left early during a provocative performance of 'Let's Get it On' by yours truly."

Laughter explodes out of me, causing Nash's eyes to surge with pride. "I would've liked to have seen that."

"Grace leaving early or my sexy performance of 'Let's Get it On'?"

"Grace." We both laugh because we both know I lied.

"Want to pair up tonight?" The mischievousness behind his eyes reminds me of the day we met at the Cubs game.

"I believe it's called a duet."

"I know what it's called." His impish smile grows, slamming my heart into my ribs with each beat.

This feels dangerous in the most exciting way.

"Didn't you promise you wouldn't hit on me again? Something about being the epitome of professionalism." My eyes narrow. "I guess that only lasted a month?"

"No, I said I wouldn't hit on you *at work*." His eyes dart past me to the clock on the wall. "It's nine-fifteen. We're well past work hours. As far as I'm concerned, this is fair-game territory."

I laugh at the loophole in his promise. "So what you're saying is, I need to be on guard tonight?"

"Not just tonight." Nash leans closer. My stomach elevates, hanging in weightlessness until his words tickle the skin on my neck, and everything drops with an exhilarating force. "I'm always interested in you. I just can't show it."

My gaze shifts sideways, giving me the perfect view of his jawline and stubble-clad cheek. He pulls back just enough for our stares to collide.

"Because I have a boyfriend?"

"You don't have a boyfriend—unless you got back together again, and I don't know it."

"No, we haven't officially gotten back together, but we will."

"Until then, I don't care about your *ex*-boyfriend."

I swallow, shifting farther back into my chair, creating more space between us. "Well, I care about him. We've been together for a long time. A relationship like that doesn't go away easily."

"It does if you take an internship in Chicago."

So true.

I look stupid defending a relationship and a man who dumped me. But I understand this breakup isn't real. It's just a fight. I'll move home in December, and we'll probably be engaged by summer once Stetson graduates from law school. That's always been the plan.

"The real reason I can't show interest in you is because I'm your boss." Flirtation fills Nash's expression. "I'll wait until your internship ends, because I honestly don't want anyone else."

Why is that the cutest thing a man has ever said to me?

"Well, let's just keep things work-appropriate tonight," I say, trying to tell myself that too.

"You don't *actually* want me to do that."

My mouth falls open in humored disbelief. "Yes, I do."

"Nah, I see the way you smile at me." His grin tips higher with cockiness. "It tells me everything I need to know."

I roll my lips together, desperately trying to cover up whatever Nash thinks he sees.

"What are we singing tonight?" Harper slams the book of songs down on the table between us.

Just in the nick of time.

"Sadie and I are singing a duet," Nash answers.

"No, we're not."

"Yeah, we are." His head flops to me with a pointed stare. "It will be the highlight of everyone's night."

Harper bounces up and down, clapping in delight. "Please, do it."

"I'll go put our names in right now." Nash leaves before I can stop him, taking Harper too.

"This is awful," I mutter. I've never even glanced at another guy besides Stetson. Now, I'm singing a duet with one.

A few minutes later, Nash returns. "We're after Victor."

"What song?"

"It's a surprise."

"What if I don't know it?"

"You know it." He takes a sip of his drink, momentarily hiding his smile.

"What if I don't want to sing with you?"

"What? Are you scared?"

"Of karaoke?" I scoff. "I'm the queen of karaoke."

"What else is there to be scared of?"

Having too much fun with you and liking it way too much.

"Nothing." I lift my chin. "I'll destroy whatever song it is."

"I don't doubt it."

Victor finishes his rendition of "Fire Ball." I had no clue he had moves like that.

"Next up is Nash and Sadie." Everyone from work cheers. "They'll be singing "Rewrite the Stars" from *The Greatest Showman.*"

"Really?" I shoot him a sharp glare.

"What?" He shrugs innocently. "It's a great song."

It may be a great song, but the lyrics hit a little too close to home. There's no doubt in my mind he did that on purpose, like a subliminal message that's not so hidden.

I grab the microphone and face the crowd, channeling my inner Zendaya as the music starts.

Nash's part is up first. He turns to me, *singing* to me. He's pitchy, and his timing is off, but I can't help smiling at his exuberant effort and the way he hams up his performance.

He's just so fun.

I'm grinning from ear to ear when my part starts, making it hard to sing. But there's no way I'm letting him outperform me. I give it my all, and by the time we're to the chorus, we both have our heads thrown back and eyes shut, holding out each note as if our life depends on it.

Nash even points the mic to the crowd, letting them sing along. At the end of the song, everyone is on their feet.

He takes my hand in his, swinging it above our heads before we drop into a bow. He slings his arm around my shoulder, pulling me in for a friendly, appropriate side-hug.

"You were terrible," he says into my ear above the crowd's cheers.

I laugh. "So were you!"

His arm drops, and we exit the stage, giving high-fives to everyone in our group.

I sit, eyeing Nash as he talks with Eli.

Everything he does is over the top and animated, and I love it.

I can't remember the last time I felt this free and had this much fun.

And suddenly, out of left field, a new life plan pops into my head—one that's so different from the one already put in place that it terrifies me.

CHAPTER FIVE

NASH

WHEN I WALK into the office Monday afternoon, most of my employees are huddled together, talking. I glance around, looking for Sadie, but she's not in the mix with everyone else. I could see her being the one person who's still working as a way to try and impress me.

But I'm already impressed. Too impressed for my own good.

Two weeks ago, it was karaoke. Sadie sang the heck out of that song, not caring how stupid she looked.

Last week, it was her presentation on recruiting better doctors. She's as smart as a whip. I might be attracted to her mind more than her looks—I said *might be*. If anything, it's a fifty-fifty tie between personality and appearance. Both are equally important and equally a turn-on.

"Who died?" I ask as I join the group.

Everyone turns to me, but it's Grace's depressed expression that catches my eye first. "Sadie's brother."

My heart catapults into my stomach. "Wait. Are you serious?" You never know with this group. But none of them would joke about something like that.

49

"Yeah, she got the call about two hours ago and headed straight to the airport," Allen says.

I hate that I wasn't here for her.

I've gotten a phone call like that. It stops everything. Suddenly, nothing else matters, and nothing will ever make sense again.

"How did he die?" I ask over my racing heart.

Josie's lips push into a frown. "She didn't say, but Harper was sitting next to her when she got the call, and it sounded like an accidental drug overdose."

Visions of my own brother's addiction dance through my mind, and my heart breaks for Sadie and her family. She doesn't even know yet how much this is going to hurt. The aftermath of his absence is worse than the initial blow.

"Should I call her?" My eyes stop on Reggie for some friend-to-friend advice.

"She's probably in the air as we speak." He lifts his shoulders. "When she lands, you can reach out and send condolences from Superior Health."

Right. Condolences from Superior Health, not me. No matter my growing feelings for Sadie, she has Stetson. Even though they're broken up, there's a history there. He's the one who will take care of her heart right now.

"We should send flowers," I look at Grace. That seems like the bossly thing to do.

Harper flashes a sad smile. "That's a great idea."

But it's not enough.

My mind and my heart are stuck on Sadie and the loss of her brother.

I know the pain all too well.

And I know sending flowers doesn't cut it.

CHAPTER SIX

SADIE

I NEVER THOUGHT I'd be speaking at my brother's funeral —at least, not when I was twenty-four and he was only twenty-six.

Everything feels numb.

The past few days, I've just been going through the motions—writing an obituary, picking out a casket, planning a funeral, finding pictures to display at the church. It's all so surreal.

But speaking and giving a eulogy is the most surreal experience of all.

I don't say what's really on my mind. Funeral talks aren't the time to air out your family's dirty laundry.

No, blaming your parents for the death of your older brother is done in the privacy of your own home. Lucky for all the guests here today, I've been doing that since I arrived in Skaneateles. There is no need to write my grievances into my eulogy about how my dad's constant demand for perfection and lack of compassion drove Tate to this point.

I have enough love and respect for my brother to keep things focused on the incredible life he lived.

My eyes drop to the typed words, reminding myself of the next story I wanted to share. "Tate was the kind of brother that would do anything to keep me safe and out of trouble. I'll never forget one night when we were kids. Tate had the idea to cut out a cardboard cat and place marbles in it for the eyes. We tied strings to it and hid in the bushes across the street from each other, holding one of the strings. Then, whenever a car came down our street, we'd pull on the strings and make it look like the cardboard cat was crossing the road. Once the headlights hit those marbles, our fake eyes would glow, and cars would slam on their brakes to avoid running over the cat. We thought we were so funny and clever." The audience chuckles, half of them probably remembering the incident. "It was all fun and games until Mayor Anderson stopped and got out of his car. Tate told me to run and hide so I wouldn't get in trouble. Then he came out from his hiding place and took all the blame so Mayor Anderson wouldn't go looking for the other accomplice. Until this day, I don't think the mayor or my parents knew I had anything to do with it." Everyone laughs again, and I force a fake smile despite my glassy eyes. "But Tate was always more worried about protecting me than himself. He was selfless like that. The epitome of taking one for the team. And I was so proud to be on his *team*."

Emotion crowds my composure. I drag in a heavy breath, hoping it's enough to get me through the last of my talk.

"No one has ever believed in me like Tate did. He was my biggest cheerleader and never let me doubt what I was capable of." As I keep talking, my gaze sweeps over the teary-eyed guests, but one face catches my eye.

Nash Carter.

My heart swells, and fresh tears fill my eyes to the brim.

I register how weird it is that Nash is here at my brother's funeral, six hundred miles from Chicago, but I can't deny how much it means to me. I want to dissect what his presence here means, but I have to finish my talk.

"Tate, your absence will forever leave a hole in my heart. Not a day will go by when I won't wish you were here so I could laugh with you and get your advice. You're my best friend, and I know you won't leave me. You'll still push me from heaven, helping me become everything you said I could be." Tears spill down my face as my eyes drop to the cherry casket in front of me. "Thanks for showing me the way and being the best big brother a girl could ask for. I love you, Tate."

I grab my paper and sit as Annie steps up to the pulpit.

I should find Stetson in the crowd for reassurance, but instead, my gaze shoots to the back where Nash sits. Sure enough, he's there, wiping his tears with the back of his hand.

CHAPTER SEVEN

SADIE

"THANK YOU SO MUCH FOR COMING," I say to Mrs. Richenbaugh as I walk her to my best friend's car. Autumn was nice enough to pick up Mrs. Richenbaugh this morning and drive her to the funeral so she could pay her respects to Tate. She always had a soft spot in her heart for my brother, even though she kicked him out of seventh and eighth-grade choir at least twice a week. But that's what was so great about Tate—you could never stay mad at him for long.

"It was a beautiful service." She squeezes my hand as I help her into the passenger side.

"It really was." Autumn opens the driver's door and takes a seat.

I don't shut the door on Mrs. Richenbaugh because she's still holding my hand.

"Did I tell you I'm getting surgery on my hip next week? I'll be out for two months."

"Yes, you did tell me that." Autumn and I exchange small smiles because Mrs. Richenbaugh keeps reminding us of her surgery even though she's here for Tate.

"I'm the music director for A Dickens Christmas, but I won't be able to go to the practices, and there's no one to sub for me. How will we be ready for the festival in December with me gone? Everyone knows A Dickens Christmas is the biggest holiday event in the Finger Lakes."

Autumn gently takes Mrs. Richenbaugh by the arm, slowly pulling her hand away from mine. "If I weren't in school, I'd come back to Skaneateles just for two months to be your substitute."

Mrs. Richenbaugh turns her head to Autumn. "You always did have a beautiful voice. Who do I need to talk to, to fly you in?"

Autumn gestures for me to close the door while she's distracted. "We'll talk about it on the drive to your house."

"Thanks for coming, Mrs. Richenbaugh." I shut the door and step back from the car, waving as Autumn reverses.

"Can you believe she came?"

I turn over my shoulder as Stetson wraps his arm around me. There's no denying he looks handsome today in his black suit with a faint gray pinstripe running through it. His dark hair is cut short around his neck and ears and slicked back in the front—very dashing and distinguished. That's always how I describe him.

Since I've been home, we've slipped back into our usual interactions. I don't know what it means, and I don't care to figure it out. Now isn't the time to have a deep relationship talk with everything else going on.

"Mrs. Richenbaugh loved Tate," I explain. "She even visited him after his football injury."

"I know. I just meant she only leaves her house for choir practice. It was nice of Autumn to pick her up and bring her to the church."

"Is everyone almost gone?" I shift under Stetson's arm so my body faces his.

"All that's left is your family."

I close my eyes, pressing my forehead into his chest. "They are the people I don't want to see right now. I think I'll stay at Autumn's house again tonight."

"I don't understand the blame you're putting on your parents. What happened to Tate was not their fault."

I whip my head up. "How can you even say that?"

Stetson gently caresses my cheek. "I know how much you idolized Tate. You would never think anything bad about him. But he had an addiction, Sadie, and he hid it from everyone. That's not your parents' fault."

"You act like he was some lowlife shooting up cocaine. He just got in trouble with pain meds, which my parents put him on and *kept* him on so that he could make a quick recovery and play football in college. They should've seen the signs. If my dad wasn't always harping on Tate about his life choices, he *would've* seen the signs."

"None of us saw them."

His words hit hard, forcing tears into my eyes. "Are you saying the same thing my dad did? That if I hadn't gone to Chicago for a silly internship, none of this would've happened? That I would've been here to see the signs?"

"No, that's not what I'm saying, and your dad shouldn't have said it either. You were pressing him on his tough-love tactics, and he lashed out in defense about you not being here." He sighs, rubbing the sides of my arms. "All I'm saying is that you don't have to blame yourself or your parents. Despite how it all got started, Tate was the one addicted to painkillers and lied to everyone about it for years. What was your dad supposed to do when he found him stealing money from him last week?"

"Help him!" I shrug out of Stetson's arms, backing away. "He could've paid for Tate to go to rehab and get clean instead of kicking him out on the street. A little compassion would've gone a long way. But no matter what Tate did, it was never enough for my dad."

"I just think you're being too hard on your parents. They did the best they could with the information they had. They wouldn't have tried tough love if they knew how it would end."

"I just..." I shake my head, wiping an unwanted tear. "I just don't think I can forgive them for turning their backs on Tate when he needed them the most."

"Is your anger all about Tate, or could some of it be about your dad not wanting you to move to Chicago?"

"They are two entirely separate things."

"Are they? Or are you blaming your dad because he blamed you first by throwing the internship in your face when you were at an all-time low?"

"No, that's not why I'm mad. I don't know why we're still talking about the internship. I already moved to Chicago. It's a non-issue."

"Not to me."

"Are we really going to have this fight right now?" Of all the days, Stetson has to choose Tate's funeral to bring up my moving to Chicago.

"I guess I just thought, after a month and a half of you being gone, you'd realize how ridiculous this is and come home."

"I'm not coming home. I made a commitment to Superior Health."

"What about your commitment to your family? To me? We're all struggling."

"Right now, I don't want anything to do with my family.

And you broke up with me, so you don't get to have a say in my life."

"I shouldn't have done that. The breakup was dumb. I just didn't want you to go."

"If you really love me, six months in Chicago shouldn't change anything."

"It doesn't change anything. But I still don't understand why this is so important to you."

"I've told you a thousand times. I want to learn from this internship and have it on my resume."

"You don't need a resume!" his voice rises. "Your dad will give you his business no matter what."

"I want to *earn* it!" Why is this so hard for Stetson to understand?

"Yeah, you keep saying that, but I think it's stupid."

"Why can't you just be supportive?"

"I let my girlfriend put our relationship on hold and move six hundred miles away."

"Let? You *let* me put our relationship on hold?" I sneer.

"That came out bad. I'm just saying, from my perspective, the internship is worthless when you can start taking over your dad's business right now."

"Nash knows his stuff. Every day I spend working for him, I'm taking away valuable information that will help me in the future."

"Yeah, you've mentioned that before. The few times we've talked on the phone, all you've wanted to talk about was your boss. Nash this. Nash that. Is there something going on I should be worried about? Do you have a crush on this guy or something?"

The United States military would spend millions of dollars for the level of defense I feel right now.

"How could you say that? He's my boss."

"I'm trying to figure out why you're different. You've been this way all week."

"My brother just died. You, of all people, know how much Tate meant to me."

His shoulders drop in defeat. "You're right. I'm sorry. I shouldn't have brought any of this up right now. We'll figure our stuff out later. None of us are handling our emotions well this week." He extends his hand to me like an invitation to join him inside. "Come on. Let's go patch things up with your parents."

"I can't forgive them, not when I know they could've helped Tate and didn't."

"I don't agree with you on this."

"You don't have to."

He shakes his head almost as if he's disappointed. Then he turns, deciding to go back inside without me.

I feel like I can't breathe here.

And I definitely won't be able to breathe easier inside.

I spin around, running toward the field next to the church.

NASH

SADIE ROUNDS the corner in a rush, colliding with my body.

Her feet trip over mine, forcing me to wrap my arms around her so she doesn't topple to the ground. Glossy brown eyes peer up at me as I steady her against my chest, holding her to me. There's one calm moment where I swear I see a flicker of relief in her eyes, something that says she's happy I'm here.

Without thinking, I pull her into a hug. "I'm so sorry about your brother."

She lets me hold her, even buries her face into my neck as she cries. I run my hand down the back of her hair over and over, comforting her. There's nothing inappropriate about this. It's just one person being there for another.

After a minute, she pulls out of my arms, wiping at her puffy eyes. "I'm sorry. I'm such a mess right now."

"You don't have to apologize."

"What are you doing here?"

"I came outside to make a phone call, but when I finished, I couldn't leave because you were in a serious conversation with Stetson. It didn't seem like a good time to jump in and say hello."

Her brows pinch together. "I meant, what are you doing in Skaneateles? Not outside."

"Oh." I shrug, embarrassed that I just admitted to eavesdropping on her private conversation. "I came to pay my respects and see how you were holding up." I glance away from her, squinting my eyes against the fading sun. Explaining why I'm here sounds crazier than it is. I lift my shoulders, darting my gaze back to her. "It just seemed like the right thing to do. Funerals are pivotal life events."

Her lips press into a closed-mouth smile. "I'm learning that the hard way."

The evening sun casts the perfect glow across her face. She looks as beautiful as ever with her tear-stained cheeks, runny nose, and crying eyes.

"I'm sorry about what you just heard." She gestures over her shoulder to where she'd been talking with Stetson. "I'm so embarrassed."

"About what?" My tone makes light of the situation. "Your *ex*-boyfriend shaming you for blaming your parents for your brother's death or the part where he accused you of something going on with me?"

"Ohhhh," she says on a sigh. "All of it."

"I have to say, out of all the conversations I've accidentally stumbled upon, that one was by far the most dramatic."

Sadie laughs. *Actually* laughs. And nothing makes my heart happier.

"Do you accidentally stumble upon a lot of private conversations?" Her smile stays even as she asks the question.

"You'd be surprised. The key is hiding around corners."

"So you weren't making a phone call, just waiting to eavesdrop."

"Guilty," I joke. "Now you know my secret."

She laughs a little more, biting back her smile until it's gone. Her eyes meet mine, and her shoulders pull back. "Just so you know, Tate wasn't some drugged-up loser."

"You don't have to explain anything to me. I'm just here to offer support."

"No, I want to." Determination fills her gaze, and I can tell it's important to her that I know who her brother was. "He didn't overdose on purpose. He wouldn't do that. He had to have taken something like fentanyl without knowing it." She shakes her head, fighting off her rising emotion. "Tate had the biggest heart and a bright future ahead of him. He was a good guy. He just struggled with this one thing and didn't tell anyone or get help. I'm sure he thought he could get a handle on it."

"I know. And I can tell from his pictures and everything you said about him that no one was better."

"Thank you for saying that." Tears drip down her cheeks, but she quickly wisps them away with her finger. "He got injured playing football his senior year and was in a lot of pain and had a lot of surgeries. I think one thing led to another, and he couldn't stop the meds. I didn't know. Nobody did. I would've never left him and gone to Chicago if I had known what he was dealing with." A stray tear skitters down her cheek, and I wish I could wipe it away, wipe away the pain I know she's feeling.

"It's not your fault."

"I just..."—she sucks in a ragged breath—"I should've been there for him, but I wasn't. And I don't want anyone thinking badly about him, you know?"

"I know exactly what you mean." I start walking and talking, hoping she'll follow. "My older brother was the funniest guy I knew—the life of every party. But he had a few demons he couldn't get past, so he drank. *A lot.*" I glance to the side to make sure she's walking with me, happy to see she is. "One year ago, we lost Nolan in a car accident that he caused. He was drunk."

She reaches out, grabbing my forearm. "I'm so sorry, Nash. I didn't know."

"You wouldn't. I don't really talk about my brother at work, and I guess everyone's learned not to bring him up."

She drops her hand, and we walk silently for a few paces. "How Nolan died, or his addiction, doesn't define who he was as a person, and neither should what your brother was dealing with."

She blinks back a few tears, discreetly wiping what couldn't be dismissed. "Does it get any easier?"

"Do you want the truth?"

"You might as well give it to me. I'm going to find out anyway."

"It doesn't get easier. You just get used to the pain constantly being there."

"But you hide it so well. You're always so happy."

"Life moves on even when you don't want it to. I've learned that grief and happiness happen at the same time. It doesn't make sense. It just works—both feelings equally take up space in your mind and heart."

"That's why you came six hundred miles to be here." Her sad smile breaks my heart. "You know what it feels like."

"I do know what it feels like."

There's a shared pain only those who've lost loved ones can understand. I see it in Sadie's eyes now—she understands my loss, and I understand hers. That's why I came. I understand her in a new way that very few people comprehend.

Our steps slow to a stop, and she turns to face me. "I'm happy you came. It means a lot."

"I'm happy I came too."

She nods toward the church. "I'd introduce you to Stetson—"

"I don't think he'd like to meet me." I smirk.

"Probably not." She laughs. "And my family...well, as you heard, I'm not really speaking with them right now."

"I didn't come for them. I came for you."

Our stares hold.

Desire, attraction, want, longing—every feeling I shouldn't feel—builds inside me. I didn't come to her brother's funeral to make Sadie's life harder or complicate her internship or relationship with Stetson, so I take a step back.

"I should let you go."

"Yeah, I need to start cleaning things up."

"Take as much time off work as you need."

"Oh, I—"

"I'm serious. Don't come back until you're ready."

She smiles. "Thanks, Nash. You're a good friend and boss."

Friend and boss.

Under the current circumstances, those are the only two things I can be.

CHAPTER EIGHT

SADIE

I PUSH the *Add a Minute* button on the microwave and stare blankly ahead at the rotating dish.

The breakroom door opens, and Nash smiles when he sees me.

"You're back."

I recognize the glow of happiness behind his expression because that's how I feel about seeing him again.

"My flight got in late last night."

He walks over to the counter, leaning his hip against it. "How are you feeling? I know it's a stupid question, but are you doing okay?"

Nash is a safe place for my grief. I learned that two weeks ago, when he showed up unannounced at Tate's funeral.

"I started bawling last night when I walked into my apartment and saw the framed pictures I have of me and Tate. That led to me crying myself to sleep and waking up this morning with a massive headache. But I'm here."

"With a homemade lunch, even." He nods at the moving microwave. "Impressive."

"I wouldn't call it homemade, but it is a comfort food."

"Oh, yeah? What food is comforting you today?"

My mouth spreads into a goofy smile. "Spaghetti-Os. I had a strange urge to eat them today."

"You must really love your Spaghetti-Os." His eyes drop to my mouth. "Look at that smile."

"Who says my smile is all about questionable noodles? Maybe I'm just happy to see you."

"I don't believe that for one second."

Our eyes lock on each other, and my stomach does the *thing* it's not supposed to do when I'm with him. His gaze slowly moves around my face, almost like he's soaking in every inch of my skin. I allow myself one brief second to do the same. His stubble is longer today. He's probably due for a shave tonight or tomorrow morning, but I like the look of this length. I imagine the coarseness under the palm of my hand and—

The microwave beeps, a long and loud noise that makes me jump. I busy myself with my food as Nash moves around me to the refrigerator.

I'm in trouble.

I just daydreamed about his stubble.

It's not that I don't love Stetson, because I do. Things are just difficult between us right now. We spent the majority of the last two weeks in Skaneateles fighting. He kept pressuring me to forgive my parents or to give up my internship, and I kept pushing back.

I'm seeing first-hand what happens when there are cracks in a relationship. You fill them with other things, like daydreaming about what it would feel like to run your fingers across your boss's stubble.

Maybe it's because Nash making an effort to come to the funeral when he didn't have to is one of the nicest things anyone has ever done for me, and I can't seem to get the image of him wiping his tears off his cheeks at the back of the church out of my mind. The fact that he'd cry for me—or my pain—moved me on a deeper level than anything else ever has.

These are normal thoughts, right?

Like, I'm not a bad person for feeling a connection with Nash or for being attracted to him—as long as things end there, which obviously they will. I'm not a cheater or anything close to it, even if technically I'm single. Stetson and I will make it through this rough patch, and we'll come out stronger than ever.

That's what I keep telling myself.

"While you were gone, we decided to take on the Serenity Care account," Nash says as he pops open a Dr. Pepper.

"That was my account. I'm sorry I dropped the ball on it." I sit at one of the tables and stir my Spaghetti-Os.

"You didn't drop the ball. You were gone on bereavement."

"I know. I just hate not pulling my weight and dumping things on others. I haven't been the all-star intern that any of us thought I would be. I feel like I'm barely contributing. I'm sure you're regretting your choice."

"Definitely not. I don't care about how much you contribute. I care about you." The realization of what he just said and how bad it sounds has him backpedaling hard. "I mean, I care about you as an *employee,* and I want to make sure you're thriving and learning as much as you can while you're here."

"I'm worried I won't be able to do the one thing you ask of your interns: pinpoint a weakness in your company, and come up with an idea to elevate it."

"Out of hundreds of applicants, why do you think I chose you for the internship?"

"I don't know."

"When I called you for the interview, you had this arrogance about you that I liked."

"Arrogance?" My eyes widen. "Are you sure you're talking about the right person?"

"One hundred percent." He smiles confidently. "You had this belief that you were going to change the healthcare industry. It might've been naive, but I liked it. Your passion was exciting, and I thought, 'This woman will keep clawing and fighting until she does something amazing.' That's someone I want on my team."

His words stun me. They funnel to the places in my mind where self-doubt and insecurities live, swallowing them up whole and replacing them with his praise.

"Sadie, I know I've said this before, but you have a ton of potential—probably the most I've ever seen from an intern. You just need to believe it too."

For years, I've been trying to prove to myself, to my dad, and maybe a little to Stetson what I'm capable of, and in a matter of two months, Nash sees everything I've been working so hard to convey.

I incline my head, narrowing my eyes on him. "You know, in a lot of ways, you remind me of Tate."

Nash's eyes light in surprise. "*I* remind *you* of your brother?"

"Yeah, I don't know why I didn't see it until now, but you have a lot of the same qualities about you. A fun-loving personality, an ability to make everyone around you comfortable, and a cockiness that is somehow endearing, not annoying." His lips lift with that one. "But beyond that, Tate believed in me more than anyone else. He never saw where I was at right then. He only saw what I could become. He never let me forget who I wanted to be and where I wanted to end up. I feel like you're the same way. You have this absolute belief in me."

"Uh…" He starts to speak, but the sound comes out gritty, as if what I said meant something to him. He clears his throat, erasing all evidence, and then flips into business mode. "That's what this internship is about, helping you achieve your goals."

I wish we could go back to two seconds ago when the conversation was real. But real conversations lead to real feelings, so I get why Nash has turned into my boss again.

My phone buzzes beside me on the table, and I glance at the screen, seeing *Mom* written in bold black letters.

Everything tightens inside me. "It's my mom."

"I'll leave so you can have some privacy." He walks to the door, throwing me a small smile over his shoulder—what a glorious thing. "I'm glad you're back, Sadie."

"Me too." I wait until he's gone before reading the text message.

MOM

> Sadie, I know you're angry with us, but it's been over a week since we've talked, and you haven't returned any of our calls. Don't you think it's time we sorted all of this out?

My eyes prick with tears just thinking about my dad throwing Tate out of their house once he found out about his addiction. What kind of parent would do that?

He died alone on his friend's couch the very next day—totally preventable.

I turn my phone face down on the table and push it away.

No, I don't think it's time I talked to my parents.

I tried a day or two after the funeral, and it just didn't work out. Tensions were too high. None of us could adequately express our feelings and frustrations without hurting someone else. We're not communicating well.

At this point, avoiding the problem with my parents is easier than fixing it.

Maybe time will smooth out the rough edges and hurt feelings. Right now, my grief is too raw.

CHAPTER NINE

NASH

"SINCE IT'S Friday afternoon and the seminar ended early, are we free to go home instead of back to the office?" Allen asks as we leave the hotel where the conference was held.

"Pretty please!" Harper leans toward me with a hopeful smile.

I glance at my watch for dramatics, but I already know it's around one-thirty, and I already know I'm not making my employees go back to work for the rest of the afternoon. That would just be cruel. Plus, I'd also love an early start to my weekend.

"I guess you're free to go." I say it like it's such a sacrifice, but I'm sure everyone figured we'd be done for the day.

"Best boss ever!" Victor slaps me on the back as he walks by.

"Yes, thank you!" Harper spins, facing me as she retreats. "I'm going to go get a pedicure."

"I'm taking a nap." Reggie salutes us before leaving.

My gaze skitters to Sadie. She has her phone out, searching Google Maps.

"Looking for something?" I step toward her, leaning in to

see if I can help with directions. A hint of her perfume carries up to me with the outside breeze. I've spent enough time around Sadie these last three months to know she doesn't wear the same scent every day.

She has a perfume wardrobe. Some days, it's a floral smell. On other days, I catch a scent of warm vanilla. Today, I sense a whiff of jasmine. All I know is, Sadie smells amazing every time I get close to her.

Her head lifts. "Isn't that big silver thing around here somewhere?"

Amused by her description, the corner of my mouth rises. "Are you talking about The Bean in Millennium Park?"

"Yes!" Her eyes brighten. "Is that around here somewhere? I'm embarrassed to say I've lived in Chicago since July and haven't seen it yet."

"I'll take you there."

"You?"

The wideness of her eyes makes me rethink my offer. "Unless you don't want me to."

"No, I'd love that. I just figured you'd have something more important to do on a Friday afternoon."

"I'm an important guy. Obviously, I have important things to do at any given moment, but I'm offering my tour guide services to you. Free of charge."

"Well, if they're free, how can I say no?"

A smile breaks loose over my lips as I tilt my body in the direction of The Bean. "We're headed this way, then."

As we walk, I keep my hands in my pockets as a signal to Sadie that this is a completely platonic tour. It's still work hours, and ever since I overheard her conversation with Stetson at Tate's funeral, I've pulled back on the flirting I had already pulled back on. Flirting twice removed. I don't think that makes sense, but it sounds good, so I'm keeping it.

"You know, The Bean is just a nickname. It's actually called Cloud Gate because the steel plates reflect the city skyline and clouds."

"I didn't know I would get commentary and facts with my tour."

"I aim to please."

"If you do a good job"—she throws me a side smile—"maybe I'll tip you when the tour is over."

Nervous laughter puffs out as I scratch the back of my head, trying really hard not to let my mind run away with how Sadie could *tip* me for services rendered.

She bounces ahead, completely unfazed by the molten pool of desire she just caused in my stomach. "Is that it?"

"Yep," I say, even though it's obvious we've arrived.

She spends her time walking around the entirety of the structure and takes a few selfies with it behind her.

"Do you want to see it from the best angle?"

"Yes, of course." An excited giggle accompanies her smile.

I gesture to the middle, walking under The Bean until I'm in the center. Then I lie down on my back, with hands clasped together, resting on my stomach.

"You can't do that." She anxiously glances around at all the tourists taking pictures.

I lift my head, staring at her. "I just did."

A hesitant smile spreads across her mouth as she debates joining me on the ground.

"Come on."

It only takes a few seconds before Sadie drops to the cement beside me, matching my position.

She sucks in a deep breath, exhaling out as her body wiggles into a comfortable spot.

"You're right. This is the best angle."

"I'll be expecting that tip now."

Her head swivels to me, with gleaming brown eyes. "You might have just earned it."

Inches separate us—separate our *lips*.

Tension builds as we gaze into each other's eyes.

Around us, people move and laugh and live, but for me, it's like the world stopped spinning.

Sadie is the only thing I see.

Intense attraction stretches, pulls, and begs me to do something. My mind is going places, wondering what it would feel like to touch her. A piece of her hair lifts with the breeze, floating over her cheek and into her lashes.

I slowly glide my fingers down her skin, removing the stray strand. Her chest lifts and falls in heavy movements, and her eyes momentarily close, but she doesn't move.

Doesn't flinch.

It takes every fight inside me to pull my hand away from touching her face, but I do. I don't want her internship to be about *this*, about *me*.

"Off the record," I say. "If I wasn't your boss and you didn't have a *kind of* boyfriend, I'd kiss you right now."

"Off the record," her words are slow and deliberate, "if you weren't my boss and I didn't have a *kind of* boyfriend, I'd let you kiss me."

But I am her boss.

And Stetson does exist in her world in some way.

And no matter how much I hate it, real life is always *on* the record. I'd never want to do anything that put Sadie in a difficult position or made her regret her actions.

So I stay statue still.

"Necesitan levantarse." A homeless man taps my shoe with his toe, breaking the moment. "No pueden estar aquí."

We sit up, staring back at the man and his hectic hand motions.

"¿Por qué no podemos estar aquí?" I ask.

Sadie whips her head to me, astonishment coloring her eyes. "You speak Spanish?"

"A little."

"What's he saying?"

"Tienen que salir de aquí." He waves us away. "Están bloqueando a todos."

He wants us to move, says we're blocking everyone, but that's not what I tell Sadie.

"Uh, he said I'm very good-looking."

Her brows drop. "No, he didn't."

The man motions for us to get up. "Apárense del camino."

"He thinks you should forget all other men and just be with me."

Sadie laughs.

The homeless man kicks his leg out, showing he's kicking us out of here. "Los estoy echando de aquí."

"He says I should kick your *ex*-boyfriend in the groin and then the head."

She laughs even harder.

"No, no." Frustration crosses over the man's face.

"Not in the head?" I ask in English.

"No entiendo lo que estás diciendo. No, Inglés. Solo Español."

"Oh, sorry. The head, *then* the groin," I clarify to Sadie. "The order of where I kick your *ex*-boyfriend really matters to him."

"I understand enough Spanish and body language to know he's not saying that." Sadie rolls her eyes, pushing my shoulder before she stands.

"Está bien?" I stand too, shaking my new compadre's hand.

But the homeless guy is still stuck on moving us along

from our spot under The Bean. "La gente puede caminar hasta aquí ahora."

"Sí verdad." I agree with him that people can walk through more easily now. "Yes, she's very pretty. I know."

"Now, I know you're lying." Sadie laughs as she tugs on my arm, pulling me away. "Come on. Let's go."

I wave over my shoulder. "Gracias, amigo!"

"Haha. You're very funny." She lets go of my arm but keeps walking.

"You think so?"

"Sometimes." She bites back her smile. "Where did you learn to speak Spanish like that anyway?"

"I lived in Belize for two years after high school."

"All by yourself?"

"No, my brother Nolan came too. We thought college was a scam and wanted to see the world. That's actually how I got the idea to start my business. We worked construction in Belize and remodeled a hospital, and they were always short-staffed on doctors and nurses. It was a huge problem. I wondered if that happened in the United States too. When we moved back, I decided to look into healthcare staffing, and the rest is history."

"I should've known you were self-made."

"Crap, you think less of me now, don't you?"

"It's the opposite. I admire everything you've accomplished. You're very impressive. You're not even thirty yet, and you have this successful business."

"I believed I could, so I did." I shrug like it isn't a big deal.

She looks straight ahead. "Now what?"

"What do you mean?"

"You're my tour guide, aren't you?"

If Sadie wants to keep hanging out, I'm not turning her down.

"I am your tour guide."

"So what's next on the Nash Carter Chicago tour?"

"Have you done an Architecture Boat Tour since you've lived here?"

"No, but I like the sound of it."

So do I.

Pretty much, I like the sound of anything as long as I'm with Sadie.

CHAPTER TEN

SADIE

"This boss of yours is so sweet. He sounds like the type of guy who would hold open an automatic door for you just to show you the respect he thinks you deserve," Autumn says through the speakerphone.

I finally broke down and told my best friend about Nash. I need some advice or someone to knock some sense into me, because touring Chicago with Nash yesterday was one of the best times I've had in a long time.

But it wasn't just yesterday. Another week of work passed, full of sparks and butterflies, and it's not even Nash's fault. He hasn't done anything wrong. He's the perfect caring boss. Professional and courteous, abiding by every invisible boundary—minus the off-the-record kissing talk—but that was off the record, so I'm not counting it. No, this is a me problem through and through.

I'm a confused mess.

"He *is* sweet!" I groan at Autumn's assessment. "Did I tell you he noticed I don't like lettuce and tomato on my tacos and ordered that stuff on the side when we stopped at a taco stand last night?"

"Wow. Sweet and observant."

"Not to mention attentive and complimentary. There's a big difference between him and Stetson."

"Stetson is a lot of things, but attentive and complimentary are not part of his MO. But that doesn't mean he's not a good guy or even the perfect guy for you."

"I know. I'm so confused about my feelings. I'm in constant turmoil."

"If Nash wasn't your boss, would you even hesitate going for him?"

Years full of memories with Stetson flash through my mind. He holds all my firsts, and I thought he'd hold all my lasts too.

"I'd still hesitate."

"Because of Stetson?"

"There's just so much history there and an already planned future. It's safe."

"But I thought the whole point of going to Chicago was because you were sick of planned-out and safe. You wanted the unexpected."

"I don't want planned-out and safe when someone else makes the decisions for me, but if I choose that life, then it's fine." I know the logic doesn't make sense, but it's how I feel.

"Well, I can go either way here," Autumn says. "I can talk you into Stetson, or I can talk you into Nash. What are you looking for?" Spoken like a true best friend.

I press my palms on the counter and hang my head. "Stetson. I know I should be with Stetson. In three months, I'll move home, and Nash will be some boss I once had."

"Okay, if you want to be all-in on Stetson, you need to stop noticing all the cute things Nash does around the office. He has an unfair advantage over Stetson because he's the new shiny guy who hasn't done anything wrong, whereas Stetson threw a tantrum and broke up with you because you wouldn't stay in Skaneateles."

I nod, agreeing with everything Autumn says.

"Stop comparing this new exciting man to the old dependable guy that's been around for years. Stetson is like your favorite pair of jeans. You know, the ones that fit perfectly to the curvature of your butt? The ones you put on and always feel your best in?"

"But lately, I feel my best around Nash."

"That's only because you and Stetson have been fighting. Your feelings for him are tainted because you're mad at him."

"I am mad at Stetson—for the breakup and my parents."

"The breakup was stupid. Everyone knows it doesn't mean anything, an empty threat to try and get you to stay. And as far as your parents go, can you really blame Stetson for taking their side with the whole Tate thing? You guys have been together since third grade. Your parents are his second parents. Your family and his family are best friends, and he's back in Skaneateles, seeing a different perspective than you."

"I know, but he should be *my* person no matter what. Is it too much to ask that he's on my side?"

"You know Stetson. His loyalty is to truth or what he perceives as truth. Maybe it's the lawyer in him. Even though he loves you, he'll tell you if you're wrong. And he definitely thinks you're wrong by blaming your parents for Tate overdosing."

"I hate how he does that." I turn around, leaning against my kitchen sink. "Do you think I'm wrong?"

"What do you mean?"

"Do you think Tate's death is my parents' fault?"

"Whoa!" She laughs nervously. "That's a loaded question and something I'd rather stay out of."

"Autumn?" I press.

Her heavy sigh filters through the speaker. "Has your dad always been unreasonably hard on Tate? Yes. Could your dad have afforded to put him in a rehab facility instead of kicking him out on the street? Yes."

I close my eyes, feeling vindicated.

"*But,*" she says, "I also don't think you should ruin your relationship with your parents over this one thing. They lost Tate, too, and are grappling with their own pain and hurt. Dividing your family over his death is wrong. They're your family, and I don't think that's what Tate would want."

Part of me knows Autumn and Stetson are right. But my grief and anger take hold of all logical thinking, and I can't do it. I can't forgive them. Not right now, at least. I need somewhere to place the blame and anger so it doesn't fall on Tate. It's easier to deal with his loss if I put him on a pedestal.

"It's not just this *one* thing I'm mad at my parents for. It's been building for a while now. You know they were against me moving to Chicago for this internship. It's like my dad wants to keep me under his thumb forever, and when Tate or I or anyone else goes against his wishes, he can't handle it. I mean, he barely spoke a word to me before I moved to Chicago as a punishment."

"Families are complicated. And you guys have some crazy crap going on in your family right now."

"That's exactly why I'm staying at your house when I come home for Thanksgiving next month, even though you won't be there. Your mom won't care, will she?"

"Nah, she'd love it. You can sleep in my room. Did I tell you that Mrs. Richenbaugh called me last week?"

"What for?"

"She's still trying to get me to fly home for a few weeks to fill in as the choir director, hold her place for her until she's fully recovered and can lead the music for A Dickens Christmas. She says she'll pay me. I'm sure it would be, like, ten dollars for the whole month."

"Wait." I straighten. "Say that again."

"Say what again? That she wants me to fly in to be her sub for a few weeks while she's gone?"

I smile. "Autumn, you are incredible!"

"What did I do?"

"I have to go. There's something I need to figure out for work."

I say goodbye before clicking off the call and running to my computer.

WAITING IN THE parking garage for your boss to arrive at work might seem a little too eager, but I can't help it.

I'm really excited about this idea.

I thought about calling Nash at home over the weekend but talked myself out of it because Nash is my boss and I'm supposed to be all-in with Stetson. So I waited until bright and early Monday morning.

His Land Rover pulls into the parking garage, and the headlights shut off.

I slowly stand from my spot on the nearest cement parking block.

"Sadie?" Nash looks concerned as he comes around his car. "Is everything okay? Are you alright?"

It's cute that he's so worried, but I push those unhelpful thoughts away.

"Locum tenens!" I bounce a little as I burst the words

out. I can't help it.

Nash's brows crease together. "What?"

"Locum tenens. It's where providers work at healthcare facilities on a temporary basis to fill in gaps or cover for people who are on vacation or on maternity leave until they come back or until full-time providers can be found."

Amusement takes over his expression. "I'm aware what locum tenens in the healthcare industry are, but why are you talking about them in the parking garage at seven-thirty in the morning?"

"That's my big idea." My smile spans from ear to ear. "That's how you elevate your business. Think about it. You're already staffing permanent doctors and nurses. But what if you also provide staffing for temporary positions? What if we work with doctors and nurses around the US and connect them with facilities that need temporary help? Superior Health would be, like, a one-stop shop for every kind of staffing need."

Right now, I hate how masked Nash's expression is. I can't tell if he hates my idea or loves it.

"Why aren't you saving this to use at your dad's business?"

"Because bringing you a killer idea is part of my internship." My shoulders lift. "My dad's company isn't set up to take on something of this magnitude. But you are."

He smiles, and it actually steals my breath. "Have I ever told you how amazing you are?"

He has.

So many times he's helping me believe it too.

"So you like it?"

"I love it! I don't know why I hadn't thought of it before." He walks toward the door, holding it open for me. "Let's go get started. You have a lot of work to do."

"Me?"

"Well, *us*—I'll help too. But from now on, this is your baby—if you're okay with that."

"I'm more than okay with that."

For the first time since I moved to Chicago, I finally feel like the person I want to be.

CHAPTER ELEVEN

NASH

A LOUD GROWL rumbles through the silence.

"Was that your stomach?" I laugh, turning to Sadie beside me.

"Yes." She taps on her phone, looking at the time. It's almost seven o'clock. "I haven't eaten anything since this morning."

"You're working too hard." I scoot my chair back. "It's Friday night. You should go home."

"And do what? It's not like I have a raging social life here in Chicago. I'd rather keep working."

Same. If I go home, I'll continue working for another three hours back at my house. I might as well stay with her.

Since Sadie came up with the idea of locum tenens two weeks ago, we've been working overtime to hopefully roll it out at the beginning of next year.

"Then let's order some food. We'll get some pizza delivered." I shoot her a smile as I pick up my phone. "Don't worry. I won't order anything like a combination or Hawaiian. We can get half pepperoni and half cheese."

She lifts her chin in satisfaction. "You know me so well."

"I'll even see if they can bring some ranch dressing with it. You'd bathe in that condiment if you could."

"What do you mean?"

I hold my phone up to my ear. "From the first week you worked here, you've drenched ranch on every type of food imaginable." My lips lift in a teasing way. "I'd love to see what would happen if you poured it on me."

Sadie slugs me in the arm. "Where's Human Resources when you need it?"

"You're looking at him."

"Then how am I supposed to report you for that comment and karaoke night?"

"None of those things are harassment at work." My smile turns wicked. "It's all after hours." The pizza place answers before Sadie can give a retort. "Delivery," I say, focusing on ordering. "They said it will be here in twenty minutes." I set my phone down.

"Who calls to order food anymore?"

"I'm old school like that."

She sits up in her chair, stretching her back. I want to watch because there's something really sexy about Sadie stretching, but I don't watch. Instead, I sit back down.

My phone dings, and I drop my eyes to the screen.

LINDY

> You should stop by for dinner. I made stroganoff. Not the homemade kind. I'm not domestic enough for that. It's Betty Crocker, but a noodle is a noodle. Eating at seven-thirty. I'll set you a place.

If I left the office now, I could make it to my cousin's house for dinner. But I'd much rather stay here with Sadie. So, I ignore the text.

"I think we've exhausted every lead today." I lean into my chair, fluffing the back of my hair.

"I wish I was going to be here in January to see how locums work out." Her lips push into a frown, and I feel for her. I'd want to see how my idea—something I worked tirelessly on—plays out in real life.

"You could always keep working here when your internship is done. And I mean that in a totally professional-boss way and not the-guy-from-the-Cubs-game way."

She laughs, but the longing returns to her eyes. "I wish I could. There's just too much waiting for me back home. Too many people depending on me."

I hate her answer because it's about everyone else. Not what she really wants.

"You don't have to decide right now. Let's just play it by year."

Amusement brings Sadie's expression to life. "What did you say?"

"I said you could play it by year."

She buckles over with laughter.

"What?"

It takes her twenty seconds to even get the words out. "It's *ear*, not *year*. We could play it by ear."

"No." I shake my head, my disbelief more than apparent. "That doesn't even make sense."

"And play it by year does?"

"Yeah, like we'll see what happens next year."

"That's not the phrase."

"I'm fact-checking you." I use my laptop to Google it.

Sadie leans in, reading the meaning out loud over my shoulder. "The term's original meaning was to play without sheet music, meaning you either remembered the music or improvised it." She turns to me. "I told you!"

Her smile widens to something full and genuine. I'm struck by how pleasant it is. I also don't usually use words like *pleasant*, but she's my intern, so *pleasant* seems like the safest way to describe it.

I'm smiling at her, and she's smiling at me. Our gazes are locked, and sparks fly between us—at least for me. Suddenly, this no longer feels like a boss/employee conversation. It feels flirty.

I scoot back. "I'm going to go to the bathroom before the pizza arrives."

"Sounds good." She rolls her chair to her spot. "I'll just be here."

That's the problem.

Sadie's here at work.

In my thoughts.

In my dreams.

In my heart.

She's everywhere.

∾

SADIE

"I'LL NEVER GET over a Chicago deep-dish pizza." I pat my lips with a napkin, savoring the taste.

"Yeah?" Nash smiles through his bite. "You like it better than New York pizza?"

"For sure! Give me all the thick bread and crusts."

Nash's cell phone rings. The sound is muffled, but it's definitely ringing somewhere in this room. We both jump to our feet, lifting papers and napkins until I find it.

"It's Lindy," I look at the zoomed-in picture of the blonde with vibrant blue eyes and a giant smile.

This is the Lindy who calls at least three times a week and the same Lindy who texted Nash earlier tonight, inviting him to dinner.

I peeked over his shoulder and read the message.

I'm not jealous.

I just liked it better when I was the woman Nash wanted, but I've been replaced by *Lindy*.

I hold his phone out to him. His fingers skim mine in the pass-off. I pull my hand back, trying not to think about how divine his touch was.

"Lindy?"

Through the earpiece, I hear her snap, "Where are you? Dinner is happening right now."

Wow, she's a feisty one.

"I should've known you'd start calling if I ignored your text."

"Well, are you coming?" I'm so glad she's a loud talker, making it easier for me to eavesdrop.

"No, I'm still at work." His eyes flick to me.

"You're a workaholic, and I hate it."

"I know you do."

"You're missing out on my stroganoff."

"Save me some. I'll eat it later."

"If you're lucky." She sounds irritated but, at the same time, not. "Okay, goodbye."

"Bye." Nash sets his phone back down. "Sorry about that."

"No problem." I begin cleaning up the pizza, working as if I don't have a care in the world. "Was that your girlfriend? She sounds lovely."

"Sadie?"

"What?"

His lips morph into quite possibly the most amused smile

I've ever seen from him. "Are you jealous?"

"What?" I scoff and puff and do all the things that I shouldn't do if I want my lie to be convincing. "No! Why would I be jealous?" I aggressively throw stuff into the pizza box—the ranch cups, parmesan packets, chili pepper packets—until Nash grabs my wrist, stopping my movements.

His eyes are so soft and green, looking up at me. "Lindy is not my girlfriend."

"You don't have to explain anything to me." I try to keep cleaning, but he tugs my arm, forcing me into my chair so we're face to face.

"Lindy is my cousin."

"Your cousin?" I wish I were better at hiding my emotions, but my small smile gives me away.

"My cousin." That same amused smile returns to his lips. "Besides, I don't need a girlfriend. I'm holding out."

Confusion clouds my expression. "For what?"

"For you." Flirtation rounds out his grin. "I thought it was pretty obvious where my romantic interest lies."

Steady beats pound in my chest, and I think my soul just pirouetted out of my body, dancing happily around me.

As much as I *love* the feeling, this is not the reaction I should have to my boss.

My eyes dart to the home screen of his laptop as a way to change the subject. "That's Switzerland at Christmas, right?"

He shifts his focus to his computer. "Yeah, the flying Santa attraction at the Christmas market in—"

"Montreux," I finish his sentence for him.

"You've heard of it?"

"You're not going to believe this, but..." I hold up my cell phone, showing him my background with a similar picture of the same magical place.

His brows inch upward. "Have you been?"

"No, but it's my dream to go there someday for Christmas to see the flying Santa with Lake Geneva in the background and experience Christmas markets, fondue, and skiing. I can't think of a better way to spend the holiday. Have you been?"

"No." He lifts his hand to his mouth, hiding a smile. "But it's my dream to go there during Christmas too. For all the same reasons."

"For real?"

"No, I just have it as my screensaver for nothing."

If Nash weren't my boss, I would think he was the perfect man for me.

And if I weren't already in love with Stetson.

That reason should've come before the boss one, but it didn't—*unfortunately*. I'm claiming *out of sight, out of mind* on this one. I haven't spoken to Stetson for a week, so naturally the boss thing would come to my thoughts first.

"Well, you should go," I say flatly.

"Maybe we should go together," he offers. "Or do you already have plans to go there with Stetson?"

"Oh, no. Going with Stetson won't happen."

"Because he's gone from a *kind of* boyfriend to an *ex-boyfriend*?" Nash's smile is hopeful.

"No, he's still just a confusing *kind of* boyfriend."

"Then why won't you go to Switzerland with him?"

"Um..."—I fidget with the corner of Nash's laptop—"Stetson is afraid to fly."

"He's afraid to fly?" The shock in his voice is pretty valid.

"Yeah, that's why he hasn't come out to Chicago to visit me. It's a long drive, and he can't miss school."

"I thought he hadn't visited because he broke up with you."

"That might be part of it, but I just say it's the flying thing to make myself feel better."

"So if Stetson doesn't fly, how will you get to Switzerland for Christmas?"

"It's not just Switzerland. I'd love to travel the world. Tahiti, Thailand, Bali—you name it, I'm interested in going." I lift my chin, masking the disappointment I've felt about this topic for years. "But you know, my friend Autumn loves to travel, so I'm sure I'll go with her. Or maybe my little sister, Annie."

My facade isn't fooling Nash. There's so much behind his stare—a promise that he'd give me the world if he could.

But I'd be blowing up my entire life plan if I opened my heart to him.

That's a lot to give for love.

CHAPTER TWELVE

SADIE

NASH IS DRESSED as a trophy or maybe an Academy Award for Halloween. The way he went all out has me smiling my face off.

He's wearing gold tights, gold shorts, and a fitted gold shirt—no comment on how good it looks on him. But the best part is the gold body paint that covers every inch of his skin and hair. From across the party, he really does look like a human-sized trophy. And every so often, he poses in the classic trophy position.

Not that I'm watching him.

I just love Halloween and respect anyone who puts effort into their costume. Where's the fun in it if you don't dress up?

I've been this way since I was a little girl, and it's like everyone close to me is boring and lazy during this holiday. Last year, I begged Stetson to dress up with me. I needed a partner so we could be Jack and Rose from *Titanic*—minus the nude drawings.

I've only been planning this year's zombie costume since May. That's why I was thrilled when Reggie announced last week that he was hosting a Halloween party at his apartment. I needed a place to wear my epic costume.

"I can't even take you seriously with all that scary makeup on your face." Nash fills his plate with a few hors d'oeuvres. I knew if I stood by the food table long enough, I'd have a good chance of *accidentally* talking to him. "You must be going for the *best costume of the night* award."

"I'm a zombie." I lift my chin, proud of the final product. "If there is a costume contest, I'll definitely win."

"I hope you do." His eyes glimmer. "Winner gets to take home the trophy."

"Let me guess. *You're* the trophy I get to take home."

He doesn't need to answer. The gloating in his eyes says enough.

My phone vibrates in my leggings, but there's so much zombie fabric hanging all over me I can't get to it.

"Hey, I was wondering. Have you ever seen a professional football game?"

I abandon the search for my phone, partly because of my costume and partly because the call ended. "No, I haven't."

"I have two tickets to Sunday's game." Suddenly, Nash is all fidgety and nervous, and it's adorable. "I thought maybe you'd like to go. You know, see Soldier Field."

"With you?"

"It's not a date. It would just be two co-workers hanging out." His lips pull into one of his mischievous grins. "Actually, now that I think about it, it *could* be a date. It's our day off, so technically, I won't be your boss that day."

"So you're only my boss when we're at work?"

"That's right. Outside of work, I'm just the cute guy from the Cubs game. Or now I can be the cute guy from the Bears game."

I laugh at his logic.

"So what do you say? Would you like to hang out with me outside of work?"

"I don't know." I scratch my ear, wanting to say yes, knowing I probably shouldn't. My eyes catch something familiar behind Nash. "Stetson?"

"Oh, come on. Don't pull the boyfriend card on me. The guy's been absent since you moved to Chicago."

"No, Stetson is here." I push past Nash and rush to the door where Stetson stands with Harper. "What are you doing here?"

"Sadie?" His brows drop. "I didn't recognize you with all that makeup."

He wraps me into his arms, spinning me around, giving me the perfect view of Nash's stoney eyes.

"What are you doing here?" I repeat.

"I missed you." He shrugs.

"Why didn't you just call?"

"I hate how things are going between us, and I felt like I needed to come here and fix everything face to face."

"How did you find me?" My eyes quickly dart to Nash. His clenched jaw says a lot.

"Your mom has your location. She gave me the address."

My head is having a hard time catching up. "You drove here?"

"Yeah, all day. I just got in town. Came straight to you. I tried calling a minute ago to give you a warning."

"I couldn't find my phone because of my costume."

"What do you think of my costume?" Stetson beams.

He's wearing a suit. Like he always does.

"I'm a lawyer. Get it?"

"Yeah, *you're* a lawyer." My smile is fake, but it's there.

He hugs me again, planting a quick kiss on my lips. The

last time I kissed Stetson was almost two months ago when I was home for Tate's funeral.

"Are you surprised I'm here?"

"Yes, I wasn't expecting you at all."

"I just know how much you love Halloween, and I wanted to do something special. It's been too long since we've seen each other."

It's the effort and the grand gesture I've always wanted him to make. So why, in the back of my mind, am I worried about Nash?

"Are you going to introduce me to your friends?"

"I only know the people I work with. Everyone else is a stranger." I spin, looking around the crowded apartment. My gaze stops on Nash again. This time, he gives me a tight smile, tipping his head as if he's happy for me that Stetson showed up, but I know he feels as blindsided as I do.

Stetson showed up like a reminder that I have a completely different life waiting for me back in Skaneateles. I'm pulled in two different directions. I love the freedom and unpredictability of my life in Chicago, but it feels like my future is in Central New York. I may push against the life plan laid out for me, but it's still the plan. It still has elements of what I've always wanted—a marriage to Stetson, taking over my dad's business, settling in Skaneateles, and raising a family.

Those dreams have been at the root of it all ever since I was a little girl.

Am I really prepared to give all that up because Nash makes me want and hope for different things?

I don't know, and I definitely don't know how I'm supposed to figure it out.

～

NASH

I'VE KEPT MY distance from the happy couple all night.

Am I pouting? Maybe.

Am I pissed? Yes.

But I don't want Sadie to know, so I pretend I'm having the time of my life across the room from her. Because, really, I have no reason to be upset. I've known about Stetson from day one. And it's not like she invited him here. He just showed up, and he'll leave again, hopefully. I don't want this weekend to be the time they get back together or rekindle their relationship.

I've been holding out on pursuing Sadie the way I want because of the internship, but there are only two months left, and I plan to start slowly shifting things between us. Hence the invite to the Bears game, which obviously she won't be going to now that Stetson is here.

My eyes drift to them. Stetson is trying to dance to the techno music but looks like an idiot doing it. Honestly, he seems like the type of guy whose ego enters the room before he does.

I will never understand why Sadie still holds on to him, especially after he broke up with her for pursuing something important to her. I mean, what kind of guy does that?

The music fades, and Stetson gets everyone's attention.

He's going to make this about him.

"Hey, I'm sorry I crashed your party. I don't know most of you, but I drove a long way to be here with my girl."

My girl?

Dude, he gave Sadie up the second he ended things.

He takes Sadie's hands, facing her. "I fell in love with you in the third grade. Back then, you had two long pig-tail braids and buck teeth, but I thought you were the cutest thing I'd ever seen."

"Awww." Harper sighs from the corner.

This sounds like the beginning of a proposal or some kind of love confession. I straighten, hanging on Stetson's every word.

"But the woman you are today is even better than anything I could've imagined. Sadie, I've shared every big life moment with you since I was eight, and I want to share every other moment with you for the rest of our lives."

Oh, crap, it's a proposal.

Stetson drops to one knee, and the weight of my feelings for her sinks my heart down in despair. He pulls out a gigantic diamond ring and holds it up. My eyes shift to Sadie. It's hard to tell with all the zombie makeup, but she seems surprised, maybe even torn.

"Sadie, will you marry me?"

I'm a guy, and even I know this is the least romantic proposal ever.

Her eyes flick to me, and everything I've ever wanted, my future happiness, hinges on her answer. I'm inwardly screaming *don't do it*, but it's not enough. She dives into Stetson's arms, saying yes on a whim.

I'm shocked.

How did Stetson go from a *kind of* boyfriend she barely thinks about when she's with me to her fiancé? None of it makes sense.

The guests cheer while I escape to the kitchen.

I'd leave, but Lindy dropped me off and took my car to her work Halloween party and will come back to pick me up.

I'm completely heartbroken and stuck.

I spend the next hour doing Reggie's dishes, cleaning up the mess throwing the party caused him.

"I've been looking for you." I turn, already recognizing Sadie's voice behind me. "I thought maybe you'd left."

"No." I chuck my dish rag onto the counter. "I've just been helping Reggie clean up a little."

"Oh."

"I guess congratulations are in order." A better man would do a better job feigning happiness or excitement.

"Yeah, it was a total shock."

"You're telling me." I hate the edge of bitterness that escaped with my words.

"I didn't know he was coming."

"You couldn't have foreseen that he'd propose to you on Halloween? The most romantic holiday of the year."

She must sense my mockery because she fires back, "I love Halloween, and Stetson knows that. It's perfect for me. For us."

"Bull crap. No woman on the planet wants to get engaged dressed like a freaking zombie."

"I put a lot of effort into this costume and—"

"Why did you look at me right before you said yes?" I step toward her.

"I...I...didn't. You must've imagined it."

My body pitches forward, closing in on her space as I whisper, "Why did you say yes?"

Her head lifts. It would be so easy to hook my finger under her chin and pull her lips toward mine—make a mess of that ridiculous zombie makeup and her stupid proposal.

"You know why I said yes."

I shake my head like her answer doesn't cut it. "You haven't even been together the last four months, and then he just shows up here with a ring, and you say yes."

"Stetson and I have a history together. I don't need the

last four months to tell me it's right. Marrying him has always been the plan."

"Whose plan?" My eyes dance across her face. "Yours or someone else's?"

"It's *my* plan. I wouldn't say yes if this wasn't what I wanted."

"I thought you were feeling..." I lean in even closer, feeling her warm breath against my lips. My words are left unspoken between us. What good would saying them now do? It would only hurt her. So I take a step back, my jaw turning hard. "Forget I said anything."

"Nash—" she begins but is interrupted by Lindy's sing-song greeting.

"Helloooo!" Lindy spins as she enters the kitchen, letting her Little Bo Peep costume twirl around her ankles.

I take another step back, resting against the counter opposite of Sadie.

Lindy's smile falters when she feels the obvious tension in the room. "What's going on here?" Blue eyes bounce to me for some answers.

"Lindy, this is my intern, Sadie." I gesture between them. "Sadie, this is my cousin, Lindy."

"Oh, my gosh!" Lindy squeals, quickly shuffling forward to hug her.

Sadie's brows jump as my cousin squeezes her to death.

"I'm so happy to meet you." She pulls back, keeping her hands on Sadie's shoulders. "Nash won't stop gushing about you."

I rub my brows in an attempt to ease the awkwardness.

"No, seriously!" Lindy laughs. "Every day, it's Sadie this and Sadie that. Or you should've heard what Sadie said today. Or Sadie looked so—"

"Lindy!" I try stopping the rolling snowball that is my

well-meaning cousin. "She's engaged. Sadie's ex-boyfriend showed up unexpectedly tonight and proposed to her."

Lindy looks at me over her shoulder. "On Halloween?"

I nod.

She turns back to Sadie with lowered brows. "No, no, no. I thought you and Nash were—"

"Lindy." I shoot a withering glare to my cousin. "What's done is done."

She morphs her frown into a smile, hugging Sadie again. "Congratulations!"

"Thanks," Sadie says.

"Well"—I heave out a giant breath—"should we go?"

Lindy knows me well enough to see I want to get the heck out of here.

"Yep, let's call it a night."

I nod once at Sadie as she stands in the center of the kitchen, then I leave without a glance back.

CHAPTER THIRTEEN

SADIE

NASH HASN'T LOOKED at me for three weeks.

The last time his eyes truly met mine was in the middle of Reggie's kitchen when he asked me why I said yes to Stetson's proposal.

I couldn't verbalize then what I know now.

Stetson is my past and my future. He's the backbone of the life plan I laid out for myself in Skaneateles. I've always known I would marry him. Everyone expects a happy ending from us. So when he knelt down on one knee, holding a diamond out in front of him, there was no other option besides yes.

And Nash keeping his distance is exactly what I needed to find some clarity.

The internship is over in a few weeks. I'll move home, and Nash will be a small blip on my radar, never to be thought about again.

"Are you having a good time, Sadie?" Josie sits in the empty seat next to mine.

Despite being the week of Thanksgiving, Superior Health's Christmas party is in full swing. Nash thinks it's better to have the holiday party before the craziness of December sets in.

Grace, Josie, and Harper worked hard all day transforming the rented hotel conference room into a Christmas wonderland. Strands of fresh garland line the walls of the room. Round tables with red and white linens create a semi-circle in front of the live band. Twinkling lights hang overhead like a circus tent, and in the middle of it all, a giant mistletoe looms over everything.

I smile back at Josie. "I'm having a great time. You guys have really outdone yourselves with the decorations."

"How come you're not dancing?"

"Oh..." My eyes shoot to the dance floor, where Nash leads everybody in the YMCA. This is his company. His party. I don't want to ruin his night by being out there with everyone. "I'm just kind of tired."

She grabs my hands, pulling me to my feet and out to the dance floor. "You can sleep on your flight home tomorrow."

"I'm driving home, not flying," I say over the music, but the closer we get to the band, the louder it is.

I maneuver my way to the outskirts of the circle, on the opposite side as Nash. The next three songs are upbeat, and I do my best to dance with my back to him, avoiding all contact.

Then the lead singer says, "Grab a partner because we're going to slow things down a little."

The piano starts, and I immediately recognize "All I Want for Christmas is You"—Michael Bublé style. That's my cue to go sit down again. At a party where everyone besides me has their significant other with them, I'm the odd man out.

Spinning around, I nearly bump into Nash.

I hate that I immediately notice how good he smells.

The reflection of the Christmas lights dot his green eyes in the most magical way. "Dance with me?"

"Uh..." I tuck my hair behind my ear, keeping my hand there as I nervously look around at all the other paired-up couples. "I don't know if—"

"Dance with me." This time, it sounds more like a command than a question. He takes my hand in his, wrapping his arm around me. His fingers skim the contour of my back before cupping the curve of my waist.

A riot of feelings pulses through my chest as I place my hand on Nash's shoulder, letting him lead us to the song's beat. We've never been this close. It's innocent—the type of dance position you'd see from awkward teenagers who are afraid to touch their seventh-grade dance partner. But even the *not*-touching is killing me.

I feel his eyes on me in a pleading way, begging me to look at him. My focus firmly stays on the wall over his right shoulder. I am zeroed in.

"I hear you're going home for Thanksgiving."

My gaze darts to him, but one glance at his soft lips, and I immediately swing my eyes back to the spot on the wall. It's safer there. "Yeah, I'm driving first thing in the morning."

"Is everything back to normal between you and your parents?" It's small talk, but not. His question is actually something real and vulnerable in my life.

"Not even close, but we'll pretend and fake it because that's what we do."

"How are you holding up without Tate? The first holidays are always the worst."

"Honestly, I'm dreading it."

I allow myself a peek at Nash.

Bad idea.

He looks so handsome when he's being sincere.

"But you'll have Stetson. He'll help get you through." His words are a peace offering, as if he's letting me know he's resigned to our engagement.

"I'll have Stetson," I say to myself just as much as I say it to him.

"Look, you two! You're under the mistletoe." Allen lets go of his girlfriend's waist long enough to point to the hanging plant.

Nash and I slowly lift our eyes to the sprigs directly above us. Our feet stop, and our arms drop.

"You have to kiss. It's bad luck if you don't," Allen's girlfriend says, keeping her watchful eyes on us as they dance close by.

I run my fingers through my hair, tucking loose strands behind my ear.

Nash's eyes dart from the ring on my finger to my face. "Sadie's engaged to another man. It wouldn't be right to kiss her."

"Aww, it's tradition," Allen barks.

Heartbeats drive through my chest, each pulse laden with worry.

What if Nash kisses me?

What if he *doesn't*?

"Nah." He takes a step back. "I'll let Stetson be the one to carry out that tradition with her."

In one quick beat of my heart, I feel the disappointment of not knowing what a kiss from Nash would feel like and the anxiety of wondering if my worn-out passion with Stetson is all I have to look forward to.

The song slows to an end, but my raging heart pounds on.

"I need some air." The announcement was more for me than anyone else.

I flee to the exit, walking down the long hallway with

awful burnt-orange carpet until I'm through the hotel lobby and outside.

Biting cold air splashes over my skin. I close my mouth, breathing its coolness in through my nose. My back rests against the side of the building, using it to hold me up. Slowly, I lift my chin, fighting the blinding streetlights for a glimpse at the night sky.

"I like you."

I straighten like a soldier called to attention and stare back at Nash. A small place in the corner of my heart hoped he would follow me outside. But corners of hearts are dangerous. That's where we hide the wants we shouldn't have.

"If things were different, I'd more than *like* you."

My head shakes as I begin my rebuttal. "Nash, I—"

"You don't have to say anything. I already know. That's why I'm putting my hands in my pockets and walking away. I just wanted to say it out loud one time. I like you *so* much." His shoulders lift, and his next words come out on a laugh. "I guess I said it twice."

"I...I can't—"

"Goodnight, Sadie." In one goodbye, he ends our conversation and walks past me down the sidewalk, calling over his shoulder. "Have a good Thanksgiving."

I stand speechless, watching him walk away until I can't see the outline of his body any longer.

CHAPTER FOURTEEN

SADIE

STETSON CONVINCED me to stay the week at my parents' house instead of Autumn's. It's important to him that I patch things up with my family, but each day I'm here, I'm more and more annoyed at how my parents act like Tate's just gone with friends, not buried six feet deep down at the town cemetery.

I want someone to cry, to show that they're struggling with him gone as much as I am, but they're all smiles in Skaneateles, and it's driving me crazy. Even Stetson is oblivious to my pain. The only time we've talked about how hard this week is was when I brought it up. I want him to care, to look across the room at me, see the sadness on my face and offer a kind smile, or at night, after all the turkey has been eaten, pull me into his lap and let me cry on his chest. Instead, I've been waiting until I'm alone and crying into my pillow.

Tears prick my eyes. It's such a contrast to the carefree conversation happening around the dinner table right now between Stetson and my parents.

"When I graduate from law school this spring"—Stetson places his hand on top of mine, barely glancing my direction, not long enough to see my emotion—"I'm going to take Sadie somewhere special to celebrate."

"Maybe the trip could double as a honeymoon," my mom squeals in delight. "I'm still waiting for you two to set a wedding date."

His fingers squeeze mine as he smiles at my mom. "No need to rush things. We've been together this long. We can wait and have the wedding when our ducks are in a row, and I'm graduated. Maybe next fall is a good time."

"You could have the wedding here on the lake if you do it in the summertime," my dad chimes in—ever the proud homeowner.

"Whatever you decide," my mom laughs, "I've already told Jay to prepare his wallet. Sadie has always wanted a big wedding."

"Sounds like she'll need to pull extra hours at the home health and hospice to help pay for it."

Everyone laughs at my dad's joke except me.

Lines deepen across my forehead as my brows lower. "I want to go to Switzerland."

"What?" Stetson asks through his chuckles.

Slowly, my face turns to his. "I want to go to Switzerland. Maybe for our honeymoon or maybe for Christmas next year."

He looks nervously at my parents and then back to me. "You know I can't fly."

"No, you *could* fly; you're just scared of it, but you could do it for me because I love to travel, and you love me."

"You think you love to travel," my dad puffs. "Just wait until you get in a three-hour customs line. You'll change your tune."

"No, I won't." My glare snaps to my dad but finds its way back to Stetson. "I want to see the world."

"Sorry, babe, but you'll have to see the world with Autumn, or you could plan a trip with your parents during a busy time for me. We've made it this far in life without traveling the world. I'm sure we can make it the next fifty years." He squeezes my hand again then lets go, returning to his own space and the easy conversation before I interrupted with hard questions about my wants and needs.

"I need to go to the bathroom." I scoot my chair back and walk away as more wedding discussions happen behind me.

My feet carry me to Tate's room. I hesitate outside, not sure I can handle the emotional agony that's sure to accompany a walk down memory lane, but I push the door open anyway. Belongings are scattered across his dresser and bed as if he'd quickly packed as much as he could when my dad kicked him out. I shed a tear for the haphazard version of Tate that was strung out on pain meds. Different from the straight-A athlete I grew up with who always had a clean room and a smile.

In a lot of ways, I wish we could reverse the clock and go back to the time before all the bad happened. When everything in life was easier. When my parents were the people I respected most in the world. When Tate had a scholarship to play football. When Stetson was the man of my dreams.

I was happy then, naively thinking I was headed in the right direction. But one day, eight months ago, I woke up and realized my life had no real progression forward, almost like I'd already reached my destination. Every decision had already been made. I was standing water. No movement. No current taking me to new and exciting places. I woke up in the middle of the night in sheer panic, thinking, 'Is this it? Is this all my life is?' It scared me, suffocating me to the point that I had to look elsewhere for air. Then, one day, my professor told me about the internship in Chicago. It was the breath of fresh air I so desperately needed. I didn't care who told me not to go or what a big mistake I was making.

I didn't want to be stagnant anymore.

Chicago breathed life into me in ways I didn't even know were possible. But slowly, I feel myself being pulled back into the standing water my life in Skaneateles offers.

I sink down on the edge of Tate's mattress, a wave of depression striking me as I glance around.

If I marry Stetson, this is all life is.

A folded brown paper on Tate's nightstand steals my attention. There's just enough writing visible under the pile of gum, Chapstick, and papers for me to know exactly what it is.

I brush everything aside, freeing it. My lips curl into a smile as I read the note from the Cubs game that Tate had saved just in case.

Bro, I'd love to take out your sister. If she's lying about having a boyfriend and you don't think I'm crazy, please give her my number.

I run my fingers along Nash's phone number, tracing the lines of his handwriting.

Life with Nash wouldn't be stagnant. It would be a raging river. A life where I'd feel confident in my capabilities and adored for who I am.

He said earlier this week that he'd more than like me if things were different, and deep down, I know I'd more than like him too. My feelings might already be there. I just haven't dared admit it.

Flutters of hope fill my chest, an anticipation that true

happiness is within reach. But with that feeling comes a deep sadness and despair.

I'd be gaining the world but giving up everything.

A new life with Nash would cost me my old one.

CHAPTER FIFTEEN

NASH

"OUR FIRST LOCUM tenens will be ready to rock and roll on January one. Good work, everyone. I think we can call it a day." I press my palms into my eyes, trying to rub away the blurriness staring at a computer screen has caused.

My employees laugh and chat as they clean up their stuff and tuck in their chairs around the conference table. I hated keeping everyone here past our regular work hours, especially the first week of December, but it's better to work hard now then ease up the closer we get to Christmas.

"See you later, Sadie," Harper calls as Sadie walks out the door.

"Bye." She smiles over her shoulder, stopping her gaze on me before turning to go.

I've done everything I could today to avoid contact with her. It's partly out of embarrassment for having a lapse of judgment at the party last week and telling her that I like her. What am I, five? And the other part is out of a broken heart. Her internship ends in three weeks, and watching her return to Skaneateles for Thanksgiving put it all into perspective.

She's leaving...for good.

The ache that realization brings is beyond anything I've ever felt.

Lindy says I shouldn't give up, that I should fight for Sadie until she's mine.

But I've been doing that since day one at the Cubs game. The last six months feel like a boxing match. In some rounds, I didn't fight as aggressively because I was trying to be the perfect boss, and then in other rounds, I went for the knockout, shamelessly flirting with her even when I knew I shouldn't.

Either way, it's the last round of the fight, and I'm throwing in the towel, accepting my loss. For the first time ever, my intuition was wrong. Sadie isn't the love of my life— the one person I'll spend forever with.

I just really thought she was.

"I feel bad that she called off her engagement," I hear Josie say to Harper, and suddenly, I'm inserting myself into their conversation.

"I know! I was so surprised."

"Wait." I step between them, desperate for information. "Who called off their engagement?"

"Sadie did when she went home this weekend," Josie says. "Didn't you notice the ring was gone?"

I grab Josie's shoulders, stopping short of shaking her for the information. "You're sure she's no longer engaged?"

Harper leans in with a knowing smile. "She didn't just call off the engagement. She broke up with Stetson for good."

The biggest bomb of excitement explodes inside my chest. My eyes skitter around the room, looking for encouragement.

"Now's your chance, boss," Reggie says.

"You know you want to," Allen chimes in.

Harper bounces up and down on her toes. "Oh, come on.

Everyone knows you're madly in love with her. She probably called off the engagement because she feels the same about you."

"You think?"

"Yes!" Josie pushes me toward the door.

Really, I didn't need any encouragement. I was going to go after Sadie no matter what. I was just letting my head catch up to my heart.

I run to the elevator and push the button four times too many until the door slides open. Once inside, my phone vibrates in my pocket, and I pull it out as the elevator jerks downward.

SADIE

> Hey, it's the girl from the Cubs game. I'd love to go out with you sometime. Especially since I don't think you're crazy, and I no longer have a boyfriend.

I laugh as I read the text, knowing from this moment on, my life will never be the same.

SADIE

I DIDN'T TELL Nash at work today about my broken engagement. There's no good way to frame something like that during office hours. 'Hey, Nash, hand me the Mountain West Hospital file, and oh, by the way, I broke up with my fiancé.'

It just doesn't come off the tongue well.

That's why I texted him from the parking garage as I walked to my car.

The door opens behind me, and Nash calls, "Sadie!"

I spin, seeing him jog to me with a huge smile on his lips. That was fast. I literally sent the text four seconds ago.

"Where are you going?" His words come out breathless.

A little V forms between my brows as they furrow together. "To my apartment."

His eyes drop to my ring finger for confirmation then flick back to my face. "You called off your engagement?"

"Yeah."

He steps closer, a languid smile on his mouth. "That's the best news I've heard in the past five months."

That small step does the sweetest things to my heart. "Just the past five months? Not in your whole life?"

"Probably in my whole life. I've just waited five months for you to be fully available."

"Am I *fully* available?" I tease. "I mean, I'm still your intern, and you're still my boss."

"Only for three more weeks." Another step closer. "But do you really expect me to wait even one more day before I make you mine?" And another step until he's standing right in front of me. "It shouldn't be a surprise."

"True." I gaze into his glimmering green eyes. "You did say you liked me."

"I said I liked you *so* much. Don't short me that extra *so*—it conveys a lot." Playful charm rounds out his smile. "And now things are different."

"And now things are different," I say, feeling butterflies take off in my stomach.

"Now I can tell you I don't *just* like you so much. I've fallen head over heels in love with you, and I think you've fallen for me too."

I've fallen for Nash so hard I'm like a teenager who belly-flops onto her bed, calls him on an old-fashioned landline, and twirls the phone cord while we talk. Everything is wrapped up in him.

I smile. "Well, I did just text you and ask you out, so..."

Nash's hand lifts, gently combing through a few strands of my hair, fingers skimming over my cheek as they glide down. It's the simplest of touches, yet it feels monumental, like the beginning of thousands of gentle touches to come.

"So, you love me too?" he asks.

"I love you too."

Without questioning myself, I rise to my tippy toes, brushing my mouth over his. A warm sensation floods my body but centers around where our lips slowly skim, graze, and move together. Three seconds in and this kiss is already better than every single one I've shared with Stetson.

Nash's fingers shift from my hair, softly cupping my cheek as his other hand wraps around my waist, bringing my body to his. Bodies flush against each other, the kiss deepens, taking the warm sensation inside me to a raging inferno. My hand goes to the back of his neck, digging fingers through the curls at his nape. The silky texture is way better than all the daydreams my mind conjured up.

Five months of forbidden passion drives this kiss forward.

Every smile.

Every longing glance.

Every forbidden touch.

Every flirtatious comment.

Every heartache of not being able to be together has built to this moment.

Nash is an exceptional kisser, just like I knew he would be. All his cockiness, charisma, charm, and playfulness combine in each tug and pull of his lips. The way his hands roam my neck, hair, back, hips, and waist in perfect precision leaves each inch of my body tingling from the warmth of his masculine touch.

Unlike all the ordinary kisses I've had, his kiss is explosive, opening my eyes to something more. It's bright colors splashed on a stark-white canvas. It's a black-and-white TV showing colorful hues for the first time.

And I know.

I want this unexpected excitement for the rest of my life.

"Phwoooooh-phwwwwwhhht!" Someone whistles behind us, breaking our kiss apart.

It's Victor and Allen.

"Way to get the girl."

I bury my face into Nash's shoulder, a little embarrassed to be caught kissing the boss, but judging by their cheers and claps, they approve.

Nash wraps his arm around my shoulder, escorting me to his car. "Come on, let's get out of here."

I smile up at him. "Where are we going?"

"You said in your text that you wanted to go out with me."

"I didn't mean tonight. Just some time in the future."

Nash leans down, pressing a kiss to the side of my head. "Sadie, you are my future, and I'm tired of waiting for it to start."

CHAPTER SIXTEEN

NASH

FLAMES pop and crackle in front of us, filling the cabin with a woodsy smell. Combine the fire's ambiance with the lit Christmas tree in the corner, and you have the perfect romantic setting for Christmas Eve.

Sadie sits between my legs, gladly letting me massage her shoulders and back after a long day of skiing in Park City, Utah.

"Do you wish you were spending Christmas with your family instead of skiing with me?"

"No." She gently shakes her limp head, probably trying to avoid interfering with her massage. "This is exactly where I want to be and who I want to be with."

I lean forward, kissing the top of her spine, then let my lips travel down her neck. Her contented sighs encourage me to keep going. I tug on the sleeve of her sweater, giving me more space to trail my kisses down her shoulder until I run into unmovable fabric I can't get around.

"But"—I straighten, continuing her shoulder rub—"have you called your parents yet to wish them a merry Christmas?"

I feel her body tense under my fingers.

"I texted them."

"Why not a call?"

"Because if I call them, I'll have to hear how Stetson is so brokenhearted. And how you manipulated me and brainwashed me into staying in Chicago with you, how my dad can't retire now because there's no one to take over his company, how I'm making Tate's death worse because now they've lost two children. Basically, a phone call would be about how my life choices have ruined everything, and I prefer not to have that fight on Christmas Eve."

"Understandable." I lean in again, dropping a quick kiss on her cheek. "I just want to make sure you're trying to mend things with your parents."

"Why?" She turns her head to the side, peeking back at me. "They were awful to me when I told them I was in love with you."

"My reasoning for you to mend things has nothing to do with you. I can't stand that your parents hate me so much," I joke in an effort to keep the mood light. "Nobody hates me. I'm the type of guy that's welcome at every party."

"Trust me," she chuckles, "the Bradley family party is one place you might never be welcomed at."

"What if I were your husband?" My hands slow. "Would they welcome me then?"

"Hah! They'd be furious at first."

"Why?" I can't help my frown.

"Because we've only dated one month."

"But we've known each other for six months."

"That wouldn't matter to them. They'd think it was more of the same—you manipulating me."

"But if I were your husband, they'd eventually have to get

over their deep hatred of the big bad boss from Chicago who stole their daughter from them. Wouldn't they?"

She shrugs indifferently. "Maybe eventually."

"Then let's get married."

"Just so my parents will like you?" She glances back with an amused smile. "I was kind of hoping the man I marry is in it for me...just a little bit."

"I could sweeten the deal. Fly you to Moorea, Tahiti."

"Hmmm," she says with a sigh. "I've always wanted to go there."

"We could have a ceremony on the beach. Next month. Just the two of us."

"Next month!" she exclaims. "If you're marrying me to get my parents to like you, a fast elopement isn't the way to their hearts."

"What's the way to your heart?"

She softly laughs. "Nash Carter, we both know you already have my heart in a chokehold."

"Then what if getting married had nothing to do with your parents and everything to do with how I feel about you? How we are together."

She twists her body to see me better but doesn't say anything.

Under the glow of firelight, she looks incredible. At this moment, I couldn't love Sadie more.

"What if I've known since the first moment I saw you that you were the person I wanted to spend my life with?" I brush a stray lock of hair away from her face. "What if I want to spend my days having an unpredictable adventure with you for as long as we both shall live and beyond?"

Glossiness coats her eyes, reflecting the dancing flames.

I slowly reach into my sock, where a ring hides, and pull

it out—no velvety box, just a simple diamond that acts as a token of my love for her.

Sadie gasps, covering her mouth with her hand.

My brows lift in what I hope is a charming way. "Marry me? Because you want to. Not because it's expected of you. Or because that's been the plan for as long as you can remember." I tilt my body to hers, brushing her lips with a quick kiss. "Marry me because you love me and want to be with me forever."

Her hand drops, revealing the happiest smile she's ever given me. She moves to me, crawling into my lap, curling her body into mine.

The answer comes out in a short breath. "Yes!"

Her mouth covers my smile before I can say anything back.

Her kiss is raw and genuine—the kind of deep connection that can't be forced or faked.

Behind every glide of her lips, there's a promise of a lifetime together.

No matter what happens in the future.

PART TWO

Forgetting

CHAPTER SEVENTEEN

Present Day

SADIE

I'VE NEVER RELATED to Ebenezer Scrooge more than I do right now.

Not in the cold-hearted, miserly, I-hate-Christmas way, but in a is-this-real-or-am-I-dreaming sort of way.

I feel for the guy. It's tough sorting through your past and present choices and seeing how they've shaped the direction of your life.

Trust me. I know.

Like Scrooge, I thought this was just a dream—more accurately, a nightmare. Any minute, I would wake up, and everything would be back to normal, exactly how I remember it.

But it finally hit me this morning. This isn't a dream. It's really happening. I've conceded to what everyone's been trying to tell me.

I had an accident skiing.

I have a traumatic brain injury.

I was in a coma.

It's a lot to take in, like the kind of stuff that makes you want to breathe into a paper bag because you're hyperventilating.

But that's not even the kicker.

The kicker is I live in Chicago permanently, and I'm Mrs. Nash Carter—life events I don't remember happening.

See, that's where Scrooge has me beat. There's no ghost visiting me, showing me how I ended up married to my boss, who happens to be a complete stranger to me.

There are *a lot* of missing pieces.

Three and a half years' worth, to be exact.

I stand in front of the bathroom mirror, searching my soul for the answers, for some kind of spark of a memory. It sounds deep, but really, I'm just staring at the unrecognizable reflection of myself.

I take inventory of the woman before me:

Pale skin, making my usually unnoticeable freckles stand out.

Gaunt cheeks—courtesy of the ten to fifteen pounds lost while in the hospital.

Overgrown eyebrows in need of a good tweeze.

A jagged scar that starts at the middle of my forehead and continues up my scalp past my hairline.

Older features.

I could blame this version of myself on the horrific fluorescent lighting in the hospital, but it would be a stretch.

Without warning, nausea rolls through my stomach, and I clutch the vanity for support.

"Sadie, you okay?" Annie peeks her head into the bathroom, smiling back at me. It's funny how time has changed my sister too. The Annie I remember—that I expect— should be finishing her junior year of high school, sitting at the kitchen table in her cheer uniform. But she's a grown woman now, studying accounting at Syracuse University.

It's hard to wrap my head around the passing of time when everything in my mind has stood still.

"I'm fine." I suck air through my nose. Drawing in a deep breath usually helps with the nausea.

"Let's get you back to bed. You've been standing a long time." Annie wraps an arm around my shoulders, leading me out of the bathroom. "These pajamas are cute." She nods toward the red seersucker set with pearl buttons and a collar.

They are cute. Very candy cane, Christmas-like.

I don't remember buying them, which shouldn't be a surprise considering the other valuable information I can't seem to recall.

"Thanks for bringing me clothes." *Clothes* is a loose description. I'm stocked with mostly pajamas and sweats. "The gaping hospital gowns were getting old."

"Don't thank me. Nash brought them."

Curiosity pulls my eyes to the open door. Nash stands just outside my room with my parents and Dr. Basu.

"He's barely left this place since the accident. I'm surprised he was willing to leave to get you some clothes."

I shrug her words away, glancing at the door again and the perfect view of my husband.

Husband.

The description feels wrong.

In my mind, Stetson Roeshine is my boyfriend. He's the one that my future self should be married to—not this Nash guy who I don't even know.

Talk about a life plan that went up in flames.

And I have no clue why or what led to it.

"At least Nash is a total babe." Annie glances into the hallway, sensing where my thoughts are. "You could've woken up from a coma married to an ugly guy with back hair thick as a fur coat."

"I don't remember what Nash's back looks like, so the verdict is still out on the fur coat."

Annie's eyes drop up and down his body in an appraising way. "Nah, he's too good-looking for a home-grown Minky Couture blanket covering his skin."

Is Nash good-looking?

I suppose I can admit that. Maybe even pat myself on the back for marrying such an attractive man.

He's dressed casually in jeans and a long-sleeve gray henley, a classic design with a modern, slim-fit cut that rewards his efforts in the gym—I'm assuming he goes to the gym. Muscles like that don't come from nothing. He combs both hands through his sandy-blond hair, interlocking his fingers at the nape of his neck as he listens to my dad talk.

It's the first time I've allowed myself to really study him since I woke up from my coma a few days ago. Avoiding him is part of not accepting this as my real life, and since my parents are enablers, it's been easy to pretend he doesn't exist.

Right on cue, Nash turns his head toward me, making eye contact. His lips lift into a sad smile—not that I have any clue about his different types of smiles, but it doesn't take a fully functioning brain to see he's having a hard time with all of this. Bloodshot eyes and overgrown stubble are the first clues.

I quickly lean back into my pillows, breaking the line of sight.

"Don't you want to talk to him? You know, see if it triggers your memory?" Annie pulls at the damp towel wrapped around my hair, letting the wet strands fall to my shoulders.

"Can't you just tell me what I missed?"

She places the towel on the dresser next to my bed and picks up my brush, gently combing through my hair. "I would if I could, but you and Nash are a mystery none of us understand."

That's not a good sign.

"Are you sure he's my husband? Like, maybe he's lying to all of us."

"Why would he do that?"

"I don't know." My shoulders lift. "Maybe for money. He's blackmailing Dad."

Annie laughs. "From what I can see, you and Nash are doing just fine on your own. He doesn't need Dad's money."

"Well, there must be another reason he's lying about being my husband. Maybe we should do some digging around."

"You sound crazy."

"I mean it." I put my hand on her arm, pausing her brushes. "Has anyone investigated whether or not he's telling the truth? Like that movie"—I snap my fingers, trying to recall the one I'm talking about—"you know, the one where she falls off the yacht and loses her memory, but he hates her, so he pretends like she's his wife."

"*Overboard?*"

"Yes! Maybe Nash is *Overboard*-ing me."

"I hate to break it to you, but you are, in fact, married to Nash Carter. I've seen the wedding pictures."

"Pictures?" The drop of my brows matches my frown. "Weren't you at the wedding?"

She stops combing, sitting down on the edge of my bed. "No one was there. You eloped."

What in the bizzaro world is happening? I would never elope.

For as long as I can remember—which I suppose doesn't

hold much weight at the moment—I've always wanted a big wedding. Everyone knows that.

"Why would I elope?"

"That's what Mom, Dad, and everyone back in Skaneateles tried to figure out."

"Didn't I tell you my reason?"

"Not really. Everything happened so fast. One minute, you were engaged to Stetson, planning a wedding, and—"

"Wait." I sit up taller. "Stetson proposed?" The thought sends my heart into a frenzy. "We were engaged?"

"Easy." Annie pats my shoulder, taming my excitement. "You were engaged for, like, a month before you called it off. Stetson and his family were devastated. We all were."

Oh my gosh. I hadn't even thought about Stetson's family or his mom. Rebecca Roeshine probably hates me for what I did to her son. *I hate me.*

And what's worse, my mind and my heart still love Stetson. I want to ask where he's at right now. Is he married? Single? Still pining for me? Am I a horrible person if I ask that? Want that?

I shake my head, refusing to believe this narrative I'm being told. "I wouldn't just drop Stetson without a good reason. We've been together since third grade. Our families are best friends. We've spent every summer and Christmas holiday together since I was little."

"But you did." Annie shrugs. "You dropped all of us. We haven't really seen you the last three years."

My mom said something similar yesterday when I asked where Tate was. She got teary-eyed and said Tate couldn't be here, but then she changed the subject by saying it had been a long time since I'd been home—another piece to the puzzle that didn't fit. I love my family. I'd never go *years* without visiting them.

"It's like I'm a different person and lived a completely different life. Nothing turned out how I thought it would." Moisture blurs my vision. "There has to be an explanation for it."

Annie squeezes my fingers. "Maybe it's time you start asking Nash these questions."

My eyes flick to the door and the one man who holds the answers.

But he's also the person I don't want to talk to.

CHAPTER EIGHTEEN

NASH

THE KEY to getting ready in your wife's hospital bathroom without her knowing is shaving in the shower. My tiny hairs get washed down the drain like I was never here.

Technically, in Sadie's mind, I never *was* here. I'm just some stranger.

My heart drops into my chest, but I decide not to dwell on the hurt.

I mean, I have.

I've cried.

No, I take that back. I've *sobbed* plenty of times over the last few days.

Always on my own and always in dark places.

But you can only wallow in despair for so many hours a day. Sometimes you have to focus on basic needs like shaving. So I leave the my-wife-doesn't-remember-me thoughts behind and run my razor over the last corner of my cheek. A small mirror hangs from the spout, showing enough of my clean-shaven face that I'm satisfied with my work.

Sadie will be back from physical therapy in less than ten minutes. I need to clean up the bathroom, get dressed, and be out of here before she arrives. She barely makes eye contact with me right now. I doubt she'd be comfortable knowing I use her bathroom to avoid the forty-minute commute back and forth between our house and the hospital.

Water droplets trickle into my eyes, so I wipe my hands down my face before opening the curtain to grab the towel. My gaze scans the small bathroom, looking for Sadie's towel, but it's not here. The options are a tiny washcloth draped over the sink or Sadie's silky pink robe. Neither are ideal.

I dry my body with the washcloth then reach for her robe, fighting to get my arms through the sleeves. When I bought the silky item for her on Valentine's Day, I pictured something more romantic than a grown man squeezing into it. I look like Cousin Eddie from *Christmas Vacation* with the robe ending upper thigh. All I need is a trapper hat with earflaps to complete the look. But it's fine. I just need to cover myself long enough to grab my clothes out of my bag. I would've brought them into the bathroom with me, but the room is so tiny, and the shower curtain only partially does its job. I didn't want to chance everything getting wet. Nobody likes damp underwear; it's a universal discomfort.

When I'm confident everything is quiet, I push the bathroom door open and dart my eyes around the room, making sure the coast is clear before I move. Thankfully, I had the forward thought to shut the hospital room door. I dash to my bag on the counter and quickly rummage through the few things I packed until I find some briefs.

I bend over, lifting one leg to put them on just as the door opens, spilling light and noise from the hallway into the room. My head jerks over my shoulder. Sadie stands frozen in wide-eyed shock. Forget about the pink silk draped over me. I have enough wits to know my hunched-over position isn't my best angle. The lower half of my bare butt hangs out the back of my robe. One month ago, my position might have been considered a form of foreplay, but judging by Sadie's repulsed expression, that's not the case today.

"What are you doing?" she shrieks, covering her eyes with the palm of her hand—not the kind of reaction I'm used to with her. I wish she'd shut the door since every nurse at the nurse's station is now craning to see what's happening.

"This...isn't..." I hop on one foot while trying to get the other through the leg of my briefs, but my big toe gets stuck on the waistband. The more I force it, the more tangled I become until I lose my balance. Panic surges as I reach for the hospital tray table, but instead of breaking my fall, it rolls back—I've never hated wheels more. Arms flail as I look for anything to grab ahold of, but my fate is sealed. I crash to the ground, landing on my stomach, taking down everything on the tray table with me.

Once all the clanging and banging stops, an audible gasp tells me Sadie is no longer shielding her eyes.

"You can see my butt, can't you?" I grunt.

"Um..." She clears her throat, confirming what I already know. I feel a draft and the bunched-up robe on my lower back. Earlier wasn't a bad angle. *This* is a bad angle. It's a full moon tonight in more ways than one.

"It's okay." I recognize Nurse Peggy's voice—so glad she could join us. "We're all professionals here. You've seen one; you've seen them all. Let's get you on your feet." Peggy is suddenly by my side, reaching for my arm.

"No!" I wave her away. "I got it!" I'm thinking of the front of the robe and how, at this point, it's not covering my man parts. "Maybe you guys could wait outside while I get dressed."

"Are you sure you're okay?" Peggy asks, retreating.

"Yep. Only my pride is hurt."

Peggy laughs. "We'll give you some privacy." But as she closes the door, I hear her tell Sadie, "You're a lucky woman. That's one cute butt your husband has."

"I thought you said, 'You've seen one; you've seen them all.'"

"I was lying." Then the door snaps shut.

I press my forehead against the cold linoleum, shutting my eyes as two thoughts run through my mind.

1. I should've done more squats to prepare for this moment.
2. This is not how I wanted to be reintroduced to my wife.

SADIE

MY SHOULDER blades press into the wall as I wait outside my hospital room.

Plot twist: I married a crossdresser.

It should be shocking, but at this point, nothing surprises me. It's a new version of Hell each day.

The door swings open, and a fully dressed Nash stares back at me with a humorous tint to his smile. "You're free to come in. No more indecent exposures. I promise."

"Too bad I can't erase the first one from my mind." I walk past him into my room. For one second, I'm immersed in the sweet smell of his aftershave, causing my senses to perk like they just got a shot of vitamin C.

"I would apologize, but it's not like you haven't seen it before."

I regret glancing back at him—his smile is far too suggestive.

"Oh, so it's typical of you to prance around in my clothes?" I crawl into my bed, situating my legs under the covers. "No wonder I blocked out our relationship." There are hints of joking in my voice alongside the clipped bitterness.

"In all fairness, I wasn't prancing." He pushes the door closed. My eyes follow until it clicks shut.

Ugh. He's staying.

"There weren't any towels in the bathroom, and I didn't want to be completely naked in case you came in unexpectedly."

"Which I did." I watch as he walks to his bag of clothes and begins packing things up.

"Unfortunate timing. Or was it?" He throws me another impish smile.

I suck in a sharp breath, feeling my annoyance build. "What are you doing in my room anyway?"

"I just needed a quick shower, and I didn't want to drive home when there's one right here."

I guess I can share my shower. After all, I'm married to the man.

He finishes with his bag and walks toward me. With each step, my heart tenses until I realize he's just picking up the stuff that fell onto the ground during his face plant.

"How did your physical therapy go?"

I guess we're making small talk.

"Great." I fake a smile to offset my sarcasm. "I got a gold star for passing off my fine motor skills. You'll be happy to hear I can feed myself."

"Oh, good." He blows out an exaggerated breath. "Your ability to hold a spoon is my top concern right now."

I don't like the glimmer in his eyes, so I turn my head, looking longingly at the door for someone to come save me, but my family has already left for their hotel, and my nurse won't come in again until the shift change.

So it's just me and Nash.

Nash and me.

"You want me to leave, don't you?"

I whip my head to him, feigning innocence. "No, I'm just tired. That's all."

"You're lying." He laughs good-naturedly, which is a better response than him being offended. "But it's okay. I'll go." He grabs the remote attached to the bed and dims the lights before putting it in my reach, then he pulls the blankets, spreading them over my body. I watch each kind gesture in silence, feeling my guilt grow. "I'll go get you more ice." He shakes my water bottle as he heads for the door.

I'm pushing him away. I know it's unfair, but it's how I protect myself. My mind drifts to Annie and all the answers she couldn't give me. I'm not sure I want the answers to my questions, but when Nash walks back into the room, I decide to try.

"I can't figure out why I married you." I didn't mean for my words to be so tactless. I quickly try to soften them. "I mean—"

"It's fine." Nash gives me another one of his easy laughs. "I've wondered that same thing for years. You're way out of my league."

Hardly. He's attractive, and by the look of his clothes, shoes, and day bag, he's wealthy, or successful, or both.

He sets the water bottle on my tray table. "Do you want the real answer of why you married me, or were you just thinking out loud?"

"It's hard to figure out how I went from being with Stetson to being married to you."

The corner of his mouth lifts. "Disappointing, huh?"

I roll my lips together. "I didn't mean it that way."

Nash slowly drops to the edge of my mattress, leaning his back against the footrail of the bed. He kicks one leg up, mirroring my position from the opposite end. I might've been uncomfortable with his nearness, but he's so calm and casual that I don't feel too anxious about it.

He cocks one brow. "After everything you've seen of me tonight, isn't it obvious why you fell for me?"

Is he implying I was shallow enough to fall for his body—more specifically, his tight butt and thighs? I blink back at him, unsure how to respond, because, at this point, falling for his good looks seems more plausible than falling for his personality.

"I'm obviously talking about my charm and wit." Judging by the gleam in his eyes, he was *not* talking about those things.

Was he this flirtatious when he was my boss? I'm one step away from calling Human Resources and slapping him with a sexual harassment complaint—if his place of employment even has an HR department.

"I'm just not convinced that we're actually married."

"Really?" He crosses his arms, leaning back even more, as if enjoying himself. "So the wedding, marriage certificate, and the joint apartment…none of that is real?"

"All of that can be real, but the marriage is fake."

"And why would we need a fake marriage?"

"Maybe you're blackmailing me. You found out something about me that I didn't want people to know, and now you're forcing me into this marriage."

I'm grasping at straws. We both know it.

Nash does his best to hold back his smile, but he's not fooling anyone. "So what is this big thing I'm holding over you?"

"I don't know. I can't remember."

He nods a few times as if he's thinking through everything I just said. "Or is it more likely that you moved to Chicago because you were bored with your bland life and bland relationship? Once you got here, your boss—that's me, by the way"—he says it like a sidenote—"charmed the socks off of you until you couldn't resist falling head over heels for him."

"No, that doesn't seem likely. I loved Stetson. Why would I leave him for you?"

The first sign of hurt dots his eyes, and I feel terrible for putting it there.

"I...uh..." My gaze drops as I scratch the back of my head. "Sorry, that came out worse than I intended."

"Listen, I know it's easier to focus on what you remember than what you don't. I get why you're hung up on pushing me away, but there's so much more to our relationship and life than those first details of how we got together. I hoped you'd want to know about the other stuff—the things that made us great together, the life we've built."

That's the stuff I'm not ready to hear.

"I can't handle everything right now. I just need a little crumb of information about how we came to be."

"A crumb of information? Okay, I can give you that." He stares back at me, and I try to find myself in his green eyes, but nothing's there. "So, back to the beginning. You applied for my internship in Chicago, and I thought you were pretty amazing, so I hired you. My gut has never been wrong."

I remember Professor Takimori mentioning an internship

in Chicago that I should apply for, but that's where my memory ends.

"So I got the internship, moved to Chicago, immediately fell in love with you, and broke up with Stetson?"

His lips press into a small smile. "It was a little more involved than that."

"I would hope so."

"Falling for you were some of the best times of my life. I'll tell you every little detail if you want." He holds my gaze, and I panic, knowing his mind replays scenes from our love story I don't remember. It's like an inside joke I'm not privy to.

I break his stare and force a yawn, hoping he catches the drift.

"No, it's okay. That's probably a big enough crumb for tonight."

"You better get some rest." He stands, thankfully taking my hint.

I nod, feeling tired now that he said something about it.

Nash slings his bag over his shoulder and walks to the door. He stops, reaching into the front zipper pocket. "I have your phone. I can keep it safe for you if it's too overwhelming right now, or maybe it will help you see that there's nothing fake about our marriage."

He extends the device out, waiting for me to answer.

"I guess a little proof might help things."

"It actually doesn't have all three years on it." He takes a step forward to place it on my tray table. "You dropped your old phone in a pool and hadn't backed things up for a while, but I think there's six or seven months of stuff on there to look through."

"That should be enough for me to decide if we're really in love," I joke.

"I promise you." His lips lift. "We're really in love."

Then why don't I feel it?

He turns, and I watch as he opens the door.

"Where do you sleep?" I blurt, not sure why I care.

"If you need me, I'll be right outside. Just like always." His smile is the last thing I see before he shuts the door.

I can't understand the comfort I feel from having Nash close by. It's confusing and unjustified. But I don't want to be alone.

Tears threaten to fall. I glance at my phone as a way to thwart them.

Not tonight.

My head is already spinning.

I can't take any more crumbs—big or small.

CHAPTER NINETEEN

NASH

FOR THE FIRST time in days, I feel hopeful.

Yes, Sadie still doesn't remember me.

Yes, I'm living in a hospital waiting room.

But we talked last night.

I cannot tell you how good it felt to spend some alone time with her. My ability to cope with this whole situation was running threadbare, but that conversation with Sadie breathed new life into me. Even if she's skeptical of us, it's a start, and I'll gladly take it.

I drag my eyes back to my laptop, trying to refocus and get some stuff done.

I've been working remotely since the accident. It's not ideal, but nobody questions it when you're the boss. Really, no one at work would give me crap for being at the hospital for Sadie. They care about her. For the last three years, she's been running Superior Health alongside me, taking us to the next level. She's one of us, whether she remembers it or not.

"One lukewarm coffee."

I turn my head just as Lindy sits in the chair next to mine.

She extends the white paper cup toward me, courtesy of the hospital cafeteria.

"Thanks." I take a slow sip. Maybe if I concentrate enough, I can pretend it came from Starbucks.

"Is Annie still in with Sadie?"

"Yeah, I think she's helping her shave or wax or something."

Lindy leans back into her chair, staring straight ahead. "You were supposed to leave on your trip today."

"I know."

Christmas in Switzerland—see the flying Santa at Noël Montreux, ride on the Glacier Express, sleep in a chalet in Zermatt, visit the Christmas markets, and go skiing at Lake Oeschinen. A month-long trip of a lifetime that we were finally going on. It's hard not to feel depressed about where we're at instead.

"At least Sadie doesn't remember her magical Swiss Christmas and therefore can't feel bad about missing it." A goofy smile covers her mouth.

Same old Lindy. Always looking on the bright side. I remember when my mom left, and Nolan and I moved in with Lindy's family. I was eleven and didn't see any good in my mother ditching me and my brother for her career. But Lindy kept saying how great it was because she'd always wanted older brothers. Her positivity eventually rubbed off on me in that situation. I hope it does the same here.

Lindy is hurting too. Sadie is the sister she never had, and right now, she doesn't even know Lindy exists. But Lindy's handling it with a smile, supporting me where she can, patiently waiting her turn to talk to Sadie.

She twists her blonde hair and drops it over one shoulder. "Where are Sadie's parents?"

I look down the hall. "I think they went for a walk around the hospital to get some exercise." At least, that's what I heard Lynette suggest to Jay. They don't typically keep me in the loop with their plans.

Tense is a good way to describe my relationship with the Bradleys. I don't recommend meeting your in-laws for only the second time when your wife is in a coma. It adds another layer to the strain that was already there.

Perception is reality, and the Bradleys perceive me as the enemy who stole their daughter from them—a tough prejudice to overcome.

"Do you think Sadie will ever go skiing again?" Lindy's question and tone are innocent enough, but a heaviness constricts my chest.

I'll never forget watching Sadie get cut off on the slope and lose control. Her body flung through the air like a rag doll until she slammed head-first into a tree. My whole world flatlined at that moment. It was like my pulse stopped right alongside hers.

"Sorry." Lindy studies my pained expression. "That was an insensitive question."

"No, don't worry about it. It wasn't insensitive, just a little too soon."

"I never think before I talk."

I nudge her shoulder. "It's one of the reasons I hang out with you. Your entertainment value is through the roof."

"That sounds like you only hang out with me because you like watching me stick my foot in my mouth."

I smile back at her. "You offer a little more value than that."

"Har har." She pushes my shoulder.

"Lindy, how kind of you to stop by the hospital again,"

Lynette says as she sinks into the chair across from us. "It's good to see you."

"Thanks, Mrs. Bradley."

"Lynette. We've been through enough to be on a first-name basis."

"I just came to check on Nash." Lindy scrunches her nose up to me. "Make sure he's eating."

"It's good he has you." Jay grunts as he sits.

"Well, now that you're fed"—Lindy hops to her feet—"I better get going. Call me if anything exciting happens." She waves at the Bradleys before taking off down the hall.

Without Lindy's carefree personality here to ease the tension, silence ensues.

Lynette's eyes drift to her husband like some kind of signal for him to start. He clears his throat, catching on to her hint.

Jay leans forward, diving into his speech. "Since Sadie will be discharged this weekend, we—"

"Wait, who told you she was getting released?"

"Dr. Basu."

I fight the negative thoughts, hating that Dr. Basu gave the Bradleys the good news before me. I'm glad her parents are here for their daughter, but I'm the one who should hear important information first.

It's like when Sadie and her parents decided without me that she'd go home to Skaneateles to spend Christmas there this year. I wasn't even part of that conversation.

But it's fine.

Sadie's alive and awake and going home. That's all that matters.

Three weeks ago, I would've given anything to hear that she was well enough to leave the hospital. I prayed every day, and I'm not even the praying type. I promised God *everything* if He would just let her get through this. I guess I can never lie, swear, or sin again now that she's awake and being released—we'll see how long that lasts.

Because of all that, I drop that I'm the last to know about her discharge and let Jay continue.

"Anyway, I made some arrangements for a physical therapist to come in a few days a week."

I expected this conversation. Jay Bradley likes to be in control. It's one of the things Sadie struggles with about her dad. But I don't need to pick a fight over logistics. If Jay wants to make all the arrangements, I'm fine with that. He forgets that we're both in the healthcare industry and that I have my own contacts, but it's not a battle I need to fight— one less thing off my plate.

"That sounds great. Thanks for doing that."

He nods, pleased with how easily I gave in. "We also booked a flight Saturday night to Syracuse. Lynette will stop by your apartment Friday to pack some things for Sadie."

"Saturday night is too soon for a flight. If she's getting released that morning, she'll be tired and should rest."

Jay's expression gets defensive. "It's only a two-hour flight."

"Yeah, but there's driving to the airport and getting through security. I think one big activity a day is plenty for her right now. She can fly on Sunday."

"But we already canceled our hotel and are booked on the Saturday night flight," Lynette whines.

"You can rebook for Sunday."

She looks to her husband for help, and he gladly jumps in.

"Well, with Annie at the hotel too, we're on top of each other. Sadie won't be comfortable there."

"She's not going to the hotel. She'll sleep at our apartment with me."

This should be obvious to them. She's been living with me for the past three years.

"Well, we just prefer to fly home Saturday night, so you don't need to worry about playing host."

"I wouldn't be playing host. That's Sadie's home." I set my jaw, showing the Bradleys that I mean to stand my ground on this one. "Why don't you guys keep your flight on Saturday night? Sadie and I will fly in Sunday evening."

That statement causes Lynette's mouth to gape open and Jay's eyes to narrow.

"We assumed you weren't coming to Skaneateles," he says. "We don't need you to. She'll be well taken care of with us."

"I'm Sadie's husband. Naturally, I'd go where she goes."

Jay shakes his head. "But she doesn't even remember you."

Losing my cool in front of the nurse's station isn't a good look, so I draw in a deep breath, relaxing my clenched fists before I dare speak. "Right now, Sadie might not remember me or the last three and a half years of her life, but eventually, she will, and when she does, she'll be furious that you used her traumatic brain injury as a way to get close to her again."

"We all know you're the reason for the rift between us." Lynette's voice shakes with emotion. "It's your fault she—"

Jay places a calming hand on his wife's thigh, stopping her from saying her accusation out loud. "We don't want to fight with you, Nash. It's obvious that you care about our daughter. But I think we both know you're out of your depth here. You haven't even been spending time with her since she woke up."

"We talked last night. Had a great conversation." I leave out how skeptical she was of me. It's irrelevant to the conversation.

They glance at each other, surprised their daughter didn't mention our encounter.

"She's starting to ask questions and wants information about her life the past few years. I'm not going to lie to her. If she asks about Tate, I'll tell her the truth."

Jay's expression hardens. "Tate is none of your business. This is a private matter that needs to come from her family."

"*I'm* her family now." It's shocking how often they dismiss me as her husband. "I'm loyal to Sadie only."

"You *were* her family." Jay shrugs, his insolence apparent. "But now that she can't remember her life with you, there's no place for you in it."

"Don't you think that's up to Sadie to decide?"

"He's right," Lynette sighs. "Sadie is the one who needs to decide where Nash fits into everything. If we shut him out and she gets her memory back, we'll lose her all over again. And I can't face that. Not when we just barely got her back."

"Fine." Jay drops his patronizing tone. "But if she doesn't want you to come to Skaneateles, I won't force it. You'll have to abide by her wishes."

Not surprising at all.

"I'll agree to that." And because I don't want to be at odds with her parents, I offer a compromise. "And I'll also agree to let you guys tell her about Tate. But it needs to be sooner rather than later."

"We were going to wait until we were back home to tell her." Lynette bites her bottom lip, trying to hide her quiver. "I think it will be best if we break the news when she's in a familiar place."

"I can support that if you'll let me be the one to talk to her about coming to New York."

They both nod, and it's settled.

Except, deep down, I know convincing Sadie to let me come might be a lot harder than I'm letting on.

So, nothing about me is settled.

CHAPTER TWENTY

SADIE

"Do you remember anything about your accident?" Dr. Hatchet, a psychotherapist at the hospital, stares back at me with a pleasant smile. How she's pulled her chair around the desk, close to mine, is supposed to ease my anxiety. But with a title that includes the word *psycho*, it's not helping much.

I can't remember anything of the last three and a half years, so why would I remember the accident? And by the way, I hate how everyone calls it an accident. It was a crash. I crashed into a tree, going twenty-five miles per hour. And I used to think I was a good skier—so good I didn't wear a helmet.

Dr. Hatchet's question is stupid, but I humor her anyway. "No, I only know what people have told me."

She smiles warmly, using it as a choreographed pause before asking her next question. "And do you have any recollection of being in a coma?"

"No." What is she looking for? A near-death experience she can write about in her medical journal? If that's the case, she'll be disappointed. There's no recollection of a pillar of light.

"Are there any memories from the last few years that have popped into your mind?"

I shake my head as my answer.

"Nothing about your husband or your life in Chicago?"

"Nope."

"The brain is such an unknown organ, and each traumatic brain injury is different. It's hard to project how your recovery will go. This memory fog might last a few days or months, or it may always be like this. We just don't know." Dr. Hatchet smiles, even though nothing is reassuring about her words. "How does knowing that your memory may never come back make you feel?"

My eyes peek up at the clock behind her. We've already been talking for forty-five minutes. How much longer is this going to go on? I try to give her a thoughtful answer—because I forgot my memories, not my manners—and because Dr. Basu won't release me from the hospital tomorrow until I'm cleared by a therapist as well.

How do I feel about my memory never coming back?

"It's okay, I guess. It means losing almost four years off of my life, but I have to move forward as best as I can." I smile, showing stability in hopes that I'll pass this test with flying colors and be released.

Dr. Hatchet sits back, narrowing her eyes. "While I appreciate your positivity in a horrible situation, I'm not sure your answer is truthful."

I scratch my ear then fidget with the lobe, tugging it down nervously. "I don't know what you mean."

"You woke up from a coma, and everything is different. You live in a different city than you expected, you have a different job, and the biggest change is that you're married to a man you don't know. You have to have some feelings about that."

"Anger," I finally say.

She nods, encouraging me along. "Who are you angry with?"

I fold my arms, glancing away. I've never been great at expressing myself and telling people how I feel. Not even Stetson got the full scope of how I really felt. The vulnerability leaves your heart wide open for someone to pierce. I'd rather keep it hidden and protected, but staying silent now might not help me get discharged.

"It's okay to feel anger," she reassures.

"I'm angry at myself."

"Why?"

I clasp my fingers together in my lap as if it will help keep my emotions in check. "I don't like the choices I made or the life I was living."

"What don't you like about it?"

"For starters, I abandoned my family. I hurt the people I loved." Stetson's face runs through my mind. "None of this is what I wanted. I had a plan, and I'm angry with myself for deviating so far from that plan."

"How do you know that the deviations were bad? Maybe those choices were the best ones you could've made at the time and made you the happiest."

"I know myself, and I know they weren't. I probably wasn't even happy the last three and a half years. That could explain why I blocked it all out."

"Why are you assuming the worst about yourself?"

My brows drop as my defenses rise. "What do you mean?"

"Why are you assuming that you'd willingly choose a life that made you miserable?"

I glance down at my fingers, not liking how her words resonate.

"What if, instead, you choose to believe that the life you created for yourself, while not the one you pictured, ended up being more beautiful than anything you could've planned?"

Tears funnel into my eyes, and I wipe at them before they can trickle down my cheeks.

"Give the Sadie you don't remember the benefit of the doubt. Trust that she made the right decisions based on the information she had at the time. And then forgive her if she didn't."

Powerful words.

But easier said than done.

I WALK BACK to my room after my session with Dr. Hatchet, feeling emotionally drained. The mental side of this has been far more taxing than the physical. Each step toward recovery is difficult and laboring. It's like I have fifty miles to go, but the pathway is through thick mud and sludge, causing me to get stuck with each stride forward.

When I get to my room, my cell phone ringing steals my attention. I freeze, fearing who might be calling me, but my curiosity kicks in, and I lunge for the device, reading the name across the screen.

Edward Cullen—a nickname given to Autumn in seventh grade when we were both obsessed with *Twilight*.

I gasp, scrambling to answer.

"Autumn?" my voice cracks as I curl into a ball on my bed.

"Sades? I didn't think I would get to talk to you."

I immediately start crying, overcome with raw emotion. "Autumn!"

"Don't cry. Don't cry."

But I can hear in her voice that she's crying too.

Autumn Cassidy has been with me since kindergarten. She's my ride-or-die. Even a cross-country move so she could attend UCLA couldn't separate us. I remember being tight all the way up to losing my memory and hope I haven't pushed her away the last three years like I did with everybody else in my life.

Thirty seconds of unintelligible conversation go by as we try to calm ourselves.

Autumn is the first to be successful. "I was honestly just calling to get an update from Nash. He's been filling me in the past month."

"Wait." I wipe my tears on the bed sheets as I sit up. "You know Nash?"

"Of course I know Nash. I was there when you married him."

"But I thought I eloped."

"If you call a private wedding in Moorea, Tahiti eloping."

I've always dreamed about going to Moorea. I can't believe I actually made it happen and got married there. It's the first thing I've heard from the last three years that I actually like.

"So you were the only one at the wedding?"

"No, Lindy was there too."

"I don't know who Lindy is." My head drops into my hands. "Autumn, I can't remember anything after college graduation. I don't remember moving to Chicago, falling in love with Nash, or breaking up with Stetson. It doesn't feel like my life. Just some story about someone else that people keep telling me."

"I know." Her voice is solemn. "It's terrible, Sades."

"I just assumed I pushed you away too. Did I? Please tell me we're still friends."

"We're still close. I'm sorry I wasn't there when you woke up. I flew in right after the accident but had to go back to California for work. I work at SeaWorld."

"What!" My hand flies to my heart. "That's been your dream job since forever!"

"I know! You freaked out last year when it happened, but it's kind of fun celebrating it with you again. And"—she squeals a little—"Silas proposed to me over Thanksgiving!"

My mouth drops open. "I don't know who Silas is, but—"

"You do, and you love him!"

"So I approve?"

"Wholeheartedly."

"Then, congratulations!" Tears fill my eyes again. "I'm so happy for you."

"You'll meet Silas sometime."

"I can't wait."

"Now, this phone call is *not* about me. How are you holding up?"

"I think I'm still in shock just trying to process everything."

"I heard your family is there. How has that been?"

Why wouldn't they be here? I'm their daughter.

I shake the thought away and just keep talking. "It's been nice to have people around me I actually remember, but they keep saying I never went home to visit them the last few years. Why did I do that?"

"There's been some friction between you guys."

"Over what?"

"I don't want to get in the middle of it, but I know for sure they aren't the biggest fans of Nash."

"I'm not either," I grumble.

"Seriously?"

"He's a complete stranger."

"No, no, no. Nash is the absolute best. When it comes to incredible husbands, he's the poster child."

"So I take it you like him?"

"Oh, I'm so on the Nash train I'm driving it, or conducting, or whatever they say about trains. He *adores* you, and honestly, you adore him."

"I don't know." I rub my temple where my head hurts. "It just *feels* wrong. Stetson's the guy I adore." Autumn is the one person I can be honest with about this. "My heart still loves him. How does that happen if I've been with another man for the last three years?"

"Sheesh." Autumn blows out a heavy breath. "I don't know how that happens—complicated stuff. It's like the wires between your head and your heart got crossed up."

"You're telling me."

"Have you talked to Nash about it? Told him how you feel about Stetson?"

"No! I've barely talked to him at all."

"Why not? He's the sweetest."

"Because it's awkward. He's like a random guy you see on the street."

"And he's seen you naked."

I smile at Autumn's joke. "If that isn't awkward, I don't know what is."

"You once told me Nash Carter was the best thing that has ever happened to you, and I saw the proof of it. Don't you owe it to yourself to discover why you believed that?"

I rest my head in my hand and close my eyes, avoiding her question.

"Will you talk to him? Please? For me."

I suck in some air. "I'll try."

"What's the worst thing that could happen? You end up falling in love with him all over again?"

Exactly.

"Let's talk about something other than my screwed-up life, okay?" I pop my head up, infusing my voice with cheeriness. "Tell me all about Silas."

"Are you sure?"

"One thousand percent. Give me all the details since I don't know them anymore."

I lie back against my pillows and listen as Autumn starts from the beginning of their relationship. It's much easier to hear about her love life than mine.

For a few seconds, I feel normal again.

When the call ends, I look down at my phone in my hands and the lit-up screen full of apps.

Instagram's icon taunts me, and I click on it against my better judgment. Instead of scrolling through the feed, I go to my page. I see myself in the different pictures—arms around Nash, kissing him on the cheek, smiling as he hugs me—and although I know it's me, it feels like I'm looking at someone else. Like I'm looking at a lie.

I return to the home page, my fingers hovering over the search button as I wrestle with morality. The devil gets the best of me, and I type Stetson's Instagram handle in and watch as pictures of him fill my screen. He looks the same, maybe even better looking than my mind remembers. He doesn't post often, but it's enough to give me a complete picture of his life. He didn't stray from his life plan. He graduated from law school. Became a partner at his dad's law firm. Spends weekends boating on Skaneateles Lake. Does a lot of outdoor recreation. The only thing that didn't end up how it was supposed to is me, and if Instagram can be trusted, Stetson is still single.

The hope that piece of information gives is scary.

CHAPTER TWENTY ONE

NASH

WITH A GAME of checkers in hand, I knock on Sadie's hospital room door before I crack it open.

"You decent?"

"Uh...yeah!"

I push the door wider as she quickly sets her phone down on the tray table next to her like a hot potato.

"Can I come in?"

Her eyes dart to the device and then back to me. "Yeah, I just got off the phone with Autumn. She called me."

There's a guilty quality to her expression. Sadie's poker face is non-existent, but I don't press because Dr. Hatchet and Dr. Basu told me to be patient with her, with us, with all of it.

"You talked to Autumn?"

"Yeah, it was nice."

"Autumn's been so worried about you. Calling every day. Texting for updates. Demanding information. It's so annoying." I hope she catches the sarcasm in my voice. The old Sadie would've.

"What a terrible friend."

I smile because she does. "The worst." I take another step into the room, shaking the checkers box. I'm hoping her love of board games will get me some alone time with her. "I wanted to see if you were up for a game."

Her eyes are hesitant, but she nods. "Sure."

The wheels on the tray table screech as I roll it between us.

"So this is going to be strip checkers," I say as I start setting up the game. "Every time you jump someone's piece, the other person has to remove an article of clothing."

I peek up at Sadie, and her expression is stiff and angry.

"I'm kidding." I laugh, but she doesn't join, causing me to clear my throat. "Jokes like that were funnier when you liked me."

"Probably." Her lips twitch, and I've never been so grateful for the hint of a smile in my life.

I glance down, continuing to place black and red pieces on the board. "The good news is, you can't remember my winning strategy, but I remember yours."

Sadie crosses her legs under her, sitting up to get serious about the game. "That doesn't seem fair."

"Your recent amnesia should be proof enough that life isn't fair."

"True."

"Ladies first." I gesture to the ready board.

She takes a second to think things through then moves one of the end pieces to the corner.

I smile.

"What?"

"Nothing." I move my piece. "It's just that you're so predictable. Memory loss has nothing on your tried-and-true checkers strategy."

"Never mind." She sits up taller, looking down at the

game. "I'm doing everything different. We'll see who's predictable."

I watch as she tries to switch things up. She looks beautiful, with her brown hair pulled up in a messy bun and no makeup exposing her light freckles. It's the Sadie I love. I want to tell her how I feel and remind her of my love, but Dr. Hatchet explicitly said to take things slow. Don't overwhelm her with information or feelings too soon. So, I leave the words on the tip of my tongue.

Her gaze jumps to me. "See? Now I have you guessing."

"Uh, yeah." I quickly glance down. The last thing I need is for her to get freaked out by me staring. But man, it was so nice to just stare. "You've got me all mixed up now."

We take turns back and forth, but it's clear her new strategy is no strategy at all. I've jumped the majority of her pieces.

As I remove her second-to-last piece from the board, I shoot her a playful smile. "I bet you're glad this wasn't strip checkers, because you'd be naked right now."

"You know comments like that aren't helping me not hate you."

"You used to love how much I flirted with you."

"I don't know." She lifts her shoulders. "It feels like a lot right now."

"I guess I hoped that after talking to Autumn, you wouldn't be so skeptical of me."

"Autumn does seem to be a big fan of yours."

"Really? What did she say?" *That I'm the love of your life? That I make you happy? That we're meant to be?*

Brown eyes flip to me with a look that says I'm not getting any information from her.

"Okay, fine. Don't tell me." I jump my last piece over hers. "That's game."

"I want a rematch." She immediately begins resetting the board. "I mean, you're taking advantage of a person with a traumatic brain injury. Who does that?"

"I can let you win if you want." My lips lift. "Take pity on you."

Her stubbornness presents itself through her lifted chin. "I don't need your pity."

"That's what I thought."

She goes silent as we play, but I don't mind. Being in the same room as her is enough.

"I'm getting released tomorrow," she announces out of the blue.

"I heard. I actually wanted to discuss that with you." I keep my focus on the game. It feels less threatening that way. "I talked to your parents, and we all thought that maybe it would be good for you to go back to our apartment, sleep there, and then fly to Syracuse on Sunday." I'm bending the facts to fit my needs, but showing a united front with her parents is better. Right now, they're her allies.

Her shoulders drop, and she sits back.

"Seeing where we live and what your life looks like might even help trigger something with your memory." I'm not trying to manipulate her. I really believe that it could help. But I also want her to have the whole picture. "It would just be me there with you, but I'll sleep on the couch."

"You'll sleep on the couch?"

I hold my hand up. "Scout's honor."

"Are you a boy scout?"

"No." I shake my head with a smile. "Empty words."

She playfully rolls her eyes, which is better than being annoyed. "It would probably be good for me to see our apartment."

"Sounds good." It's tough to keep my excitement in

check, but I have to because I haven't even asked her the biggest thing yet. "And then the next day, we'll fly to Syracuse together." My eyes dart to Sadie, checking to see if she understood the *together* part.

Her raised brows are the first clue she did.

"Oh." She pulls at her ear like she always does when she's nervous. "I didn't know you were coming with me."

"I'd like to—if you'll let me." I hold her stare, pleading with her to look at me how she used to.

She drops her eyes, breaking our locked gazes. "I might be in Skaneateles for a long time, not just the holidays. Don't you have to work?"

"Before all this happened, we booked a month-long trip to Switzerland for Christmas, so I already had planned not to work much the next few weeks."

Her head pops up in interest. "We did?"

I love the glow of excitement in her eyes. "Yeah, we were supposed to fly out yesterday."

"I've always wanted to go to Switzerland during Christmastime." Her words are almost reverent.

"I know."

Her lips lift, and that slight smile means more to me than anything else has since she woke up. I want to stay in this moment, but I know I can't.

"So"—I look down, moving my next checker piece—"as you can see, it's not a big deal if I spend the next few weeks in New York with you."

"I don't know. I'll have to think about it."

"Okay."

"It's not that you're not welcome." Her expression floods with guilt. "You're my husband, so obviously, you're welcome. It's just kind of awkward, you know? I don't really know you."

"Maybe me coming home with you would help change that."

She bites her lip as she stares back at me.

I can't imagine not being with her, but I play it cool. "Think about it, and let me know what you decide." I add a casual shrug to counteract the desperation inside.

"I will."

If the silence for the rest of our game is any indicator, she's going to tell me I can't come.

SADIE

ONCE NASH leaves, I pick up my phone again, needing some advice. I shoot a quick text to Autumn and stare at the screen, waiting for her to reply.

SADIE

> Nash wants to spend the holidays in Skaneateles with me at my parents' house.

EDWARD CULLEN

> It would be weird if he didn't want to come. He is your husband.

SADIE

> Yes, on paper, he's my husband, but under these circumstances, having a stranger hang out with me for a month is worse, isn't it?

EDWARD CULLEN

> Nash is not a stranger. He loves you.

I should've known Autumn would answer this way. Can you call it advice when the person you ask is so obviously biased?

SADIE

> Usually, when someone you don't know loves you, they're considered a stalker.

EDWARD CULLEN

> Your marriage wasn't one sided. You loved him.

I loved him.

I still can't reconcile that in my head.

SADIE

> Where's the proof? Even though my mind can't remember, shouldn't my heart?

EDWARD CULLEN

> There's proof all around. You just have to be willing to look at it.

My head pushes back into the pillows, and I close my eyes. Autumn is right. I can find proof if I want it.

The pounding in my chest almost convinces me not to, but I decide to switch my phone to a text thread between Nash and me. I scroll, reading each message, trying to picture our life together. The last text was from the day before the accident. Nash asked if he should bring home tacos. The few before that were about our skiing plans and renewing our car insurance. But even with all the day-to-day stuff, it doesn't take long to get to the proof Autumn talked about.

SADIE

> You looked pretty sexy when you left this morning. I've been thinking about you all day. Can't wait for you to get home tonight. (kissy emoji)

NASH

Is that an invitation?

SADIE

Maybe.

NASH

In that case, I'm leaving the conference right now.

And another day.

NASH

Hey, I just wanted to say how beautiful and talented I think you are. I'm so blessed to have you in my life. I love you!

SADIE

Aww, thanks, babe! I love you too. I don't know where I'd be without you.

Probably married to Stetson.
I scroll up a little more.

NASH

You're hot.

SADIE

Aren't you supposed to be paying attention to the board meeting right now?

NASH

I can't concentrate with you sitting across from me. If I sit up a little taller, I get a glimpse of your cleavage.

SADIE

Haha. You're the worst boss ever!

NASH

But the best husband?

SADIE

One thousand percent the best husband.
(heart eyes emoji)

I can admit the flirting back and forth over text is cute
—something that would make me smile if I saw it in a
movie. Stetson and I never did things like this. We were
busy with school and work. It was hard to find time to
look at our phones. When we did have a chance to text, it
was short and to the point, very business-like, until we
could be together in person. That was where the magic
happened.

These messages don't seem like me, but at the same time,
I can hear my voice behind them. I read a few more, looking
for myself in each one.

NASH

I just booked that chalet in Zermatt with a
private Jacuzzi.

SADIE

That's perfect because I just bought a new
black bikini.

NASH

Unnecessary purchase. Clothing is
prohibited.

SADIE

Just wait until you see it on me. I think you'll
let me keep it. (winky emoji)

NASH

As long as I get to be the one to take it
off you.

SADIE

Deal.

> I still can't believe you're taking me to Switzerland for Christmas. How did I get so lucky?

NASH

> You're incredible and deserve to have all your dreams come true.

SADIE

> You're the dream! I've never been happier in my entire life. Thanks for putting me first. Love you!

I stare at the words on the screen.

That message was just two days before I got hurt.

I've never been happier in my entire life.

I don't understand how that can be true when my family wasn't an integral part of my life. They were always the most important thing to me. Happiness could never exist without them, but then again, I said it did—a hard reality to wrap my head around.

Tiredness seeps in, and I tell myself I'll just read a couple more.

SADIE

> How did your appointment with Dr. Wyman go? I've been thinking about you all day. (heart emoji)

NASH

> It was rough. You know how I feel about therapists.

SADIE

> I know.

NASH

I hate opening up everything I tried so hard to forget.

SADIE

For what it's worth, I'm proud of you for going and talking to her. I know it's hard, but it will be worth it in the end.

NASH

Maybe, but for now, I just feel emotionally exhausted.

SADIE

Take the rest of the day off work. I'll hold down the fort here.

NASH

Nah, I'm already on my way. Taking a day off work is only fun if you're with me. I'll feel better when I see you and hug you. You're my rock.

SADIE

And you're mine.

I feel like an intruder spying on something I wasn't supposed to hear—something so intimate and tender it's deeply personal. Seconds before, Nash was just a man who knew how to flirt with his wife, but after reading this last exchange, he became dimensional.

My eyelids get heavy, and I succumb to their weight. *Who is the real Nash Carter?* This is the last thought that goes through my mind before everything goes dark.

CHAPTER TWENTY TWO

SADIE

"ARE you sure you'll be okay?" My mom holds my shoulders, staring into my eyes. Her wild gaze conveys her concerns, and it's obvious she wants me to blink twice as a signal I'm being held against my will by my captor. The captor in question: Nash Carter.

No one was more surprised than me when I decided to stay with Nash tonight in our apartment *and* agreed to let him come to my parents' house for Christmas. Well, no one *other than* my mother. Lynette Bradley's jaw fell to the unsanitary hospital floor when I announced the plan. I lifted my chin, showing more confidence in my decision than I felt—I had to. Once my mom reeled in her shock, she listed all the reasons it was a bad idea to include Nash in my recovery here in Chicago and back home.

My family is firmly in the "We Don't Like Nash" camp. I was too—maybe I still am—but after reading those texts last night, I decided I owed it to myself to see where my choices three years ago led me today.

For better or worse.

"It's only one night." I plaster a reassuring smile on my face. "I'll see you guys tomorrow evening."

My mom leans in, shielding Nash from her words. "I wish I had the same confidence in him that you do."

I wouldn't say I have confidence in him. It's more about the confidence I used to have in myself and my ability to make solid decisions. But waking up with my life turned upside down has made me question everything. Part of leaning into Nash is discovering how I ended up down a path that doesn't make sense and seems so unlike me.

"If you feel uncomfortable with him at all—"

I tune out my mom's words, darting my gaze to Nash as he loads the back of his Land Cruiser with our bags. His expression when he heard he was coming to Skaneateles will be burned in my mind forever—barring another bout of amnesia. Teary green eyes, a broad smile filling his entire face, raised brows in surprise. A look that genuine is hard to replicate.

"Oh, I'm sure Nash isn't that bad." I shift my attention back to my mom. "I married him for some reason."

"And yet, we still don't know that reason." She steps aside so I can hug my dad and Annie.

"It will be so good to finally have you home again," my dad says as he wraps me into his arms. "We'll get the house decorated for Christmas, and your bedroom will be ready for you."

"Thanks."

Annie is next. Her hug isn't as fragile as my parents'. She tugs me in, swaying our bodies together back and forth. "I'll see you tomorrow night."

"You're picking us up from the airport, right?"

"I'll be there."

Awkwardness fills the air as the five of us stand on the

hospital curb by our cars, staring at each other. My parents don't want to watch me leave with Nash, and my nerves about the situation prevent me from initiating the final goodbye.

Nash looks at me with raised brows. "Are you ready?"

There's more behind his words than just asking if I'm ready to leave the hospital. His stare is loaded with questions about being ready to open myself up to the life I created with him and see the person I've become.

It would be easier to leave here with my parents, fly back to Skaneateles, and pretend everything in Chicago with Nash never existed. A huge part of me *wants* to do that. But I owe it to the woman behind those text messages to see what made her so dang happy.

NASH

I NEVER CARED if there was silence between me and Sadie in a car ride. We were comfortable enough for that sort of thing. But today, the lack of conversation feels quieter than silence.

It feels deadly.

For our future, at least.

Sadie has a lot on her mind, so I don't want to force her into talking if she doesn't feel like it, but I also worry that if we don't talk, she'll assume we're incompatible.

"Was it—" I begin just as she says, "Have you—"

We both laugh nervously.

"Sorry." I grip the steering wheel tighter. "You first."

"No, you go."

"I was just going to ask if it was hard to say goodbye to

your family. I mean, I know it was. I just wanted to know if you're okay." I hope the reason she's not talking has nothing to do with me and more about her being sad about her family.

"They're what I remember, so having them with me is comforting, but it's only until tomorrow. I'll be okay for twenty-four hours without them." Her face turns to me. "Have you been to my hometown before, you know, with me?"

My lips lift. "Yeah, I've been there with you."

I don't have the heart to tell her I wasn't there under the circumstances she thinks.

"Good." A wave of relief washes over her, and instantly, she relaxes into her seat. Her eyes brighten. "So you know my brother Tate?"

"I've met him once. He's the only person in your family who liked me right off the bat."

"Really?" She purses her lips in disbelief.

"Is that so shocking?" I laugh.

"I guess not. It's just, out of everyone in my family, I'm the closest to Tate. I've worshiped the ground he walks on since I was a little girl."

"I know." This entire conversation rips my heart to shreds, but I promised Sadie's parents I wouldn't say anything about her brother.

"Do I talk about Tate a lot?"

"Yeah, but you don't have to feel bad about it. I love hearing all the crazy stories about the two of you. It's one of my favorite things to listen to you talk about."

"Really?" Her smile widens into something adorably innocent.

"Yeah."

"I can't wait to see him when we get there." She adjusts in her seat, glancing out her window. "I miss him so much."

The words were more to herself than me, so I let them hang without a reply, hating how, in a few days, that happiness over seeing her brother again will be wiped away.

"Do you have siblings?"

I smile, glad she's willing to let down her walls enough to get to know me a little better. "I have a brother."

"What's his name?"

"Nolan, but he passed away four and a half years ago."

Her expression falls. "Oh, I'm so sorry. Can I ask what happened?"

With anyone else, I wouldn't want to talk about this kind of stuff, but Sadie has always been the one person who makes it easy to work through my pain. Grief connects us, cutting the same.

"You don't have to tell me if you don't want to. It's none of my business."

"Of course it's your business. Everything important to me has always been important to you. It's one of the things I love about you."

"Uh." The mention of the word *love* has her tucking a strand of hair behind her ear to deal with the anxiety of the declaration.

"Nolan was an alcoholic," I say, trying to keep the open dialogue going. "He was drunk and crashed his car into a tree. Luckily, it was late at night, and nobody else was involved in the accident."

Unprompted, Sadie reaches out, placing her hand on my shoulder and keeping it there. The same small gesture she did years ago when I told her about my brother. It feels like a milestone compared to two seconds ago, when the thought of me loving her made her fidget nervously.

"I'm really sorry." Her brown eyes are full of her signature sincerity.

"I know you are." I stare at her for as long as a person driving a car can until they have to look back at the road.

She moves her hand away, and my skin goes cold without the warmth of her touch.

"Do you have any other family besides Nolan?"

"My dad took off before I could walk, and my mom dropped us off at my aunt's house when I was eleven so she could pursue her career. I grew up with my cousin, Lindy. She's like a sister to me."

"Autumn mentioned something about Lindy. So she's your cousin?"

"Yeah, you and she are really tight."

Sadie's eyes widen. "We are?"

"Yeah, next to Autumn, she's your best friend. I used to joke that you liked her more than you liked me."

Her gaze drops to her hands, and I know she's grappling with another piece of information she doesn't remember.

"Lindy is one of those people who's instantly lovable. She's also an open book, so you'll know everything you need to know about her within five minutes of meeting her."

"I don't think I'm ready to meet her just yet. I can only handle getting to know one stranger at a time."

"I beat you in checkers three times last night. I'd hardly call us strangers," I joke. "But you don't have to worry about Lindy. She'll be here for you whenever you're ready."

Instant relief washes over her. "Okay."

Our house comes into view, and I park the car in front. "This is us."

Sadie slowly climbs out, studying the brownstone apartment. Four steps and a rod iron railing lead to black French doors. Bay windows on each floor stack one on top of the other. Forty-year-old trees line the streets, shading the front.

"Which level is ours?"

"All three."

"All three?" she gapes. "Why do we need a house this big? Do we have seven children I don't know about?"

"No, not yet." I walk to her side, gazing up at the brick building. "It's more space than we need right now, but you fell in love with this place the second the realtor showed it to us."

"It is charming."

"Come on, I'll show you inside." I lead the way, unlocking the front doors and pushing them open.

She stands in the entry, taking in the living room. "There's a Christmas tree."

I set the bags down on the floor. "Lindy put it up for us even though we lived at the hospital."

Hesitantly, she takes a few more steps inside, like a guest.

"I know it doesn't feel like it, but this is your house. What's mine is yours and vice versa. I just want you to feel at home and comfortable."

"It's really nice." She runs her fingers down the arm of the brown leather couch. "Is this your furniture?"

"It's *our* furniture." I smile. "You decorated the place."

"I did?"

"Well, you and the decorator, Lawrence."

"Ah. That makes more sense. I've never been good with design."

She walks around the room, looking closely at the pictures on the shelves.

"That's our wedding day," I say, following her.

"In Tahiti. Autumn told me," she explains but doesn't have any other reaction to the best day of my life.

"And that was the first day we moved in." I point to one of us sitting on a blow-up mattress, holding Spaghetti-Os cans.

"Where's this?" She stops in front of a picture of her ziplining backward, spider style, with another man.

"That's in Costa Rica. The tour guide said you had to go down the zipline tandem with him, and for some reason, he made you lay flat on your stomach and then straddle him. He was so pleased with himself when he zoomed past me with your legs wrapped around him." I smile, lifting my shoulders. "I don't know. We thought it was hilarious, so we put the picture in our house."

She nods a few times, barely cracking a smile. "How long have we lived here?"

"Almost from the beginning of our marriage." I follow her into the dining room and kitchen. I don't want to hover, but since she's asking questions, I feel like it's safe to linger. "We remodeled the kitchen ourselves."

"It shows."

I think that was a joke, but I can't be sure.

"You wanted neutral tones, plus you wanted to knock down the wall between the dining room and the kitchen to open the place up more."

"And do I usually get what I want with you?" She flips me a teasing glance that sends a thrill through my stomach.

We're making headway.

"Usually." I return her smile.

She opens a few cupboards and drawers then turns to face me. "I knew you were rich, but I didn't know you were *this* rich."

"I wasn't. Not when you married me, at least. But we've had some good luck."

"What changed?"

"I fell in love, married a brilliant woman, and made her my business partner."

"Me?" she scoffs. "What did I do?"

I cross one foot over the other as I lean against the kitchen counter opposite of her. "Locum tenens."

"Loco what?" she shakes her head, not understanding, which isn't a surprise because all of this happened during the lost years of her life.

"Locum tenens, where physicians fly around the country to fill in for other clinicians when they're on vacation or maternity leave. You didn't make up the concept, but once you learned about it, you brought the idea to me and helped add it to our business model."

She frowns. "That seems a little presumptuous of me to give my boss business advice."

"It wasn't like that. It was part of your internship, and you were right. It completely elevated our company."

"*Our* company?"

"We're equal partners. Your name as a co-owner is listed on all the official documents."

She blows out a breath, letting her lips vibrate against each other. "I guess I expected some kind of prenup—you know, since you built your business before you knew me. It's only smart to protect yourself and your assets."

"I didn't feel like I needed protection. I trust you completely, and I trust what we have together."

Her jaw hardens. "Sometimes things change."

"But how I feel about you never will."

"You can't be that sure. From the sound of things, I'm a different person now than I was before. I have a jagged scar across my forehead and sunken cheeks. I don't know if I'll ever be the person you loved and married."

"When I married you, I vowed to enter a contract of mutual decay."

"Like, you said that in our vows?"

"No," I sputter. "I just mean that no matter how we change or deteriorate, we promise to love each other through it all. The good and the bad. If this is your bad right now, I'm not scared, and I'm not going anywhere. I love you no matter what."

Sadie glances away, just like she always does when I talk about my feelings for her. She pushes off the counter. "I guess I should be happy. I have always wanted to run some kind of healthcare business. That's the motivation behind my degree and what brought me to Chicago for your internship in the first place. I just always thought I would run my dad's home health and hospice business."

"Are you disappointed you're not?"

"I don't know." She shrugs. "There are a lot of things that didn't turn out how I expected."

"Like me?"

"You're definitely a curve ball I wasn't expecting."

The corner of my mouth rises with an edge of playful charm. "But if you're patient and sit back on a curve ball, it could be a home run."

"Or a swing and miss."

"We're not a miss, I promise."

Sadie stares at me, unconvinced, and all I want to do is show her how great we are together. I want to shove a million pictures of us into her hands, play our wedding video on every TV, or pull her into my arms and kiss her neck and lips the slow, sensual way that drives her crazy. But I can't. So I say instead, "You know, we met at a baseball game."

"I thought you were my boss."

"I was. But the Saturday before your first day at work, I hit on you at a Cubs game."

Her brows draw inward as she tries to make sense of it all. If Dr. Hatchet were here, she'd tell me that overwhelming Sadie with facts about our life is a bad idea. She'd tell me to give her time to put the pieces together herself when she's ready.

I'm failing miserably at that.

"Listen, I'm kind of tired." She rubs her hands down her face. "Could we do the whole house-tour thing later?"

"Sure. I'll show you to our room so you can get some rest."

Disappointment falls through me, but I hide it. I wore her out with too much information. Things would be so much easier if Sadie were as eager as I am to fill in the gaps, but I have to keep reminding myself this is going to be a *long* recovery process. She sets the pace, and I follow along for the ride.

There's nothing fast or easy about rediscovering three and a half years of your life that you lost.

CHAPTER TWENTY THREE

SADIE

THIS AIRBNB—WHICH is really my house—has amazing Egyptian cotton sheets, excellent-smelling body wash and shampoo, and the loveliest view of the Chicago skyline. While I'm more comfortable here than in the hospital, it doesn't *feel* like home. Just a VRBO I'm a guest at.

Shouldn't I feel like more than a guest?

There are glimpses of me. I can confidently admit that I did live here just based on the handwritten notes stuck to my bathroom mirror, the endless supply of Chapstick in my nightstand drawer, my Syracuse University sweats that have withstood the closet cleanouts, and the copies of my favorite books lined up on the shelf. And if we remodeled this place ourselves, I'm ashamed to say I'm the one to blame for the two showerheads in the walk-in shower. I've always thought something like that would be romantic. But the reality of showering with Nash makes me want to cover my face in embarrassment.

The proof of life should be comforting, but instead, it depresses me, adding more unknowns to my plate.

After a long, hot shower, I walk around the room, taking

in hints and clues about our life together. Framed above our bed is a brown note with a scribbled message across it. I climb on the mattress to get a better look at what it says.

Bro, I'd love to take out your sister. If she's lying about having a boyfriend and you don't think I'm crazy, please give her my number.

This is obviously something special between me and Nash to be the focal point behind our bed, but it means nothing to me. My head shakes as I drop down to my butt, leaning my back against the headboard. I'll have to ask Tate about it when I get to Skaneateles. I assume the note was written to him since it said *sister.* I could see Tate loving a bold move like that from Nash just to get my attention.

But even as small pieces fit together, this life still feels like a dream with no chance of waking up in sight. I stare aimlessly ahead when Nash knocks on the door.

"Come in." It is his bedroom, after all.

His light hair is the first thing I see, followed by a timid smile. "I heard footsteps and the shower, so I figured you were awake now."

"It's a great shower." I nod toward the bathroom.

"Right?" He takes a small step inside the room. "We went back and forth on where to position the double shower heads, but in the end, you were right as usual."

"I figured the double heads were my idea. I've always wanted something like that."

His expression pulls to something playful. "Even more so after you married me."

I laugh as I crawl to the edge of the bed, purposely avoiding eye contact in hopes he doesn't see my blush.

"Are you finding everything you need?"

"I don't even know." I comb my fingers through my damp hair, swinging my legs over the mattress to a sitting position.

"The more I dig, the more questions I have, and the more overwhelmed I feel."

"Maybe I can help." He slides his hands into his pockets, taking another step into the bedroom. "For starters, why are all my pants cropped and wide-leg? Is this the actual style now, or just some fashion statement I was trying to make? And according to the t-shirt in my closet, Taylor Swift has released three new albums. THREE NEW ALBUMS. Do you know how many hours of songs I need to listen to just to get caught up? And apparently, there's a new *Top Gun* movie, unless that movie poster in the back of the closet is lying."

"Wow. That's a lot to unpack." He laughs, joining me on the edge of the bed. I recognize his cologne probably because I picked up the bottle on the bathroom counter and smelled it. A man wouldn't douse himself in a fragrance his wife wasn't a fan of, but man, I did not expect to like the way Nash smells so much. Despite the awkwardness of our situation, a nose-dive into his neck doesn't seem like that bad of an idea, but I'll just use the bottle on the counter whenever I need a whiff.

"As far as I know," Nash says, pulling me out of my cologne frenzy, "the wide-leg cropped pants are in style. And as a side note, you look very cute in them."

I bite my lip, containing my smile.

"And you have a Taylor Swift shirt because we went to her concert in Paris a couple of months ago. It was pretty epic."

My shoulders sink. "I missed Paris and a Taylor Swift concert?"

"You didn't miss it. You were there, and you fully enjoyed yourself. We sang our hearts out. And until you have time to listen to the new albums, I can tell you what songs are your favorite."

"And what about *Top Gun?*"

"Excellent movie. I'm jealous you get to watch it again for the first time."

"I don't have time to watch it again because I'll be busy relearning everything I can't remember."

"A lot of it you'll figure out as you go. Like, does it really matter right now that Queen Elizabeth died, and you don't remember?"

"What?" My posture falls. "The queen is dead?"

"I was just giving a random example."

A wave of emotion I can't explain slowly pools inside me, funneling into my eyes. "How did she die?"

Nash studies me, watching as I unravel. "Are you okay?"

"No." I shake my head, fighting against the building tears. "Queen Elizabeth is dead."

Somehow, it's the final straw.

It's not logical.

It's not normal.

But it's happening, and I can't stop it.

Tears spill out of me in a steady stream as my chest heaves up and down.

"Shhh, it's okay." Nash wraps his arm around my shoulder. "Just breathe."

"I'm...try...ing," I say through heavy gasps that are too substantial to rein in.

This breakdown isn't about the Queen of England, a new *Top Gun* movie, or a weird clothing style I don't understand. It's about everything else. Everything I've been holding in—all the overwhelm, confusion, newness, unknowns, anger, and disappointment—unleashes, and emotion fills the gaps. Uncontrollable sobs decimate whatever composure I had.

Nash pulls me into his side, allowing me to cry on his shoulder, and I wonder if I've ever been this vulnerable in front of him. Has he ever comforted me on this raw of a level before? By how his hand gently runs down the side of my head, smoothing my hair repeatedly, I feel like he has.

I feel like he knows exactly what to do.

I don't get caught in the weeds of whether or not I'm ready to share this level of intimacy with him. I'm too exhausted and sad to be bogged down by that. I simply let him comfort me on a human level because I need it. He doesn't speak, just allows my tears to flow—a stark contrast between him and Stetson. Stetson's a fixer. By now, he'd have given me ten different solutions for how to feel better. But in this instance, the silence is nice. Maybe even needed.

After a while, Nash pulls me back into the pillows, cradling me in his arms. I cry on his chest for what seems like an eternity and even feel the moment one of his own tears trickles down onto me, wetting my hair. I'm not sure if he's crying for me or for himself. Either way, the heartache is too much to bear, and I don't want to feel it anymore.

Sleep is the easiest way to hide from the pain.

THE GOOD-SMELLING cologne was the first thing I noticed.

Then, one after another, more information falls into place.

The coarse stubble against my cheek.

The weight of an arm draped over my side.

The hard chest rising and falling with my own breath.

Everything clicks, and I panic.

My eyes fly open, and I lurch forward, escaping from Nash's arms to my feet. The sudden movement jolts him awake to an upright position.

"What? What happened?" His head swivels, assessing

potential danger despite his groggy confusion. Wild green eyes land on me. "Are you okay?"

I fold my arms over my chest like protective armor and glance away. "This wasn't the sleeping arrangement you promised."

"Uh..." He looks around at the crumpled bed and morning sunlight blaring through the windows until he grasps the situation. "It was an honest mistake. You were crying and..." Guilty eyes fall to the mattress where, seconds ago, our bodies were intertwined. "I just fell asleep, and the cuddling and all of that was an accident. Like muscle memory."

"I don't care if some stupid certificate says you're my husband," I snap. "You're a stranger, and I don't want your arms around me. Do you know how invasive that is?"

My words break him.

I feel the force of his hurt pierce my soul. Crestfallen, he drags himself off the bed.

"I'm sorry," I blurt, as if backpedaling can somehow fix the damage I caused. "I just meant—"

"You don't have to apologize." There's a smile, but nothing about his expression says it should be there. "It's my fault."

"No, I just..." I cover my face with my hands.

"It's fine." I hear his footsteps shuffle to the door. "I'll make some breakfast, and you can go through your clothes and find things you want to take to Skaneateles. It's all fine."

I don't drop my hands until Nash is safely out of the room, and I'm alone with my guilt.

CHAPTER TWENTY FOUR

NASH

THE MORNING after the accidental cuddle has been tense. Whatever headway I thought I was making with Sadie was all erased the second we slept together, and all we did was *sleep*. I would never dream of doing anything more under our current circumstances—I didn't even dream of cuddling. But when you've been married for three years and fall asleep on a bed, it just naturally happens.

I wish it didn't, based on the silent treatment she's been giving me.

It hasn't been complete silence. In a lot of ways, Sadie's like a toddler, needing help packing and finding the suitcases, not knowing where her passport is, or even thinking about needing identification to fly.

Helping her isn't annoying. I want to help. I meant what I said about loving her through everything life brings. It's just hard. I never counted on Sadie not remembering me. It's a level of tragedy most hearts aren't prepared for.

I know I wasn't.

Sadie slept most of the short flight to Syracuse, which I

was happy about. Going home for the first time in three years will be mentally exhausting for her tonight.

Annie waited for us at the curb when we exited the airport. Sadie's face lit up for the first time today when she saw her. I sat in the back of the car as the two of them chatted and pointed out landmarks that had changed from what Sadie remembered.

Snow already covers the ground of her small hometown. Annie drives us down Genesee Street, showing off the Christmas decorations, giant wreaths, holiday garlands, and lights that adorn the quaint shops.

"I was thinking about the Dickens Christmas Festival the other day," Sadie says as she cranes to see out the window. She glances over her shoulder, filling me in. "Skaneateles does this thing every Christmas where they bring Charles Dickens' *A Christmas Carol* to life through street performances and carolers. It's a huge deal here."

"I think it's been going for thirty years or something like that," Annie adds.

"Who are the street performers? Where do they come from?" I ask.

"There's everything from Dickens himself to the entire cast of the story and even someone who plays Queen Victoria, since that was the time period when Charles Dickens wrote it."

"Did you know Mom was an assistant costume director this year?" Annie's eyes momentarily leave the road and dart to Sadie.

"She was?"

"Yeah, she did it last year too."

"That's weird." Sadie glances back out the window. "She's never cared about helping A Dickens Christmas before."

"Now that she and Dad are empty nesters, she has a lot of extra time on her hands."

"That makes sense." Sadie keeps her focus on the passing town. "Where does Tate live now?"

Through the mirror, Annie's panicked gaze shoots to me.

"Hey, is that Skaneateles Lake? I thought it would be completely frozen over by now." I point opposite Sadie's window, trying to distract her from her last question. I would never lie to her, but I promised her parents they could be the ones to tell her about Tate. They better do it soon, because I refuse to keep this up much longer.

"Yeah, that's the lake we live on. Some parts probably have a thin layer of ice, but you can still take a boat out."

Annie offers me a grateful look as I exhale a tight breath.

We turn down a beautiful road lined with tall trees, frozen over with frost. When I came to Tate's funeral three years ago, I only went to the town church. I never saw where Sadie grew up.

The two-story white house sits right on the lake with a small boathouse off to the side. Windows wrap around the exterior, showing off the beautiful view. The Bradleys have it decorated perfectly for Christmas. White lights line the rooftop, glowing in the dimming sunlight. Two skinny Christmas trees stand on the porch, splitting the front door evenly. A giant garland with bows droops over the door, adding Christmas charm. The whole place is full of so much Christmas magic I'm surprised Sadie stayed away during the holidays. And that's just the outside. I can already see fully decorated Christmas trees through several of the windows.

Sadie stands in front of her house, taking it all in.

I walk to her side, holding our luggage. "It's magical."

"My mom always goes all out for Christmas." She sucks in a deep breath. "It's really good to be home."

SADIE

"WHERE'S NASH?" I ask my mom as I sit on my bed, letting her unpack my suitcase like I'm a ten-year-old.

"Your father took him to the boathouse to show him around."

I twist my body, glancing out the window, but instead of seeing Nash and my dad, I see the Roeshine's house thirty yards away. I won't be able to avoid them this holiday season. Our families celebrate together. I'd be lying if I said I wasn't anticipating seeing Stetson again—that is, if he even wants to see me.

"I put Nash in Tate's old room," my mom says, cutting into my thoughts.

I spin back around, facing her. "I don't see why we have to share the same bathroom."

"It's a Jack and Jill. You and Tate shared it."

"Yeah, I know what kind of bathroom it is, but you replaced the doors with rolling barn doors that don't lock."

My mom fondly looks at the new addition. "Aren't they pretty? We did that about two years ago when we cleaned out both of your rooms."

I shoot her a flimsy glare. "Pretty doors without locks don't help me in this situation."

She smirks. "Are you afraid Nash will sneak in while you're showering and see something he's already seen before?"

"What happened to the mom leaving the hospital yesterday who was so worried about me staying with Nash?"

Her shoulders lift. "You stayed with him and came home in one piece."

"Yeah, but I thought you hated him."

"I don't hate him." She folds one of my sweaters and tucks it into a drawer. "I just don't know him."

"Neither do I."

"Since you invited Nash here"—*invited is a generous way of saying it*—"we might as well try to get to know him a little better."

I'm not sure I like this change in my mom. It was easier knowing I had people on my side who were one hundred percent okay if I just walked away from my life in Chicago and all the people in it. No questions asked. Who's going to drive the getaway car now?

"I am trying to get to know him." I scoop up one of the pillows on my twin-sized bed and hug it to my chest. "For example, I learned this weekend that Nash has no family besides one cousin he's close with...and *me*."

My mom and I share a look, neither of us saying out loud what we're both thinking. *If my memory doesn't come back, can I really abandon this marriage if I'm the only family Nash has?*

"I've met his cousin, Lindy. She's very nice."

"You have?"

"She spent a lot of time at the hospital."

I can't let my mind wonder about Lindy. I'm not ready for more people expecting me to remember them and then being disappointed when I don't.

"At least Nash has one person he's close with." My mom uses her hip to close the top drawer. "Dinner is ready downstairs. I made potato cheese soup and even left out the broccoli just for you."

"That sounds amazing."

She places my suitcase on the top shelf in the closet. "And for dessert, homemade cinnamon rolls."

I smile as she walks out of the room.

This is home. Not Chicago.

I can't believe I ever abandoned this place.

CHAPTER TWENTY FIVE

NASH

"Wow, you rolled out the red carpet for me. Christmas dishes for dinner tonight?" Sadie traces the edge of her soup bowl.

"It's a special occasion." Jay smiles. "You're finally back home where you belong."

A coded statement from my father-in-law, but I keep my thoughts to myself.

Sadie's eyes skip to me like she heard it too. "I know everyone says it's been a long time since I've been home, but it doesn't feel that way to me."

"Too long." Lynette holds the pan of cinnamon rolls in front of me, offering up seconds.

"No, thanks. I'm stuffed. That meal was delicious."

Sadie tilts her head to the empty chair across from her. "Where's Tate? He's usually good for third and fourths. I thought he would be here or at least call to talk to me by now."

Annie's chair scrapes the wood floor as she stands. "I'm tired. I think I'll head upstairs."

"So soon?" Sadie's eyes follow her.

"Yep." Annie keeps walking, not looking back.

"What was that about?"

Jay and Lynette exchange glances, and I know what's coming, what made Annie hurry and leave the dinner table. Jay told me earlier they would address the Tate situation after dinner. I wish I could save Sadie from this moment, from experiencing the pain all over again.

"Sadie, we need to talk to you about something," her dad begins. "We've just been waiting for the right time to tell you."

Creases slowly form across her forehead. "Okay."

Lynette grabs Jay's hand, giving him the strength to start.

"A few months into your internship, we found out that Tate was addicted to pain medication. It was an addiction that he'd been hiding from all of us for almost eight years. Something that started after his football injury in high school."

Lines deepen as Sadie's brows drop, but she doesn't interrupt.

"We found out about his addiction because he'd been stealing money from us and using it to buy Oxycontin."

She bites her bottom lip nervously, and all I want to do is reach out and take her hand, but I can't—not yet, at least.

"So we got him help, right?" Her eyes move back and forth between her parents, looking for answers. "Right?"

"We wanted to, but everything blew up when we caught him stealing, and we all said things we shouldn't have. Tate ended up leaving that night," Jay's voice cracks with emotion.

"Where did he go?" Panic tears through Sadie as she tries to keep up.

"At the time, we didn't know, but he drove to Syracuse and bought more painkillers from a dealer on the street. But the pills he had weren't just Oxycontin. They were laced with fentanyl."

"No." She shakes her head, visibly upset.

"Tate didn't know," Lynette defends her son. "They looked the same. He didn't know."

Jay draws in a breath, fortifying himself for the final blow. "We got a call the next morning that Tate had passed away on his friend's couch. He'd overdosed."

We all silently wait for Sadie to react, ready to pick up the shattered pieces as best we can.

A single tear falls down her cheek. "Was it suicide? Did he leave a note?"

"No. Tate's friend said they didn't know they'd bought fentanyl." Lynette's shoulders lift. "It was just an accident."

"I want to see his grave," she says after a few seconds of it all sinking in.

"Honey, it's so cold out," Lynette tries to convince her.

"I want to see it."

"We can go tomorrow," Jay offers.

"Are you really not going to take me to his grave?" She pounds the table with her fists. Dishes clatter at the sudden movement.

"I'll drive you." I place my hand on her shoulder as I stand. "Let me get your coat and a few blankets."

Sadie pulls in a ragged breath, numbly sitting at the table.

Jay stands too, following me out of the kitchen to the stairs. "Nash, you're not going to start up all that nonsense again about tough love and it being our fault that Tate's gone, are you?"

"I was never the one who thought that."

"I know, but I'm sure all these years, you didn't help defend us to Sadie."

"The last thing I want is to drive a wedge between you guys. She can draw her own conclusions about Tate's death, but it won't come from me and never has."

I don't wait for his response. I run up the stairs, gathering enough warm stuff from Sadie's closet to keep her outside for as long as she needs.

I help put her coat, hat, and gloves on while she stands unmoving. The ride to the cemetery is silent. I rush around the car to open her door and help her out. Then I lean back down to grab a few blankets. The only other time I was here was at Tate's funeral. I hate that I'm back under similar circumstances.

Slowly, I lead Sadie to his headstone. The moonlight illuminates his name, making the nightmare more real. I lay down a couple of blankets over the skiff of snow, and she falls to her knees, blankly staring at his memorial.

I expected tears and anger and all the emotions I've talked her through over the last few years, but this time around is different. She's different, and I don't know how to help ease this new version of her grief.

After thirty minutes, she stands, gently touching the edge of his tombstone. "We can go now." Smoke puffs out as the words escape her mouth.

My arm wraps around her shoulder, gently leading her back to the car. Her parents are by the door when we get home.

"Sadie?" Lynette starts. "Are you—"

"I can't talk about it." She shakes her head, walking past them.

I follow her up the stairs, but when we get to her room, she shuts the door, blocking me out. In the safety of her room, the tears come. From my spot outside her bedroom, I hear the gut-wrenching sounds of my wife falling apart.

It's agony in its purest form.

I try the handle, needing to get to her, to comfort her, but the door is locked. My head presses against the wood as I listen to her muffled cries.

All I can do is wait outside until she trusts me enough to hold her pain. Slowly, I slide to the ground, leaning against the wall. It's there in her parents' dark hallway, in the middle of Skaneateles, New York, that I allow myself to fall apart too.

SADIE

TATE IS GONE.

It took most of the week lying in bed for the reality of that to sink in.

I'm mourning the loss of my brother while mourning the loss of my life, and it just feels *so* heavy, like a crushing weight I can't avoid.

My mom, Annie, and Nash rotate, bringing me food and sitting beside me. This week has been a blur of depression at a level I've never experienced before. At least, I don't think I have, but maybe it was like this the first time I found out about Tate.

I sit on my bed, hugging my knees to my chest with my head pressed against the cold window. So far, my day has consisted of watching snow flurries swirl from the sky onto the lake. Even the soft knock on my bedroom door doesn't break my focus.

Nash enters. He walks to the nightstand beside my bed, placing a steaming cup of hot cocoa on the coaster. I don't even acknowledge his presence, just keep looking out the window.

"I brought you something you might like." He sits on the edge of the mattress. "If I were in your position, I would want to see this, but now I'm second-guessing everything. It's stupid."

His back-and-forth nerves are enough to pull my attention away from the snow flurries. My eyes flick to him and the phone in his hands.

"I have a link to Tate's funeral. I thought you might want to watch it. Get some closure like people usually get in normal situations."

The pounding in my heart shows how scared I am, but I take the device from his hands anyway.

His lips press into one of his sad smiles. I'm getting used to that one. I've seen it the most. "I'll just be in the other room if you need anything."

The door shuts behind him.

I'm all alone, free to come undone.

Sometimes, the best way to get through the pain is to feel it, so I sink into my bed and push the link.

A picture of Tate flashes on the screen—the one I took at the derby a few years ago. He looks happy, and my heart breaks, thinking about everything he hid behind the facade.

The camera pans the room as the funeral procession begins walking down the church aisle. I smile at the large crowd there to pay their respects. Of course Tate would have standing room only at his funeral.

Rows of white flowers fill the front of the church—he loved white flowers, said they were the most perfect. Every detail of his funeral was beautiful, and seeing that somehow eases my grief. Nash was right. Experiencing Tate's funeral again does bring a small measure of closure.

When all the talks and tributes are done, the crowd stands as the family follows his casket out to the cemetery. The camera pans the room again, and that's when I see a familiar face, wiping tears off his face.

I grab my chest, where my heart aches with a discomfort I can't quite name.

Nash came to Tate's funeral.

It couldn't have been more than a month and a half into my internship, but there he was, six hundred miles away from Chicago, supporting a woman he barely knew.

Something about that kind of loyalty touches my soul.

And for the first time since I woke up from my coma, I understand, at least a little bit, why I fell in love with Nash.

CHAPTER TWENTY SIX

NASH

"You just twist the ropes together until you get your desired thickness." Lynette stands over my shoulder, teaching me how to make homemade candy canes.

Since Sadie's been hiding in her room all week, Lynette and I have been spending a lot of time together. She's different than I imagined, different from the picture Sadie painted of her mom. Lynette is warm and service-oriented. Motherhood is the center of her life, and I like seeing her in her element. She's a mother figure I never had.

"Twist them like this?"

"Yep, you're a natural." She smiles down at me, patting my shoulder. "And then when you're out of rope, you form it into a cane shape to harden."

"Hey, look at me." My head kicks back, examining my work. "I'm a candy-cane-making pro my first time." I hold my gloved hands up, waving them back and forth. "I might just keep these heat-resistant gloves. You never know when they'll come in handy."

"Nash Carter, you'll have to get your own gloves. Those

are mine." Lynette returns to her spot at the counter, pulling out another red and white piece from the warm oven.

"How did you learn to do all of this?"

"I just taught myself. Jay worked long hours when he first started his business. So, I lined up my three little kids and started baking. Anything to keep them busy, especially during the holidays."

My eyes cast over my mother-in-law, noticing the similarities between her and Sadie. "Your children are really lucky to have you as their mom."

She pauses her work, glancing up at me with glossed-over eyes. "I don't think any of them would say that."

"A few bumpy years doesn't take away all the good things you've taught them or the love you've shown. They're lucky to have you, even if they don't always admit it. And someday, if Sadie and I are blessed with children, the things you taught her will be passed down to my family. I'm thankful to you for that."

She wipes a tear with her wrist, keeping her cooking hands free from contamination. "I don't mean to get emotional." She laughs nervously. "It's just..." Her head shakes as she forces a smile. "I really appreciate you saying that."

"What do you appreciate?"

For the first time all week, Sadie is dressed and out of bed.

"Hi!" I stand, moving to kiss her on the cheek but realize too late that a kiss isn't appropriate.

"Uh..." She pulls back, dodging my advances, and now I feel like an idiot.

"Sorry for that." I cringe. "Habit."

"No, I'm sorry for pulling away. I wasn't expecting to..." Her words drift to an awkward silence.

A nervous laugh falls over my lips. "Should we just start over?"

"That would be great."

I pull out a stool for her. "Your mom and I are just bonding over homemade candy canes."

My eyes flick to Lynette, who pretends not to have witnessed my clumsy interaction with her daughter. Each day is a new level of humiliating circumstances.

"Bonding, huh?" Sadie's brows rise.

"We're hosting the neighbor bash this Sunday, so I just thought I'd get a start on making some of the candy for that."

"I can help too," she offers.

"If it's okay with your mom"—I glance at Lynette and then back to her—"I've been dying all week to go into town. Maybe you can show me around a little."

"Oh, the doctor said I can't drive—"

"Naturally, I would drive us." An amused smile covers my lips.

"It's also the weekend, so things will be crowded with A Dickens Christmas."

"That's what I want to see." I smile, trying to coax her into saying yes. "Come on. Be a tourist with me."

She bites her bottom lip, hesitating. *Always* hesitating.

"I think getting out of the house is a great idea." Lynette grins, and I appreciate the support. I need all the help I can get to win back my wife. "You can take my car. The keys are on the hook by the garage door."

"Okay," Sadie half-heartedly agrees…but she agrees.

"WHAT ARE you going to show me first?" We walk

together down Genesee Street, passing charming shops and restaurants.

If she were the old Sadie, we'd be holding hands, but I won't let that depress me. At least she's out of the house.

"Me?" Her head jerks back. "I'm not in charge."

"This is your town, and you're my tour guide, so technically, you are in charge."

"Yeah, but I have a traumatic brain injury and a deceased brother I just learned about. Don't I get a hall pass on life for at least a month or two?"

I feign a sigh. "I guess I can put you on the injury reserve list, which means I'm now in charge of our afternoon." I glance up and down the street. "Where do we start with the Dickens stuff? I want the whole experience. Don't cheat me out of seeing Ebenezer Scrooge."

"I don't know if the schedule is still the same, but carolers usually gather at the gazebo at two o'clock for a sing-along."

My eyes drop to my watch. "That's in, like, twenty minutes!"

Sadie's lips twitch, fighting a smile.

"What?" I smile back.

"I've just never seen a grown man so excited about small-town Christmas stuff."

"Well, *you* just don't remember it. I'm like this every year."

"Good to know."

"So..." I point in both directions. "Which way to the gazebo?"

"This way." She nods to the right. "You'll be happy to know there are free refreshments on the way. Roasted chestnuts and eggnog."

"We'll skip the eggnog because I know you hate it, but roasted chestnuts on an open fire? That's a Christmas classic."

She stares at me for a long second. "I do hate eggnog."

"I know, Sadie." My smile spreads bigger. "I *know* you."

CHAPTER TWENTY SEVEN

SADIE

MY HEAD'S been on a constant swivel ever since we got into town. It's not like I expect to see Stetson at A Dickens Christmas. Locals don't hang out here, but you never know, and it's the unknown that has me tied into knots.

"Man, they can sing," Nash says over the song.

I lift my lips, trying to fake as much interest in this event as him.

The performers hit the last note of "Deck the Halls," and the crowd claps and cheers.

"These actors are amazing!" Nash gawks. "I really feel like I'm in the Victorian Era."

Instead of searching for Stetson, I should be soaking up my stranger-husband's pure enjoyment. It is cute watching him. There's a simple happiness about Nash that I admire, especially right now when dark clouds seem to constantly hover over me, choking out the sunlight.

"There's Scrooge." He points to the other side of the gazebo. "Come on, let's go talk to him."

He grabs my hand, pulling me through the crowd of people. I glance down at our joined fingers. Shouldn't there be a spark of something? A flicker of butterflies? A feeling that tells me this is right? Because I just don't feel it.

"Scrooge!" Nash drops his hand from mine, extending it to the actor. "Merry Christmas."

"Bah humbug!" Scrooge huffs, pushing Nash's hand away as he rushes past us.

"Where are you going?" he asks the old miser.

"Bob Cratchit! I'll skin him and turn him into a jacket when I find him. A Cratchit jacket!"

Another happy smile from Nash as he points to the actor. "I love this guy!" His eyes go wide, and he abandons Scrooge, distracted by something else more exciting. "Is that a horse-drawn carriage ride?"

I follow his gaze. "Yeah, you have to pay for it, though."

"We were going to do that in Switzerland."

"We were?"

If I hadn't gotten in the accident, I'd be celebrating Christmas in Switzerland right now. That information slipped my mind this past week with everything else going on.

"We were going to do *everything* in Switzerland. It was the trip of a lifetime."

"I'm sorry you had to cancel it because of me."

"Don't be sorry."

He steps closer, tucking a strand of hair behind my ear. The tips of his fingers graze the side of my face and ear, sending a shudder of anxiety down my spine. My muscles tense at his touch, and I hold my breath, waiting for the sensation to end.

"I know we'll go again."

Nash's optimism fills my chest with more anxiety. My memory may never come back, and if it doesn't, I can't see myself traveling the world with him.

"But until we get to Switzerland, we have the horse-drawn carriage in Skaneateles." His arm swings out to me in a dramatic gesture. "Come for a ride with me."

It's not really a question.

And I don't want to seem like I'm not trying to be happy or that I'm not grateful I'm alive and walking around, because I am. But no amount of gratitude can fill the void inside me. It's not just my mind that's hollow. It's my heart too—clinging onto a life from three and a half years ago that doesn't exist anymore.

"Okay," I give in, lightly placing my hand in his.

Nash leads me to the horses and makes all the arrangements with the driver.

"He offered me a blanket to keep you warm, but I told him it wasn't necessary." He winks. "I'll keep you warm with my body heat."

I don't know if it's panic or disgust on my face, but whatever it is, it makes Nash laugh.

"Relax! I'm kidding. There are blankets under the bench seat."

I climb into the carriage, scooting over to the side as much as possible without making it look like I'm trying to avoid sitting by him. He spreads one of the blankets over me and then sits down. I try not to be annoyed by how close he is to me compared to the rest of the open bench seat.

The horses begin their steps, jolting the carriage forward. The clap of hooves on the pavement has a calming rhythm. I shift in my seat, trying to relax and lean into the beats.

On the sidewalk, the Ghost of Christmas Past says a famous line from *A Christmas Carol* to a watching crowd. "I told you these were shadows of the things that have been, that they are what they are, do not blame me!"

The words strike deep into my soul as my eyes drift to

Nash. He's what remains from the choices I made years ago. I can't go back and change marrying him or avoid the path I put myself on. The thought weighs like a brick in my heart, tanking it down into my ribcage.

"I'm glad you came out today." He smiles back at me. "I'm worried about you."

"I'm worried about myself," I mutter.

"Did you watch Tate's funeral?"

"I did. It was helpful. Thanks for finding it for me."

"You're welcome."

"I saw in the video that you were there. Gutsy to come all that way when you knew I had a boyfriend."

"You didn't have a boyfriend."

"What do you call Stetson, then?" I scoff.

"An *ex*-boyfriend. Stetson broke up with you the week before you moved to Chicago because he was upset you accepted the internship and were moving away."

My brows lower in absolute shock.

I can't believe Stetson would do something like that.

I'll have to ask Autumn about it later. My current husband isn't likely to give me the details I'm seeking. But I had to have been heartbroken or just really mad.

"Besides," Nash continues, "I didn't come to Tate's funeral to steal your heart away from Stetson. I came because I knew firsthand how difficult losing a brother is."

"Oh, right." A dawn of recognition hits, and guilt wraps around my stomach. "I forgot your brother died too."

"It's okay."

"You probably think I'm so selfish that I didn't remember, that I only think about myself."

"You've been through a lot in the last month and a half. You *should* be thinking about yourself. And a lot of information is being thrown at you right now."

"I know, but I'm sure this is hard for you too, and I'm not giving a lot in return."

His green eyes soften. "My love for you isn't a transactional thing. It's constant. No matter what."

I glance down, blinking the sting of tears away. It's overwhelming to be loved that much and not feel the same. I don't know how to reconcile that in my mind.

"But I will say," Nash's tone lightens, "you're different."

"How so?"

A playful smile smears across his lips. "For starters, the old you was obsessed with me, and this version...not so much."

"Obsessed with you?"

"That's right." He leans back, resting his foot over his knee with all the confidence in the world.

In the hospital, Nash's cockiness rubbed me the wrong way, but now I think it's more about him being comfortable with who he is.

I envy that so much.

I've never felt more *un*comfortable with my own identity.

I shake my head. "I'm not the type of woman who'd be obsessed with a man. In this thing, I think your memory is failing *you*."

"I would believe you or maybe question myself, except I have three years' worth of data to pull from that proves otherwise."

"Like what? I mean, besides the obvious that I married you."

"You kissed me first."

My mouth drops open. "I did not!"

"You did." He smirks. "I was kind of bummed about it— not *bummed*. I'd been dying to kiss you for months, but I just wanted that masculine moment where I dip you and kiss the crap out of you. You took that moment from me because you were so obsessed."

I roll my eyes, unsure if I believe a word coming out of his mouth.

"I'd give you a few more examples of your obsession, but I don't want to embarrass you."

"That's just your excuse since you have nothing else to say."

"Trust me." He gazes at me with glimmering green eyes. "A highlight reel plays in my mind every night."

I push his arm. "Oh my gosh!"

He leans away, laughing, and I feel like if we can't be lovers, maybe we could at least be friends.

But in my heart, I know Nash would never be satisfied with just friends.

And I might not ever want more.

CHAPTER TWENTY EIGHT

NASH

I STICK to the corner of the Bradleys' family room as I wait for Sadie to come downstairs. It's their annual neighbor bash, where every family on their street is invited to their home for cider and desserts. I thought this was a casual get-together, but I'm quickly learning with each guest that arrives how underdressed for the occasion I am. Jeans and a flannel button-up are not party attire in Central New York. I think the last lady that arrived came in a fur coat—tacky but fancy. I thought about changing, but I want to be here for Sadie when she comes down. Something like this might be overwhelming for her.

"Why are you hiding in the corner?" Annie smirks as she joins me. "Are you nervous about the Roeshines coming tonight?"

I drop my brows, faking indifference. "Who are the Roeshines again?"

"You're hilarious."

If things had been different between Sadie and her family, I feel like Annie and I could've been good friends and in-laws.

"Why would I be nervous to meet Stetson's family? I'm not the one who broke their son's heart."

"Yeah, but you're the one who stole Sadie away."

"Nah." I sip my warm cider. "Sadie is the one who should feel uncomfortable, but thanks to her memory loss, she doesn't know what she doesn't know."

"So true." Annie holds her glass up, agreeing with me.

"I doubt Stetson's parents would be mean to her about something that happened three years ago, anyway."

Annie leans in like an old friend you gossip with. "The big question is, does Stetson come alone tonight or bring a date?"

My brows climb halfway up my forehead. "Stetson is coming?"

"Yeah, he always does. I assumed you knew that."

"I just figured a street party with his parents' neighbors on a Sunday night wouldn't be a top priority."

Annie shoots me a wry smile. "Look who's nervous now."

I turn my head, staring directly into her eyes. "Not nervous. I'm the one who got the girl of both of our dreams. It's not awkward for me tonight."

"But you're also the one she can't remember."

Sick burn, Annie. Sick burn.

Suddenly, my shirt collar feels like it's choking me. I take another sip of my drink, masking my discomfort.

"Speak of the devil himself," Annie says as Stetson and his parents walk through the door. He's going stag tonight—a huge disappointment for me.

The Bradleys rush to greet them, hugging and shaking hands like old friends do.

"Stetson looks like someone who got in trouble with the law, but his dad talked to the judge and got him out of it."

She chokes on her drink. "He totally does!"

"Annie!" Lynette calls, waving her over to them, somehow forgetting about her son-in-law.

"Duty calls." She spins, walking backward as she says, "Good luck tonight. May the best man win."

I'm the best man, right?

I mean, I know I am, but does Annie think so?

A hush falls over the room, and every pair of eyes drifts to the stairs.

Sadie slowly walks down each step, wearing a white long-sleeve sequin mini dress. I've never seen her in sequins before, but the fitted dress and the short hemline flatter her silhouette in the best ways. Her hair is pulled up with two curtain bangs left in front, probably hoping it would cover her new scar.

She's gorgeous—a Phoenix rising from the ashes.

I leave my spot in the corner, making my way to her while she scans the room. Her search stops as soon as she sees Stetson by the front door. Brown eyes light up with a glow she used to reserve only for me. It's not even a slow smile that spreads across her lips. It's quick and animated, shredding my heart apart. I watch their reunion play out in front of me from across the room. Each moment is a torturous clip.

"Hi," she says to Stetson when she reaches the bottom of the stairs. The enchantment behind her expression is painfully obvious. "I didn't know if you would come."

"Haven't missed a neighbor bash since we moved here in third grade." His eyes drop down her body. "Wow, you look incredible. It's been years since I've seen you. You're a real sight for sore eyes."

"For me, it feels like we saw each other just the other day."

"I heard about your accident. We've all been praying for your recovery."

A dazzling smile covers her mouth. "Your prayers must have worked."

The way they stare at each other like star-crossed lovers makes me sick.

Lynette points to Mr. and Mrs. Roeshine. "Sadie, you remember Lewis and Rebecca?"

"Can you say things like that under the current circumstances?" Lewis laughs, hugging her like a daughter.

"You're actually people I do remember," Sadie jokes as she moves to hug Stetson's mom, and I try my best to ignore the cutting sting her words caused in my heart.

Rebecca Roeshine is full of nothing but glee. "We are so happy to have you back home."

"Yeah, we are." Stetson's gaze has a little too much intensity behind it for my liking.

I step into their circle, arm extended. "I'm Nash." *The better man. The husband. The man she really loves.* "It's nice to finally meet you."

His jaw flinches as he shakes my hand. "Likewise." The smile on his lips seems innocent enough, but his words are laced with condescending charm. "Didn't Sadie tell you the dress code for this party? We go all out for Christmas." He points over his shoulder. "I'm sure I have an old shirt and tie next door you can borrow."

"Nah, I'm good."

Sadie stands between us, fidgeting with her ear.

"It was nice to see you." Stetson flashes her a smile as he begins to walk away. "Let's catch up sometime."

"I'd love that!" Her eagerness is my worst nightmare. She blatantly follows Stetson's departure with her eyes.

I suck in a deep breath, reminding myself of everything between us. Once upon a time, she had Stetson, but she *chose* me instead. Now isn't the time for jealousy.

"You look amazing." I draw her distracted attention back to me. "I've never seen you wear sequins before."

"Oh." Her eyes drop down her outfit. "This is Annie's dress. Thanks to my recent weight loss, I can fit into it."

"I can go upstairs and put on a tie if you want. I didn't know this was such a formal affair."

"No, it's fine." Her gaze darts across the room like she's keeping tabs on Stetson's whereabouts.

"Do you want some cider?"

"Uh..." She brings her stare to me, forcing a smile. "Yeah, let's get some cider."

Out of habit, my hand goes to the small of her back, guiding her like I've done a million times before. Except, this time, she stiffens at my touch, causing me to drop my arm.

Besides when she woke up and said she didn't remember me, no moment has hurt as much as this one.

SADIE

STETSON.

I hoped he would be here tonight. I dressed as if he would.

Seeing his face—his smile—brings to life all the feelings my mind so easily recalls.

What I can't find with Nash is at the forefront of my heart with Stetson. It doesn't make sense, but it's there, and it's easy.

"Did you try my mom's homemade Oreos?" It's a pathetic opening line after breaking a man's heart and not seeing him for three years, but that's what I start with when I join

Stetson at the dessert table. "I have a feeling she made them for you."

He grins, and oh, I've missed that smile. "I've already had three. You know they're my favorite."

"I remember."

He shifts his body in my direction. "What else do you remember about me?"

"Everything." I laugh, but when his brows hike up, I modify my answer. "Well, not *everything*. I don't know how I woke up married to some random guy instead of you."

He fights the smile my words bring. "I honestly don't know either."

I glance to the side where Nash is conversing with my neighbor who lives two doors down.

A moment of freedom.

"Do you want to...maybe..." *Why is this so hard to say?* "Get out of here or something? Catch up like you said?"

"I'd love to."

So would I.

I spin to leave, not glancing back to Nash.

CHAPTER TWENTY NINE

NASH

"It's like I wasn't even there," I tell Lindy. I just needed someone to talk to, and calling my cousin seemed like the best option.

"I'm sure it wasn't that bad."

"I'm telling you, she was flirting with Stetson right in front of my face without a thought of me."

"What did you do?"

"What could I do?" I lift my shoulders. "To Sadie, he's still her boyfriend."

Lindy blows out a long, sad breath. "That's messed up."

"But it gets worse. She left the party with him and isn't back yet."

"She didn't *leave* with him. She probably just went to talk, get some closure on that chapter of her life."

"I hope so." I spread my fingers over my brows, trying to rub some of my frustration away.

I thought about jumping in a car and hunting them down, but Dr. Hatchet's words keep replaying through my mind.

Give her space to figure things out.

Let her discover who she is.

Don't pressure her to be who you want her to be.

I guess running off with her ex-boyfriend—no, *ex-fiancé*—is part of Sadie discovering who she is.

I just have to sit back and watch it happen.

And it sucks.

"But besides the ex-boyfriend—who is the current boyfriend in Sadie's mind—how is everything else going?"

I drop my hand. "Her mom seems to like me more, and the same with her sister. Then yesterday, we spent the afternoon together doing Christmas stuff in the town village. But it's just not the same. She's so standoffish. I can see it in her eyes."

"She just needs some time to get to know you better."

"What if she doesn't need time? What if she just doesn't like me?"

"Nash, you're impossible not to like," Lindy counters.

"I have a wife that may not agree with you."

"Then change her mind."

I scoff, feeling like Lindy's answer dismisses how hard this is.

"No, seriously, you did it once before. You can make her fall for you all over again."

"How?"

"Fight for her. Show her all the things about you that she likes. Remind her of your chemistry. It's not like you're starting from scratch. You know everything about Sadie. You know what she likes. You know how to turn her on. How to drive her crazy. Do all of that."

"So you're saying I should try to win back my wife?"

"Absolutely."

Isn't that what I've already been doing since she woke up?

"Nash, you don't have any other choice. You either win Sadie back, or you come home without her."

A sobering thought.

So I better win her back.

~

SADIE

NASH SITS at the bottom of the stairs when I get home. His elbows rest on his knees, hands clasped together. He looks up the second I walk through the front door. My heart pounds. It's hard to answer to a man you feel has no say in your life.

This is a pit-in-my-stomach, heat-crawling-up-the-side-of-my-neck situation. I feel like a teenager who got caught staying out too late, or in this case, a wife who got caught spending time with her ex-boyfriend.

"Hi." It comes out more like a whisper. I don't know if that's because the house is dark and everyone has gone to bed or because of the guilt rising in my chest.

"Hi."

I walk to Nash, sitting down beside him. "I was with Stetson."

"I know."

"We were just catching up."

He nods several times and then looks at me. "Did you get all the answers you were looking for?"

My gaze meets his. The dim lighting makes it almost impossible to see what's behind his stare. "Not all of them." I shrug. "But enough for now."

The silence between us thickens, constricting my breath.

"It was Tate's death, wasn't it? The reason I stayed away from my family for so long."

"That was part of it."

"Last night, I opened up the text messages between me and my mom—at least what was still saved on my phone."

"And?"

"There were only four or five in the last seven months, and one was on Mother's Day, and one was on her birthday." A sneer puffs out. "I mean, how did I get so callous that I barely texted my own mother?"

"You weren't callous. You were just trying to deal with your own emotions."

"Stetson said I started to change when I got the internship and moved to Chicago."

"Is that his excuse for breaking up with you?"

"He knows that was a mistake." Regret and longing are behind my words. "A lot of things might've been different if he'd been more supportive of the internship."

I probably wouldn't have married the wrong man.

"He said after moving to Chicago, Tate happened, and the friction between me and my parents just got bigger and bigger, and then—" I stop myself, but it's too late.

Nash finishes what I didn't say. "And then me."

"I'm not blaming you. I know I'm the one who made these decisions, but it doesn't seem like me. And then talking to Stetson and hearing how I just dropped him out of the blue. I don't know. It just doesn't make sense. Nothing went how I thought it would go." I shake my head, pushing my hair back from my face out of frustration.

"It's all so confusing, and I don't expect you to understand, but the last thing I remember is planning a future with Stetson, and then I wake up, and everything is completely different, and I don't know how I got here, and I'm just..." Emotion swells in my eyes. "I'm mourning the life I thought I would have."

The life I wanted.

"It's just so depressing looking at how everything turned out so wrong."

"You were always the one thing that turned out right in my life." His head shifts, and his chin drops slightly, enough for me to know what I said hurt him.

Hurting Nash is all I seem to do.

"You're right," he says with a heavy breath. "I don't understand everything you're going through. And maybe you'll wake up in two months, and your memory will come back, and everything that doesn't make sense now will fit together. But until then, I want you to know you were happy. *We* were happy. Our life together wasn't what you planned, but it was our life, and you loved it."

I swallow, feeling the weight of his words in my chest. I blink a few times as a tear or two falls.

"I promise you'll be happy again." His lips lift. "All of this will sort itself out."

Yeah, it will sort itself out, just not how I want.

I've been waiting for this nightmare to end so I could go back to how things were—the life I remember. But maybe it's time I need to face the facts.

My old life doesn't exist anymore.

CHAPTER THIRTY

SADIE

"STETSON HAS A GIRLFRIEND," I announce to Annie as we sit at the kitchen bar, addressing envelopes for my mom's Christmas cards. "Her name is Savannah, and she's a paralegal at his office." I peek at my sister to get an idea of how she's taking this information, but her expression is masked, telling me nothing, so I glance back down to the envelope I'm writing on. "They've been dating for two months."

"Is that what he told you last night at the party?"

"Yeah—well, when I left with him."

"What did you expect? He couldn't wait around forever."

"I know. I just..." The thought stays unfinished because I don't actually know what I want. I just know Stetson having a girlfriend limits possibilities.

"Maybe it's for the best." Annie shrugs. "You're not single either."

"No, I suppose I'm not."

We write silently for a few seconds, focusing so we don't make a mistake, and send the Bradley family Christmas card to some random person.

"This is for you." Nash enters the room, handing Annie a crumpled-up piece of paper.

"What is it?"

He shrugs as if he doesn't know, even though he obviously does. He takes a seat at the dining table and flips open a magazine.

Annie looks at me with lowered brows as she unfolds the paper.

I lean closer, reading the note over her shoulder with her.

Hey, I'd love to take out your sister. If you don't think her husband would mind and you think I'm a decent guy, please tell her to go out with me.

I smile, remembering the note hanging above our bed in Chicago.

"This is how you guys met, isn't it?" Annie asks.

"It's part of how we met." His eyes go to mine. "I thought maybe we could go on a date."

"A date?" My brows inch up.

"Yeah." His smile has charm written all over it. "Just because we're married doesn't mean we stop dating each other, and in our current situation"—his lips pull to a grimace—"where you have no memories of me, I thought a date might be the perfect way to remind you why you fell in love with me in the first place."

"Awww."

I look at Annie and the goofy smile stretched across her mouth.

"What?" She stares back. "That's adorable."

It is adorable, but my mind automatically goes to Stetson. My answer might be different if he didn't have a girlfriend, but he does, making my life with Nash my only option. I should at least try to make it work.

"Okay, I'll go on a date with you."

"Perfect." He leans back into his chair, a happy smile lighting his face. "I'll pick you up tonight. Wear something nice. This is a serious date."

"You're one to talk, flannel boy," Annie sneers.

Nash's eyes whip to her. "Hey, I don't appreciate that joke."

But he laughs easily anyway.

THERE'S A KNOCK on the barn door that connects Nash's room to our shared bathroom.

I roll the door open. "I'm just about done in here."

His eyes slowly travel down my body and the black body suit of Annie's she convinced me to wear. The top is like a bralette, and the middle is sheer, giving a glimpse of my torso. Then she let me borrow a chunky tan cardigan and black wide-leg pants. She said it was the perfect combination of sexy and classy.

Judging by Nash's expression, it's leaning a little too hard on the sexy side.

He drags his wide eyes back up to my face, not bothering to do anything about his slacked jaw.

"It's Annie's." I panic. "Is it too much?"

"It's the perfect amount of much." His lips turn into a flirtatious smile. "Trust me."

The first flutters of butterflies bounce around my stomach, catching me off guard, but was that because of *him* or because it was nice to feel wanted?

"Um…" I glance down, quickly gathering my stuff off the counter. "I'll get out of here so you can get ready."

Like a whirlwind kicking up dust everywhere, I pile everything into my arms and spin out of the bathroom, pulling the barn door on my side of the room shut with my big toe. The force is too much, causing the whole thing to bang shut and roll back open five inches.

I drop my stuff on the makeup vanity in my bedroom and take a seat. My eyes catch the outline of Nash behind me. From where I sit, I have the perfect view through the mirror of him in the bathroom. That five-inch opening—thanks to the barn door—provides a lot.

He holds one of those cordless electric shavers. Leaning closer to the mirror, he turns his cheek like he's about to shave but stops and slides off his shorts so he's only in his briefs. Then he goes for his shirt.

His arms get caught in the sleeves, making the entire action take longer than it needs to, *and* making his muscles ripple as he fights to free himself from the fabric. Once over his head, he tosses the shirt on the floor in his room.

Now, he's only in his underwear, slung low on his hips. His body pitches forward as he begins to shave. It's all *very* appealing. And another piece to why I married this man falls into place.

Well done, Sadie.

I congratulate myself on choosing a husband that's physically so attractive it hurts my eyes.

I mean, I literally have to look away to make the pain stop.

But now I can't concentrate on putting my makeup on. I reach for my phone, shooting a text to the one and only Edward Cullen.

SADIE

Nash is shaving in the bathroom...in only his underwear. And because I accidentally left the barn door slightly ajar, I can see him through the mirror.

EDWARD CULLEN

Oooh, fun! Talk about a great start to your date.

SADIE

Is it fun? Maybe I should go shut the door. Tonight feels like a first date, and as far as I can remember, I don't typically watch my first dates get ready in their underwear.

Actually, now that I think about it, the only first date I've ever been on was when I was fifteen and went to homecoming with Stetson. That's kind of sad.

EDWARD CULLEN

He's your husband. I say pay your thanks to Jack and Jill for their lovely bathroom design and watch the man undress.

My eyes skitter back to him.

SADIE

He does look really good.

EDWARD CULLEN

Talking about how good another woman's husband looks gives me the ick, but I'm really happy you're figuring out you're attracted to the man you married. That's a big step for you.

Nash turns his head, catching my eyes on him. His mouth hitches upward. "I can open the door wider if you want."

237

I press my lips together so hard. There's no way I'm letting this man see my smile. I stand, walking directly to the bathroom. And let me tell you, the closer I get, the better he looks.

"I'll give you some privacy," I say as I pull the door shut.

The way his cocky smile drags across his mouth is, unfortunately, the last thing I see.

CHAPTER THIRTY ONE

NASH

"I ASKED your dad where the best place to eat in town was, and he said Antoni's Cucina," I say as we walk down the sidewalk to the restaurant.

"You asked my dad, and he actually gave you a recommendation?"

"Shocking, huh?" I hold the door open for her, feeling the warmth from inside crash over us. "Your dad and I are becoming fast friends, connecting over our healthcare businesses and our shared love of you."

Sadie's lips purse as she thinks over what I just said.

"May I help you?" the host asks.

"Yes, I have a special reservation under Nash Carter."

"Ah, yes, Mr. Carter, we have everything set for you on the patio."

"The patio? Won't it be freezing out there?"

"Let's just see how it goes."

Sadie walks ahead of me, and this time, when I put my hand on the small of her back to escort her, she doesn't flinch.

The host leads us out back, where a private table is set up

in front of a stone fireplace with a raging fire inside. Blankets are draped over the backs of our chairs, and freestanding patio heaters are pulled over beside our table.

Sadie smiles as she looks around at the string lights and romantic candlelit dinner. I knew she'd like this.

She loves extra effort and romantic settings that feel private and unique. This was the best I could do in Skaneateles, but it turned out better than expected.

The host helps us into our seats, dropping the blankets over our legs like he would with the napkins, and then hands us the menu before leaving.

"Wow," Sadie gushes. "This is pretty cute."

"I'm pretty good at this."

"I'm beginning to see that." She smiles, and there's a spark of the old Sadie underneath it all. "So what did we do on our actual first date?"

"It was Christmastime three years ago, so we went ice skating at Maggie Daley Park Skating Ribbon. Instead of a rink, it winds around like a ribbon. Then we got some hot cocoa and made out in front of the Chicago Christmas tree."

"No, we didn't."

"We did." I can't help my satisfied smile. "I think someone even yelled at us to get a room."

An embarrassed laugh puffs out. "Okay, what about after that?"

"We went back to my place, and that's when things really heated up."

She holds up her hand, stopping me. "I get the picture. You don't need to say what else we did."

"We roasted s'mores on my balcony," I say with a growing smile. "Good grief, it was a first date. Get your mind out of the gutter."

Her eyes roll as she laughs. "So if our first date was the

beginning of Christmas and we've been married almost three years, when did we get engaged?"

"Got engaged on Christmas Eve and married almost one month later."

"Why so fast? That's a crazy timeline."

"We were madly in love, so why wait?"

"Uh..."—her eyes go big—"to get to know each other better, to make sure it's right."

"We'd been getting to know each other at work for six months."

"Yeah, but there are more reasons than that to take things slow and plan it out."

"You were sick of all the life plans. That was one of the things you liked about me—the unexpected excitement of not knowing what life will bring, just enjoying the adventure as it goes along." She says nothing as my words sink into her heart and mind. "We both knew it was fast, but we didn't care if it made us seem insane. We knew what we had was a once-in-a-lifetime kind of love, unmatched by anything else."

I want to tell her it could be that way again and that it *still is* that way for me, but I don't. Those are things that Sadie needs to discover on her own.

"Besides, I knew you were the one the second I saw you."

"So you're claiming love at first sight?" Skepticism coats her words.

My head tilts, and I smile. "At first sight and every moment after."

~

SADIE

AFTER DINNER, Nash and I walk down the Skaneateles pier to the end, where the village Christmas tree is lit. Its magical lights cast a glow across the lake like a lighthouse.

He leans his head back so he can see the star on top. "And now, for the rest of my life, nothing short of a Christmas tree next to a lake will do."

"It is beautiful, isn't it?" My teeth chatter as I try to get the words out.

"Are you warm enough?" His hands glide up and down the sides of my arms, creating a friction of heat.

"It's a little cold."

"I could help with that if you want." His eyes twinkle like the lights on the tree.

"Was this your plan all along? Keep me outside all night until I get cold enough to beg you to warm me up?"

"I mean, it's not a bad idea." His hands stop their frantic movement against my arms, and the mood shifts.

Nash steps a little closer, and the glimmer in his eyes turns into something warm and loving. He wraps his arms around my body, pulling my chest against his. Instantly, heat rushes through me. I don't know if it's real or from a flicker of desire, but I like it.

"You look beautiful tonight." His gaze skitters around my face. "Did I tell you that yet?"

"Only about four times."

Slowly, he leans forward, and my breath catches the moment his warm lips press against the scar on my head. They linger over the jaggedness like a reverent tribute to my recovery. As he pulls back, his fingers brush my cheek lovingly.

"Your hand is cold." I lean away from his body, opening up my jacket, inviting his arms into my warmth.

A subtle smile tugs the corner of his mouth upward at my invitation. He readjusts his arms, slowly sliding his frozen fingers around my stomach and waist. The sheer fabric of Annie's shirt is a blessing and a curse. I feel his hands on me as if I were wearing nothing.

"Can I hug you?" There's something really sweet and innocent about his question that moves my heart.

I nod, and suddenly, I'm encircled by Nash's body. His face buries into my neck and hair. Hot breath spills over my ear as he sighs in contentment. My eyes close, and I melt into him. In return, he squeezes me tighter, like I'm the only thing in his life he holds dear.

We stay in that all-encompassing hug for a long time, both taking something we need from the other. For me, it's the safety and comfort amidst so much uncertainty. And for him, it's me. Just *me*.

His arms loosen, letting me know he's pulling back. "I better get you home. I'm sure you're tired."

His hands glide over my waist again on his way out from underneath my coat. I don't know if it's the curiosity about whether or not we have chemistry, the genuine care and concern Nash has for me, or even the fact that Stetson has a girlfriend, but I grab his wrists, stopping him.

"That's it?"

"What do you mean?"

"I thought you were going to seize your masculine moment, dip me back, and kiss the crap out of me."

He stares at me, debating like only a gentleman would.

Both hands cup my face in preparation, and my heart buzzes with apprehension. Softly, Nash caresses my cheeks, still gazing longingly into my eyes. "Your last first kiss?"

My heart pounds, bringing anxiety with it.

I only remember kissing Stetson. Would this really be my last first kiss?

The softness behind Nash's gaze eases my concerns, and somewhere deep inside, I feel secure giving him this intimate piece of me.

Anticipation builds and builds, and just when I feel like I'll snap in half, his hands wrap around me, tilting me to the side. It's a dip like he promised, but not in the traditional way. His arms cradle me against him as our bodies slant to the side together. My hand goes to his neck, and the other holds his back. His movements are deliberate, as if he knows this situation requires patience and time. The tender smile covering his lips is the last thing I see before his mouth presses to mine. I close my eyes, giving myself to his kiss.

It's a gentleman's kiss—soft and slow—a token of something real, pure, and ideal. I feel the warmth of his love and affection from my toes all the way up to my treacherous, forgetful mind.

His arms pull me in tighter and tighter like a treasure he never wants to lose. The way he holds me says so much about how he values me. It's achingly beautiful—something every woman should experience in their lifetime. I'd consider giving up another three and a half years of my life just to be kissed like this again.

Nash brings me up straight again, tugging and brushing his lips over mine a few more times before he pulls back.

"I've missed you," he whispers between us.

His words pierce and squeeze my heart in ways I can't understand. I don't return the sentiment, because I can't. I'm still just trying to figure it all out.

But there's one thing I do know: Nash Carter has set the standard high.

CHAPTER THIRTY TWO

NASH

"YOU'RE in a good mood this morning." Lynette smirks from her spot at the stove.

My cheerful rendition of "Santa Bring My Baby Back to Me," in my best Elvis Presley voice, probably gives me away to Sadie's mom.

"Things must have gone well on your date last night."

I can't contain my smile. "They did, although I'm sure that's not what you want to hear."

Lynette's eyes return to the pot in front of her, stirring the soup for dinner tonight. "Nash, I'm not against you. I just want my daughter to be happy and to have a relationship with her."

I push my laptop away, focusing on our conversation. "Now that I've been in Skaneateles with your family the last two and a half weeks, I feel bad about everything Sadie's missed the past three years. I should have done more to mend the rift between you guys." I lean forward, hoping she feels the earnestness behind my words. "I did try, and I sincerely want you to know that taking your daughter away from you wasn't my intention at all. I encouraged her to call you, but I could have done more. I gave up easily when Sadie pushed back, and I shouldn't have."

Lynette stopped stirring halfway through my speech and faced me, giving me the perfect view of her misty eyes. "I appreciate you saying that. It means a lot." She wipes her hand on her apron and walks to where I sit at the dining table. "For a long time, I placed a lot of blame and anger on you, as if it were your fault for everything that went wrong between us and Sadie. It was easier to blame you than to face my own missteps in our relationship. But I was wrong in doing that. You're different than I thought, Nash. You're a good man. I see what Sadie likes about you."

She reaches her hand out, placing it on top of mine.

"So, is this, like, a truce?" I smile.

"I think so. Moving forward, maybe we could work together."

"I'd really like that. I don't know my own mother very well, but I'd like to know you."

"I'd like that too." She squeezes my fingers before returning to cooking dinner.

"If we're allies now," I say, "maybe I could ask you for some advice about your daughter."

"At this point, I think you know Sadie better than I do."

"That might've been true three months ago, but I'm in uncharted water now." I walk to the barstools around the island and take a seat. The closer proximity to Lynette seems appropriate for such a delicate topic. "Last night, we went on this incredible date. We had so much fun, and it felt like how it used to be. I saw Sadie's walls come down, and we even kissed." Lynette's lips twitch with surprise. "But now I don't know where to go from here. Obviously, I want to build on the momentum. So, I thought I could take her to Syracuse tonight and do something fun and different—unless you have a better idea."

"Give her some space." Lynette leans against the counter. "Just because the date last night went well doesn't mean everything between you two is fixed."

"But we kissed." *A really great and romantic kiss.*

"And now Sadie has to process what that kiss means, and you need to give her the space to do that. I know it's not what you want to hear, but one good date isn't a declaration of her love. She's grappling with a lot of emotions."

My head hangs. "You're right. I know you're right."

So, space it is.

~

SADIE

"GREAT WORK today," Heather, my physical therapist, says as I walk her to the door. "That was our last session."

My brows lift. "Really?"

"Yeah, you've passed everything with flying colors. From a motor skills perspective, you've made a full recovery."

"That's great." I try to show enthusiasm as I open the front door for her. "Thanks for everything."

"No problem, and good luck with the rest of your recovery." She spins, walking down the front steps.

My eyes drift to Nash, down by the firepit, chopping wood. I'd be lying if I said him chopping wood wasn't attractive. The manliness behind each lift and swing of the axe is something worth watching.

So I do watch—at least for a few seconds.

There's a proven attraction with Nash. After our kiss the

other night, I'm not doubting that. It was nice. Hands down, the best first kiss I've had.

But a great kiss isn't enough to build a life on.

It's the emotional connection that's not coming as easily. It's hard to force feelings you don't feel. And how long do you give yourself to find those feelings before you decide they're not coming and never will? I don't know. I just know it's too soon to decide anything yet. I woke up from my coma less than a month ago. I need more time to sort through it all.

When Nash notices Heather's car pulling out, he lifts his head, seeing me by the front door. An immediate smile drops over his mouth, and he waves. I wave back then shut the door.

I'm glad he's keeping himself busy. The last thing I need right now is him following me around. There's already too much pressure on my feelings.

Sometimes, it's nice to have some space, even if space is what scares me.

If I really loved Nash, shouldn't I want to be with him all the time?

CHAPTER THIRTY THREE

SADIE

"WHAT'S IN THE BAG?" I glance over my shoulder to the giant garbage bag sitting in the backseat of the car.

Nash's mouth curls into a mischievous smile. "It's a surprise."

"Can you at least tell me why we're dressed in snow clothes? You know I can't go sledding, right? I have a traumatic brain injury."

"Don't worry"—he squeezes my knee, sending a thrill shooting up my leg—"it's not sledding."

He turns the car into Clift Park, and I see the crowd of people standing around.

"The snowman-building contest?"

"We're going to destroy this thing." Signature cockiness rounds out his grin. "Queen Victoria is not going to know what hit her."

"Queen Victoria?"

"Yeah, she's the judge who decides who builds the best snowman." He climbs out of the car, gathering all our supplies.

I join him by the trunk, where he pulls out a ladder. "How did you even know about this?"

"I follow A Dickens Christmas Facebook page. They have the entire schedule of events posted there." His words are matter-of-fact, as if I should already know all this as a local.

"Never pictured you as a small-town guy." I scratch my head, realizing I have absolutely zero information to back that up with.

His flirty eyes shoot to me. "How do you picture me?"

"You can't turn snowman building into a sexual thing."

"Watch me." He pats my butt as he walks past, heading for the registration table.

I stand frozen, my mouth gaping, eyes blinking.

Nash swings his body around, the full force of his charming smile slamming me in my chest. His shoulders lift even as he carries the bag of supplies in one hand and the ladder in the other.

"Let's go, babe!" he calls, walking backward a few paces before turning around again.

I have no idea why Nash manhandling that heavy ladder with one hand is so dang attractive, but it is.

My feet stumble forward, following after him.

"You're on one today." I push the sticks Nash brought into the sides of the snowman.

"What does that mean?" he grunts as he rolls the head through the snow.

"You're extra flirty."

"Nah, this is how I always am." His head lifts, showcasing a goofy grin, and somehow, I know he's telling the truth.

"Did I like how flirty you are?"

"What do you think?" Another big smile accompanies his words.

I'm guessing life with Nash was full of fun, playfulness, teasing, banter, and lots of flirting. I can see why I'd like that, be happy even. There's a vibrance about him, an energy that's addicting.

He rolls the ball to my feet. "Now we have to get the head on the body."

"I think you overestimated how big to make this thing." I look down at the giant snowball and then around at the other pairs building regular-sized snowmen. When finished, ours will be the biggest by far. "Is this even possible?"

"Sure. That's what the ladder is for."

Dragging it over in front of our snowman's body, he shifts it into an A-frame. Slowly, Nash rolls the head up the side of the ladder. The rungs shave parts of the round circle, but overall, it's mostly an effective method. Once at the top, he lifts the ball on top of the other two giant circles.

A victorious smile paints his mouth, and both hands raise high above his head, pumping up and down like Rocky. He gives a big whoop, still pumping his arms as he glances around the park at the other builders.

I bite my lip, trying to hold in my laughter.

He's cute.

A man who doesn't take himself too seriously.

Two feet hit the ground as he hops down from the top of the ladder. "Now we just need to put the stuff on his face. Accessorize him."

I dig through the bag, holding up three cans of Spaghetti-Os. "I'm not sure what I'm supposed to do with these. You didn't bring the typical snowman items."

"These are our buttons." He grabs one of the cans from my hands, turning it so the metal top is facing forward, then pushes it into the snowman's body, spinning it round and round until the can tunnels its way into the snow. "They have sentimental value."

"Spaghetti-Os? Really?"

"Really."

"Okay." I reach into the bag, pulling out the classic coal for eyes, ropes of licorice for the mouth, a pipe, a scarf, and a Cubs hat. This one, Nash doesn't have to tell me. I know enough about our past to know the significance of the Cubs hat. "I'm assuming this is for his head."

"Yep."

"Won't the hat be too small?"

"It'll be perfect." He moves the ladder away from the snowman and puts it right in front of me. "Climb on my shoulders, and you can do the honors."

My brows drop in suspicion. "Your shoulders? Why not use the ladder?"

"What would be the fun in that?"

His flirtatious eyes dare me to play along with his game, and there's no reason for me not to. I need to try and build my connection with him.

"Fine."

Nash holds the ladder steady as I climb the first few steps until I'm tall enough to swing my leg around him. Once sitting firmly on his shoulders, I lock my legs around his body for support. His hands go to my thighs, holding me to him. That same thrill from when he grabbed my leg in the car dances up my body.

"Do not drop me!" I warn as he slowly walks us toward our masterpiece of snow.

"Don't worry. I've got you."

I spend the next few minutes placing all the accessories until I'm satisfied.

"He looks good! Our little Cubsman."

"We're totally going to win."

"We probably will. And you'll have to tell little six-year-old Cindy Lou Who over there that two grown adults took her trophy."

"Eh, she'll live."

Nash slowly bends his knees, giving me a chance to get off his shoulders, but just as my foot touches the ground, he loses his balance, sending us both falling backward into the snow, laughing.

Before I can react, Nash flips around and crawls over to me. The weight of his body presses against mine as our legs tangle together. His green eyes scan my face as his soft lips lift into a smile. He brings his hand to his mouth, using his teeth to pull off his glove—the action oddly sexy. He takes the glove from his mouth and chucks it to the side.

The back of his hand gently brushes down the side of my face. My breathing gets heavier, moving in tandem with the wild heartbeats inside my chest. I don't know what his next move will be, but I want it no matter what it is.

"I love your freckles." His finger plays dot to dot on my face between a few of my more prominent flecks. I close my eyes, relishing in the feel of his touch.

Warm lips press against the corner of my mouth. I peek my eyes open, catching his own half-closed gaze as he slowly moves to kiss the crow's feet at the edge of my eye.

Is Nash an outlier—a man so sweet and perfect that he's too good to be true?

Or does he just love me *that* much?

I arch my back, pressing my body into his, wanting, *needing* to feel the flame between us. My chin lifts, coaxing his mouth to mine.

Instead of a kiss, my lips are met with a smile. His tongue clicks in mocking disapproval.

"This is a family-friendly event. I don't want Cindy Lou Who's dad to have to cover his daughter's eyes. I mean, what do you think this is? The Chicago Christmas tree on our first date? You think we can just make out in front of all these people?"

I purse my lips together, hitting his arm playfully before pushing his body off. "You're the one who laid on top of me."

Nash sits in the snow beside me, shooting me a wicked smile. "Don't act like you didn't want me to."

I turn away, hiding the red blush creeping up my cheeks.

But he's right.

I wanted everything he was offering, and that thought terrifies me.

CHAPTER THIRTY FOUR

NASH

PER LYNETTE'S ADVICE, I'm on this pattern where I wait three days between every date I have with Sadie before taking her on another one. Luckily, today is a date day. Since it's midweek and nothing is happening in town, I had to get creative.

"It's really hard to walk with you covering my eyes." Sadie's hands reach out in front of her as if I'd let her walk straight into a tree.

"Almost there."

She shivers, giving me the satisfaction of knowing my whispers against her neck affected her.

I guide her to the edge of the dock in front of her house and count to three before pulling the blindfold away from her eyes.

"Tada!" I say proudly, gesturing to the small red boat in the water.

"You put a Christmas tree inside my dad's boat?" Her sideways smile gives me the impression she might think I'm crazy.

"Romantic, right?" I climb inside, literally rocking the

boat back and forth. "I got the idea from that women's Google site."

Her eyes narrow. "Women's Google? Is that a new thing that's happened in the last three years that I don't remember?"

"No, you know the thing where you, like, pin stuff?"

"Oh." I nod in understanding. "You got the idea from Pinterest?"

"Yep." I reach out to help her, but she doesn't accept it.

"You put the Christmas tree in the center of the boat."

"Yeah, mostly for balance but also so we could face each other and see the twinkling lights."

"Well, if you help me in, how am I going to get around the tree to sit on my side of the boat?"

"Great question." My hands go to my hips, assessing my design flaws.

"I'll just climb in myself." Sadie holds onto the edge of the dock as she lowers into the boat.

I can barely see around the tree to where she sits opposite of me, but it's fine. It's romantic, like I said.

"Watch this." I tap the remote on the battery-operated lights, making the tree glow. It's the perfect ambiance between the moonlight and the fairy lights around the tree.

"Very impressive." She leans her head to the side so I can see her smile.

"Thank you. I'm impressed with myself." I grab the oars and begin rowing us away from the shore. "There's a blanket by your feet if you're cold."

"You've thought of everything."

"Yeah." It's my turn to lean my head out so she can see me.

I didn't think of everything, or else I would've thought

about how a tree in the middle of the boat would put miles between us.

Stupid.

I blame Pinterest for this.

I keep rowing, trying to engage in conversation, but it's useless. The tree is a problem.

"I've had enough of this." I stand, finding my balance between the rocking of the boat.

"What are you going to do?"

"For starters, I'm moving this stupid thing." I try and lift the fake tree, but one of the legs is stuck under the seat.

Sadie half stands, reaching to undo it.

I can't explain what happens in the next few seconds. All I know is that inertia takes over, and before either of us can stop it, our weight tips us—*and the stupid tree*—into the icy water.

A thousand tiny pinpricks stab my skin, and my breath freezes inside my chest the second I hit the water. The force of the fall slams my body into the ground, letting me know I can touch here. My feet scrape against the bottom as I come up for air. All I can think about is Sadie. She gasps beside me, finding her feet in the three feet of water.

"Are you okay?" I huff as my lungs thaw.

Her heavy breaths and frantic movements to get back in the boat let me know she's at least alive and not frozen to death.

"I'm...going to kill you...Nash." Her teeth chatter as she tries to get the words out.

I do my best to push her butt to hoist her back in the boat. Her body flops over the edge, and instead of climbing in, I decide to push the boat fifteen feet to shore.

"It's a memory. You need more of those."

"Not one this cold."

"Use the blanket," I say through my clenched jaw.

"I think my clothes are frozen to my skin."

"Almost got it." I give a final push, hitting the boat's bow onto the rocks. "Come on!"

She stands, and instead of helping her out of the boat, I pick her up and cradle her in my arms. My adrenaline kicks in, giving my frozen body the strength to carry her into the house. By the time we get inside, we're both laughing through our shivers.

"I hate...your tree...idea."

"This isn't how I saw it going," I say as I climb the stairs.

I push her bedroom door open with my foot and carry her the rest of the way to the bathroom, where I sit her down to turn on a warm shower.

She faces the mirror as she takes off her shoes and socks. "My hair is icicles!"

"Forget about that. We have to get you warm." I begin peeling layers off of her as we both laugh.

"I can't believe you dumped us in the lake." She smiles, letting me pull her jacket off.

"Epic fail."

I start to lift up her shirt but stop as our eyes lock. Suddenly, everything goes warm. The steam from the shower floats around us, shifting the mood to something entirely different, as if a fire has been lit inside our bodies.

Her frozen hands slide under my shirt, pressing against my chest. It's the lighter fluid exploding the flame inside me. I drop my head, kissing her more passionately than I probably should, but she returns the desire, melting her wet body into mine.

Passion and excitement collide, intensifying everything. Her hands roam up and down my torso in a way so satisfying it's maddening. I pull Sadie closer, feeling like no amount of her is enough.

My arms wrap around her waist, lifting her body to sit on the bathroom counter, knocking things over in the process. This kiss is different than the other one we shared on the pier. Hot and frantic desire replaces the slow gentleness from before.

This kiss rivals some of the best kisses of our marriage.

My body craves the next step so badly, to feel like we're one again.

I know the survival guide stuff. I know we need to remove our wet clothes and use direct body heat to raise our core temperatures. I could easily justify my carnal desires, pass it off as something innocent. We're married, after all. It's nothing we haven't done before, but no matter how much I want that—*heck, maybe even need it*—I know Sadie is not ready to add physical stuff to the emotional complications already in the mix.

So I stop.

The kind of control and willpower it takes to stop drains my soul. I'm a battery pack with nothing left to give.

My lips pull back, and I press my forehead against hers. I grab her hands out from under my shirt and hold them between our two bodies.

"I want this. I want *you*," I breathe.

"So do I." She presses her body into mine, trying to reignite what burned hot seconds ago.

"No, you don't. Not like this. Not until you're sure *I'm* what you really want."

I kiss her on the cheek and exit the bathroom, rolling shut the barn door on my side, hoping for a day when Sadie truly feels like my wife again.

CHAPTER THIRTY FIVE

SADIE

I ENTER the kitchen the next morning in a bad mood, quickly silencing the light chatter between my mom and Nash. I open cupboards, stare aimlessly inside, then slam them shut again.

"Can I help you find something?" my mom asks. I can feel her exchange a glance with Nash behind my back.

"Don't you keep any cold cereal around anymore?" I huff, whirling around to face her.

"No, but I can buy some today."

"It's fine." The eye roll I give says otherwise.

"Did something happen to make you so upset?" My mom's voice is soft, as if her words are walking on eggshells.

"I started my period this morning," I announce as I swing the refrigerator door open and grab the jug of orange juice. I figure since Nash is my husband, he can handle sensitive topics like this.

"That does happen once a month." My mom smirks like I'm being some dramatic teenager.

"Yeah, but it used to not happen to me. Not since I got an IUD put in five years ago. So now, I need to figure out if it's not in the right place or if something is wrong from the accident. It just feels like another thing added to my already full plate."

"Well, we can call Dr. Lucero and make an appointment for later today just to check things out."

"Um…"—Nash shifts uncomfortably in his chair—"that's probably not necessary."

My glare lands on him.

Nash isn't who I'm mad at.

I'm mad at myself.

I don't know what would've happened if he hadn't stopped things in the bathroom last night. Actually, I do…a *giant* mistake.

Everything is confusing right now, but kissing Nash is pretty straightforward. It feels good. I like it. It allows me to escape the murky mess in my mind—just forget about it all. So basically, I'm self-medicating my messed-up life with Nash's lips. Something that's not fair to him or to me.

"Why isn't going to a gynecologist necessary?" There's a bite behind my words that I'm not proud of.

"Probably because, a month before the accident, you had your IUD taken out."

My head rears back. "Why would I do that? I love my IUD."

He walks to me, grabs the jug of orange juice from my hand, refilling his glass. His eyes flick to mine. "Because we wanted to have a baby."

The words carve a hole in my chest, hollowing me from the inside out.

Nervously, his gaze skips to my mom and then back to me. "You were going to track your cycle for a few months, and then we were going to hit it hard in Switzerland." Uncomfortable awkwardness fills the room, especially after everything that transpired last night. "That sounded bad." He shakes his head, getting flustered. "Basically, we were trying to have a baby. That's why you started your period unexpectedly."

A baby?

I don't know how I should feel.

I want to be a mother, but Stetson was always the dad in the plan. Replacing him with Nash is a blow my mind wasn't prepared for this morning. I don't know if I'll ever be able to fully wrap my head around that.

"I guess that explains that." I force a tight, closed-lip smile and walk out of the room.

CHAPTER THIRTY SIX

SADIE

"THIS IS JUST a little something from our family to wish you Merry Christmas." My mom hands a basket of baked goods to my dad's secretary, Deborah.

"Oh, Lynette, you've outdone yourself." She points to one of the candies wrapped in waxed paper. "Is this your famous caramel?"

My eyes drift around the space as the two women chat.

This was supposed to be my office. Deborah should be my secretary by now—another part of my life plan that didn't play out how I wanted it to.

"Sadie?" My dad waves me into his office, keeping his hand on the door until I enter, then he shuts it. "I'm glad you came here today with your mother. I wanted to talk to you about business."

Running my dad's company was the dream. I worked for him all through high school and college, and that's where my mind is still at, even today.

"This operation is small potatoes compared to what you and Nash built in Chicago." He takes a seat in his massive leather chair behind his desk. "But we're profitable and growing at a steady rate."

"I don't know what Nash and I built in Chicago."

"That's right." He shakes his head, forgetting what I forgot. "Nash has told me a lot about it—about the locum tenens you introduced."

"He has?"

"Yeah, he's been down here a few times, comparing notes, sharing information. He knows his stuff."

Why didn't I know my dad and Nash were talking and hanging out? It's not like Nash and I are constantly together. I guess it's expected that he'd fill his empty days in Skaneateles with other stuff. I just didn't think about it. In a lot of ways, Nash only exists when he's with me, like a side character in a plot you only see when they're in the scene with the main character.

"But as impressive as Nash is, I've been more impressed with what he's told me about you and your ideas."

My heart lifts. Impressing my dad in a work setting was always at the forefront of my mind.

"I think I was unfair to you all those years ago." He clears his throat, erasing the hint of emotion I thought I heard.

"How?"

"I didn't put enough trust and belief in you." He puffs out a humorless laugh, another mechanism to hide his vulnerability. "I probably micromanaged you to death, and I just wanted to say I'm sorry."

There's only been a few times in my life when I've heard my dad utter the actual words, *I'm sorry*. His apologies usually dance around it but never include it.

"I'm so proud of all you've accomplished. I really am." He smiles even as his eyes fill with moisture. "You're smart, and even though you can't remember everything you've accomplished in the last three years, you still should feel proud. I'd be honored to have someone like you take over my business any day of the week."

I blink back at him, almost like I'm watching in real-time as years of arguments, frustrations, and complicated feelings fall away from our relationship one brick at a time.

"Thank you," I finally manage to get out. "And I feel like I owe you an apology too. I don't remember all the ins and outs of why I pulled away from you so much, but I know it wasn't fair of me. I'm sorry I didn't stick around and figure it all out. I wish I had."

He wipes a tear.

I saw him cry once at his mother's funeral when I was a little girl and once in the video of Tate's funeral.

And now I've seen him cry over me and the lost years between us because we were too stubborn to forgive and forget.

"Let's do better moving forward?" I offer.

"I'd like that."

I'd like that too.

That simple admission releases years of weight holding me down. I can't remember how it held me back. I just know deep down that it did.

CHAPTER THIRTY SEVEN

NASH

THIS IS the one event on the calendar I've circled ever since I heard about A Dickens Christmas—December 23rd—the Fezziwig's Christmas Ball, just like in *A Christmas Carol*—but Skaneateles style.

You dress up. You dance. You fall in love.

At least, that's how I'm hoping the night goes. But Sadie has been standoffish the last few day, ever since the night we fell in the lake, and even more so when I told her we wanted to have a baby. I don't know if it's all connected or if there's something more going on. I just know every wall and guard that I've been working to tear down has been raised again.

But I'm holding my breath, hoping for the best tonight.

"My lady." I bow, kissing Sadie's knuckles as I help her out of the car.

Her lips lift, but it's not a smile. Not really.

"Shall we?" I offer her my arm, and she loops her hand through.

"Are you going to talk in Victorian-style language all night?"

"I doubt it, since I don't know anything else besides what I've already said. Wait." I hold my finger up as another word pops into my head. I lean in closer, whispering into her ear. "You look ravishing tonight."

That gets a lip twitch. Not a full smile or a laugh. But at least there was a twitch.

Sadie does look ravishing in her fitted maroon off-the-shoulder dress.

"You're the most beautiful woman here."

She eyes me. "Thanks. You look nice too."

"At least this time, I'm in a suit and tie instead of a flannel button-up." I hold the door open for her. English-style music plays loudly, and stomps and shuffles scrape across the wood floor as groups learn a new dance.

"This looks fun." I glance around the room, taking in the Christmas garland and giant red bows.

"There's Annie and my parents."

It's not until we start walking toward them that I see Stetson and the pretty blonde beside him. She's not as beautiful as my wife, but she seems nice enough.

Sadie's feet trip up. I glance down to see if she stepped on her dress or something, but when my eyes lift, I follow her gaze to Stetson and his date, and I know the reason for her falter.

I press my hand against the small of her back, coaxing her forward again until we join the circle of Bradleys and Roeshines.

"What a party, huh?" I say in an effort to shatter the tenseness I know she feels.

"Oh, Sadie, you look absolutely lovely," Stetson's mom gushes.

"Thank you." She smiles as her eyes drift to Stetson.

"This is Savannah." He gestures to the woman beside him. "And this is Nash and Sadie."

"It's so nice to meet you." Savannah extends her hand, and I visibly see the moment Sadie masks the unrest she feels, replacing it with a smile.

"Same to you."

"Savvy and I are going to hit the dance floor. We'll talk to you all later."

"Do you want to dance?" I ask, trying to pull Sadie's attention back to me.

"Not right now." She shakes her head, eyes darting in Stetson's direction before returning. "I think I'll just sit at a table."

"I'd love to dance," Lynette speaks up.

"I would too," Annie says.

"Will you do me the honors?" I hold my hand out to my mother-in-law as I smile at Sadie, proud of myself for coming up with another old-fashioned saying, but she doesn't notice. She focuses on the dance floor and the couple swinging in and out.

"I'd love to!" Lynette puts her hand in mine, glancing back over her shoulder. "Jay, you'll dance with Annie, won't you?"

"Of course."

"You'll be okay by yourself?" I hesitate, wanting to make sure Sadie doesn't feel abandoned.

"Yep." She smiles.

Something tells me Sadie doesn't need anyone to keep her company. She seems pretty preoccupied with Stetson and his date.

∽

SADIE

"Do you mind if I join you?" Stetson asks, pulling out the chair beside me.

I lost track of him and Savvy twenty minutes ago. I honestly thought they left.

"Where's Savannah?" My eyes follow his broad shoulders as he takes a seat.

"She's dancing with her little brother."

"She's beautiful. I'm happy for you both." *Biggest lie I've ever said.* Actually, I wasn't lying about the part where I said she was beautiful, because she is.

"You're not happy." He smirks. "I can see it all over your face."

"Are you happy for me and Nash?"

His eyes flick to the dance floor, where Nash stomps around in a circle, holding hands. "No, but I can answer yes if you want me to."

I should tell him to lie like I did, put a final stamp on my heart that everything between us is over, but I don't.

"Do you remember the one Fezziwig's Ball we went to?"

"How could I forget? You shoved your tongue down my throat in the coat closet. I didn't know people could kiss like that. It totally freaked me out."

He laughs. "I wasn't very smooth back then."

"And are you now?" My gaze holds his.

"I thought so until you left me for another guy."

Everything about me plummets. "I'm so sorry I did that to you."

"You don't have to apologize. Like I said the other night, I could've done things differently. I should have put you first more instead of taking for granted that you'd always be there."

"Regrets are the worst, aren't they?" I blow out a breath, feeling the weight of so many decisions I don't remember making but still regret.

"You know what I really regret?" He smiles. "That I didn't dance with you that night at the ball."

"You were too worried about setting up our kiss in the coat closet."

"I guess so." His eyes stare into mine, and like it's fate, the music changes—violins playing something slow. Stetson holds out his hand. "Should we rewrite history?"

There's nothing I've wanted more since I woke up from my coma.

I slip my hand in his, letting him pull me to my feet and out to the dance floor. One hand goes to my waist as the other holds mine in the air between us. I place my fingers on his shoulder, barely touching him. Slowly, he waltzes us around the dance floor.

I've danced with Stetson at every school dance since I was a teenager. We didn't typically dance like this, but the whole thing feels natural and familiar—something I've been missing the last few weeks.

As the music continues, his hold around my waist gets tighter, and our bodies effortlessly move closer, our chests skimming each other. I should look away from his blue eyes, but I can't. His stare stirs up feelings that I want to feel.

"Hey, man." Nash taps Stetson's shoulder. "That's my wife."

The entire room can probably hear my racing heart over the music as I glance between the only two men who have ever owned my heart.

Nash steps forward, exuding confidence and territorial claim. "I'm cutting in."

"Of course." Stetson drops his arms, stepping back from my body. He gestures to me. "She's all yours."

And it's those exact words that break my heart as Stetson walks away.

CHAPTER THIRTY EIGHT

NASH

ORANGE, red, and yellow flames sway together, funneling up to the moonlit sky. If I squint my eyes, the bonfire looks like it's in the middle of Skaneateles Lake instead of on the edge of the Bradleys' property.

I take another long and slow sip of my drink, letting the strong liquid burn my throat as it goes down. I'm not trying to get drunk, but I'm definitely trying to take away the constant, dull ache that's been in my chest all night at the ball.

Who am I kidding?

That ache took residence in my heart the moment Sadie looked at me in the hospital with void and hollow eyes.

"I saw the fire out here and thought I'd come join you." Jay pulls up a camp chair beside me. "That is, if it's okay with you."

"Of course." I smile up at him. "It's your house. I'm just enjoying the scenic view."

He grunts as he lowers into the chair. "This has always been one of my favorite things to do. Nothing like a lakeside fire on a cold winter's night."

I lift my glass to him. "I wish I had a drink for you."

"Nah, you need it more than I do."

I sniff out a laugh, wondering if he saw the way Sadie looked at Stetson tonight too.

"You know, Lynette and I were talking on the way home from the ball about how you remind us of Mr. Fezziwig from *A Christmas Carol*."

My brows cinch together, not understanding.

"You remember his character, don't you?"

I shake my head.

"He was Scrooge's old boss and the complete opposite of him. Instead of being a Christmas crank, he was jolly, giving and full of life."

I scoff as I watch the flames move in front of me. "I don't feel very full of life tonight."

"There's a lot more to Fezziwig's character than just liking Christmas more than Scrooge. You see, Mr. Fezziwig was his opposite in every way. He showed how a selfless and caring boss can create a sense of family and community in the workplace by being kind and generous. And in a lot of ways, that's what you've taught me."

My eyes shift to Jay, surprised by where the conversation is going.

"Especially when it comes to Sadie. I haven't always believed in her like I should've. I did as a daughter, but as a formidable business partner, not as much. I wish I could've been more like you, not so worried about the bottom line and more accepting of new ideas and different methods of running a business." His lips push into a sad frown. "I think if I would've been more like that—more like *you*—I wouldn't have lost my daughter for so many years."

"In some ways, I'm glad you weren't like that, because then maybe she never would've stayed in Chicago with me."

Jay chuckles. "I think she still would've. You two are meant to be together." He shifts his gaze to me. "It might take her some time to realize that, but her heart will eventually find its way back home."

He smiles at me, and for the first time in my life, I feel what it's like to have a father look out for me and give me advice. I never knew until this moment how much I wanted that.

My eyes water over. "Jay, you're a good man."

"So are you. No matter what happens, you'll always be part of our family."

"I could use a little bit more family in my life."

"Then it's settled." He stands, patting my shoulder before leaving to go inside.

I shift my gaze back to the fire, blinking away my tears.

CHAPTER THIRTY NINE

NASH

ANNIE CARRIES a tray of snacks into the living room, setting them on the coffee table. She steals a bite of Chex mix before bouncing onto the sofa.

"Where's Sadie?" She looks at her mom. "I thought we were going to watch a Christmas movie together. That's always our Christmas Eve tradition."

Lynette's hands twist and move as she crochets a scarf. "I don't know. She left the house just before lunch and didn't say when she'd be back." Her gaze flicks to me—the same edge of concern I feel lingers in her eyes.

"Wait. I thought she couldn't drive."

"She finished the medication that made it so she couldn't drive. She's all clear now."

Annie's eyes hover in suspicion. "Where would she even go? It's Christmas Eve."

I've wondered the same thing the last two hours.

"Probably just went for a drive. Clear her head a little bit." Jay doesn't even look up from his book.

"What if Sadie crashed the car and is dead in a ditch somewhere?"

"Annie!" Lynette gasps. "What a terrible thing to say on Christmas Eve."

"What?" She shrugs. "We're all thinking it."

We *are* all thinking it.

I jump up from my spot on the couch. I can't sit here any longer, pretending to watch a Bowl game.

"Maybe I'll just drive around and see if I can find her."

Jay sits up. "Do you want me to come with you?"

But I'm already at the door, grabbing my coat from the hook. "No, I'll be back soon."

The snow crunches under my feet as I rush to the car. I turn on the ignition, flipping the heater to full blast. My hands clutch the steering wheel, but I don't move. I don't know where to go to look for her.

Then I remember her cell phone. If Sadie has it with her, I should be able to see her location unless she turned it off sometime over the last month. I open the Find My app and pull up her device. She's still in Skaneateles on Lane J. I shift the car into drive and head in that direction.

It takes about twelve minutes to get there. I turn onto Lane J and see her car parked down the street at a house. It's not until I drive by that I recognize the place. Jay showed me a picture of it once before—a real estate property he and Lewis Roeshine purchased five years ago as a rental and then eventually as a home meant for Stetson and Sadie.

Now it's just Stetson's house.

The worst feeling rips through me, destroying my whole world.

Sadie is with *him*.

My mind jumps to all kinds of conclusions as anger, hurt, jealousy, and pure anguish drag my heart in different directions. I want to knock on his door and demand answers or at least an explanation, but I don't.

I turn my car around and leave, numbly driving until I find myself at the cemetery. The place is empty despite being Christmas Eve. A wreath and fake poinsettias sit at the foot of Tate's grave. I stare blankly at his carved-out name, finally deciding to speak.

"I'm losing her," I say out loud, the admission crushing my soul. "It's happening right in front of me, and there's nothing I can do about it."

Silence.

"She looks at him the way she used to look at me." Tears rush to my eyes, and I swear under my breath, blinking them away.

More silence.

"I love her—more than the day I married her. You don't stop caring for someone just because they stop caring for you. And I'm scared I'll stay in love with her the rest of my life even if she doesn't love me back." I clear my throat to hold off my growing emotion. A humorless laugh comes out with a grunt as I wipe a lone tear. "I'm sorry, man. I wanted to take care of Sadie for the rest of her life. I *planned* to take care of her forever." I drop my shoulders in the saddest defeat. "I just wanted to let you know."

CHAPTER FORTY

SADIE

THE SKY DIMS as I pull into my parents' drive.

I lost track of time, not realizing it was almost five p.m.

I run to the side door when I see the back of Nash's head.

He sits beside the firepit, watching flames snap into the sky.

He's waiting for me to come home.

Guilt sweeps through me like a tornado.

Slowly, I walk to him, building my case of defense with each step.

I sit down, hoping he'll speak first, but he doesn't say anything, and I know I have to start.

"Sorry, I lost track of time."

His gaze shifts to me. "I miss you." Sadness coats every single one of his features, tripling the guilt I thought I felt before. "Even though I've spent every day with you since the accident, I still *miss* you. I miss the way we were."

I lift my shoulders. "And I can't even remember it."

"I've been trying to show you. Remind you."

"I know." A chill runs up my back, and I shove my hands in my pockets. "But it's not the same. *I'm* not the same. You want me to reignite a flame I can't find."

"You can't find the feelings right now, but that doesn't mean they won't return with time."

"Do you know how much pressure that is? It's overwhelming." Stinging tears pierce my eyes. "It's hard to figure out who I am with that kind of pressure. I feel like I can't breathe inside your arms with you watching and waiting for me to fall back in love with you."

For the last month, I've been sheltering Nash from the feelings inside my heart and head, but it's time for everything I feel to be in plain sight. My words need to unravel the unspoken realities between us.

"So if you don't love me, do you love him?"

I don't have to ask who *him* is.

"I'm confused." I wring my hands, feeling the gravity of the moment. "The last thing I remember is loving Stetson. Then I wake up, and everyone says I have a different life with someone new. It's just hard to wrap my head around those changes." I drop my eyes, trying to find the right words to explain. "Imagine someone picked out a random woman on the street and told you that you needed to have feelings for her and share the rest of your life with her, but in your mind, you really—" I stop myself because I don't want to hurt Nash more than I already have.

"But in your mind, you love someone else. That's what you were going to say, wasn't it?"

"I don't know. Like I said, I'm different. He's different. *Everything's* different, and I'm just surviving."

"And now you have me that you have to deal with. Some random guy that's in the way."

"I'm trying, Nash. I really am." The tears unleash, wetting my cheeks. "I'm straining for feelings, but they're not coming easily or as fast as you want. And I'm sorry." My shoulders lift as more tears freely flow. "Loving you shouldn't be this hard."

"I didn't feel this way alone, you know." His eyes stare directly into mine, showing emotion and heartbreak. "Once upon a time, you loved me too."

"I'm not saying that I didn't love you or that our marriage wasn't everything I wanted at the time. I'm sure it was. But…" Emotion builds, pausing my words. "My feelings aren't where yours are. And I'm so tired of pretending and trying and failing and disappointing you. I can't do it anymore."

Tears fill his green eyes as my words sink in. "And what if your memory comes back, and you remember everything that we shared together? Then what?"

I shake my head, unable to give him an answer. Either way, the outcome is tragic.

Defeat clouds his features. "So I'm supposed to love you from a distance?"

"Nash, please," I plead with him, begging him to understand and to be okay with what I need.

"Don't worry about me." He forces a smile—the saddest smile that ever existed. "I can let you go *and* still love you."

His eyes drift across my face as if committing me to memory. He stands, pulling me to my feet, wrapping me in his arms. Even his embrace feels broken.

Nash holds me for a long time, almost like he has to convince himself to let me go. "Despite losing you, I still feel like the luckiest man alive because you were mine for a little bit."

His head pulls back, and his hand goes to my face, caressing my cheek.

"Nash, you're the perfect guy," I say through trembling lips. "I see why I fell in love with you and stayed in Chicago with you. You were worth changing all my life plans for. I understand now how my life got here, and I don't regret it."

"I don't regret it either."

The way he kisses my lips—soft and quick—I know it's our last.

Nothing has ever killed me more.

MY DAD PEEKS through the bedroom window. "Nash's Uber just left."

Another tear trickles down my face, rolling into my ear as I lie on my parents' mattress.

"The hardest part is over now." My mom sits beside me on the bed, running her fingers through my hair. "This is how you grow as a person, by making difficult choices."

I stare blankly ahead, numbness taking over.

What if Nash is the love of my life, and I just let him walk away?

PART THREE

Finding

CHAPTER FORTY ONE

NASH

IT'S BEEN one month since Christmas Eve, and the night I was forced to walk away from everything important to me.

Technically, I wasn't *forced*. But leaving was the right thing to do, no matter how much I wanted to stay and keep fighting for us.

But no matter how hard I fight, I can't change what her heart has already decided.

Sadie doesn't love me.

At least not anymore.

She holds my whole world in her hands, and I just have to wait for her to decide what to do with it. Until then, I promised Lindy I wouldn't text or call Sadie to see how she's doing.

Or to see if she's changed her mind.

Lindy said Sadie would contact me if she wants to talk. So, I haven't reached out.

Everything hurts—my heart, my mind, my entire soul.

It's a type of loss similar to death. I'm grieving Sadie like I grieved Nolan.

Our home feels empty without her here. My happy life discarded. The bright, shiny future, all those best-laid plans put in place, don't work without her.

So when Jay's text comes through one night after work, I feel my last shred of hope evaporate as I read the words.

JAY

Nash, Sadie has decided to file for divorce. I'm so sorry.

She's made her decision, throwing me to rock bottom.

I fall onto my bed, curl into the fetal position, and sob for the love I lost.

~

SADIE

"IT'S AN EXTREMELY generous settlement," Stetson says as he reads through the divorce papers.

Settlement feels like such a weird word, something you'd use for a business deal, not a loving three-year marriage to a man as kind and sweet as Nash.

"He's offering a fifty-fifty split of all the assets, even his company, Superior Health."

My eyes lift. "Superior Health isn't mine. It's his."

"You're a co-owner. So technically, you're entitled to fifty percent of it. He was stupid to list you as a co-owner or not have you sign a prenup."

I said the same thing to Nash a few months ago in his kitchen—*our* kitchen—the day he brought me home from the hospital. I said all those things before I knew him and understood the kind of love he has for me. I regret those words now and the way I mocked him.

"I expected some kind of prenup, you know, since you built your business before you knew me. It's only smart to protect yourself and your assets."

"I didn't feel like I needed protection. I trust you completely, and I trust what we have together."

"Sometimes things change."

"But how I feel about you never will."

"You can't be that sure. From the sound of things, I'm a different person now than I was before. I have a jagged scar across my forehead and sunken cheeks. I don't know if I'll ever be the person you loved and married."

"When I married you, I vowed to enter a contract of mutual decay."

"Like, you said that in our vows?"

"No, I just mean that no matter how we change or deteriorate, we promise to love each other through it all."

I shake my head, trying to stop my mind from thinking back to that day and what Nash said. The promises he vowed to keep that I couldn't carry anymore.

Am I weak to divorce him?

In some ways, it's taking the easy way out, but in other ways, it's the most difficult thing I've ever done. How do you look at a man desperately in love with you and tell him his love isn't enough? Tell him that, despite giving you the world, you're still searching for something more.

It's pure torture.

But Nash let me do it because it's what's best for me. No questions asked. No huge guilt trip. He loves me enough to let me go graciously. I'll forever be grateful for that. I'm not going to punish him now by taking half his company.

"I don't want Superior Health," I say to Stetson.

"But do you know how much money you'd be giving up?"

"I don't want it. Take it out of the settlement."

"I know you feel bad about how everything went down between you two, but you've beat yourself up about it enough. You don't need to buy his forgiveness by giving up hundreds of thousands of dollars."

"I'm not trying to buy his forgiveness. I just don't want it."

It's not mine. Not really.

I give Stetson a pointed look. "Take it out and take out the Chicago house. He can have that too. Then I'll sign the papers."

There's an edge of annoyance behind Stetson's voice. "If you say so."

It's the right thing to do.

I may not love Nash the way he wants me to, but I still want what's best for him.

~

SADIE

I SIT IN THE backseat of my parents' car, staring up at Nash's brownstone in Chicago. Even though I know he's not here, I stay in the car while my family loads boxes into the U-Haul trailer. All the furniture and house stuff remain with him. My dad asked Nash to pack up anything that was only mine, like clothes and belongings. Now that the divorce is final, this was the last step in severing our life together—a hard step.

"That's all the boxes." My mom opens her car door and climbs inside.

I hear my dad shut the back of the U-Haul and lock it.

"Let's get out of the city, and then we'll find a place to eat dinner." She looks back at me with a smile. "Does that sound okay?"

"It's great." I put on a brave face even though sadness holds my heart.

Nash and I are really over now.

It's what I wanted—a necessary step in moving forward with my life—but what kind of person would I be if I didn't feel sad about how it all ended? Sad about the turn of events that upended both of our lives?

My parents said I didn't have to drive to Chicago with them. They thought coming here might be difficult for me. It's been easier to let them handle cleaning up the messy details of abandoning the life I don't remember. But once Nash mentioned to my dad that he'd be out of town for a meeting the weekend they planned to come, I decided it was a safe trip I could make.

I'm not ready to see Nash. It's all too raw.

Even though losing my memory isn't my fault—just an unfortunate accident with sad consequences—the aftermath is hard to face.

Despite my 'no regrets' policy that I keep reminding myself, doubts still creep in.

Did I try hard enough to love Nash back?

Did I give up too easily?

Did I break him?

Those questions plagued me at first, but now that it's been three months and things are final, I feel like I'll finally be able to move on with my new life.

At least, I *hope* I'll be able to.

As the car pulls away, I glance back at the house that was an important part of the life we'd begun to build together. The house that was once my home.

The warm glow from the porch lights is the last thing I see as we drive off.

NASH

"You can't sell your company." Lindy folds her arms, a severe expression lining her brows.

"Why not?" I dig inside a grocery bag, pulling out a box of noodles.

"Because it's *yours.*"

"Exactly. It's mine, so I can do whatever I want with it, and I want to sell it."

Her eyes follow me to a cupboard where I put away a few items. "Superior Health is your whole life. It's all you have now. Why would you want to get rid of it?"

Because it reminds me of Sadie.

Because it doesn't give me joy anymore.

Because I need to start fresh with a new life.

"Going public and selling the company was always the plan."

"But after you sell it, what will you do?"

"I don't know." I lift my shoulders. "Maybe move somewhere different. Travel the world." I smile, trying to be as convincing as possible. "It's going to be great. I can do whatever I want."

But my heart knows *none* of this is what I want.

SADIE

"I SWEAR I've seen my Syracuse cap and gown somewhere in my closet." I hop up from my spot on the living room floor and head for the stairs.

"That would be great if you still have yours," Annie says. "Then I wouldn't have to buy one for graduation."

"Maybe you want your own," my mom tells Annie as I climb the steps.

"I'll just see if I can find mine."

I rush to my bedroom closet, flipping on the lights. I swipe through hanging clothes until I'm sure the gown isn't there. Then I move to the boxes. The first one I open is nothing but books. It takes all my effort to push that heavy one aside to get to the others behind it.

I peel back the packaging tape and open the next box. Laying on top is a framed picture of Nash and me, wearing fancy clothes at some ceremony. He's looking at me with the most adoring eyes imaginable. I trace the edges of his face, feeling nostalgic, then gaze over my beaming smile as I point to an award I'm holding. I pick up the frame, trying to get a closer look so I can read what the award was for, but I notice the actual certificate in the box directly under the frame.

Staffing Industry Magazine: Forty Under Forty. Presented to Sadie Carter.

I know that magazine. It's one of the leading magazines in the healthcare staffing industry. Every year, they choose forty outstanding people under forty who have made an impact in the business. They're usually young, ambitious, and successful.

And last year, I was one of the winners.

I sit back as the shock sets in.

I won an award.

Not Nash or my dad, but *me*.

The feeling is incredible.

My eyes drop to the next paper in the box. It's a printout of a screenshot of a text from someone named Harper, dated the exact date of the award.

HARPER

> I wish I could've snuck a video of how Nash looked and smiled at you a few times throughout the award ceremony. You could see how much he loves you and how proud he is of you. It was the sweetest!

> If I could've figured out how to discreetly record him, I totally would've. He was so proud!

My eyes mist over. Nash really was my biggest champion and cheerleader. When I first woke up from my coma, I was angry at myself for how far off course my life had seemed to go. But I didn't realize then how every decision I'd made led me to become a better, more complete version of the woman I always wanted to be.

And Nash was a huge part of that.

He gave my ambition new wings.

I dig my phone out of my back pocket and write the text I should've written months ago.

SADIE

> Thank you for always believing in me. I don't know if I'll ever fully understand all the ways you enriched my life, but I do know that you gave me wings to fly, and I'll always be grateful to you for that.

I bite my bottom lip, nervously waiting to see if he replies.

The dots dance, speeding up my heart.

NASH

I just wanted you to be happy.

One tear falls.

SADIE

I know.

I think about ending the conversation there but decide to give him a little more so he doesn't worry or wonder.

SADIE

I'm working for my dad again at his home health and hospice and doing well there, implementing a few new things. Annie and I are going to Cancun for her college graduation trip. I can genuinely say I'm finding myself again. Thank you for allowing me to do that.

NASH

I wish you all the happiness you're looking for.

SADIE

Same to you.

SADIE

"HEY, STETSON!" My mom waves at him as he walks down the dock toward our boat, holding a cooler. "We're glad you're coming with us today."

"First boat outing of the summer." The smile on my dad's face is the same one he's had my whole life whenever we're on the lake. His love of boating is the reason we live where we do.

My mom reaches for his cooler and brings it into the boat. "No Savannah today?"

"Uh, no. We broke up last week." His eyes flip to me. The pointed meaning behind his stare stresses me out.

Stetson dating Savannah for the last six months was best for my mind and heart. Right after the accident, murky feelings clogged my mind. I didn't know how I was supposed to feel, who I was supposed to love, or who I wanted to be with. I remembered loving Stetson, but just because that was fresh in my mind didn't mean it made sense now, three and a half years later.

I needed time to sort through everything, and his dating Savannah gave me that time. But now that the buffer between us is gone, my chest feels heavy with pressure. Just like I told Nash six months ago, I can't figure out who I am while in a relationship with someone. There are so many missing pieces to my puzzle. I'm just barely starting to get them all sorted out. I can't add more to that process.

That's why I spend the next two hours doing whatever I can on the boat to avoid alone time with Stetson. If my dad needs a rope untied, I'm on it. When it was time for the first surfer in the water, I volunteered. But there's nowhere to hide when Stetson walks to the bow to sit with me.

He hands me a bottle of water. "You've been avoiding me."

"No, I haven't." I take the drink, putting it in the cup holder beside me.

"You're a terrible liar." He laughs as he sits down next to me. "What did you think about my news?"

"What do you mean?" The clarification is unnecessary. I know exactly what he means.

"About me and Savannah."

"Oh." My response is too big and dramatic to be sincere. "I'm sorry to hear you broke up. Savannah is great."

"I'm not sorry." His eyes glimmer in a way I've only seen a few times from him since moving back home to Skaneateles. "I've been wanting to end things for a few months."

Months?

The way that statement ties my stomach in knots freaks me out.

"I just needed to make sure you were in a good place."

"Me?" I swallow. "What do I have to do with anything?"

"Sade, you know what I mean. There's nothing in our way now." He reaches out and grabs my hand. "We can finally be together. Our story can pick up right where it left off."

I glance down at Stetson's fingers interlaced through mine—a familiar gesture I can remember. But despite the familiarity, things are different. Our story can't pick up from here because it didn't stop here. It kept going, and even though those years are gone from my mind like a book with a chunk of pages ripped out, they still happened, shaping who I am today.

I'm not the same woman anymore. I don't know if I'm the old Sadie or the new Sadie. Probably somewhere in the middle. And part of being in the middle is trusting the decisions I made almost four years ago when I broke up with Stetson. I've been thinking about this a lot lately, since I found that award hidden in a box in my closet. I no longer second-guess the choices I made back then or hold them against myself.

I think about the words the hospital therapist said to me the day before I got discharged. *Give the Sadie you don't remember the benefit of the doubt. Trust that she made the right deci-sions with the information she had at the time. And then forgive her if she didn't.*

I'm slowly learning to take the doctor's advice and trust that the old version of me knew something I don't understand today. I don't want to relearn everything I already learned.

I'm not going back.

Only forward.

I move Stetson's hand to his lap and pull my fingers out from under his. "You've always been a constant in my life, and your friendship over the last few months has meant so much to me."

His chin lowers as if sensing what's coming next. "But?"

"I can't keep living in the past just because that's what I remember. I need to pave a new way forward. Try new things and learn about the years I can't remember until I find who I really am."

"I can help you discover who you are."

"You can't. Only I can do that for myself."

"I hoped I was your new way forward." Rejection colors his eyes. "I thought you were ready to take on more. Maybe explore a relationship and a future. Live life to the fullest."

"My life looks different now, but it can still be full even with much less than I once had or wanted."

"I feel like this is what you do. You pull men in then change your mind and push us away."

"That's not fair."

"What's not fair is you leading me on for the past six months."

My brows drop. "I didn't lead you on."

"You came to my house on Christmas Eve, begging for

who knows what. Then you divorce Nash—a pretty obvious sign that you were choosing a life with me over him."

"Divorcing Nash had nothing to do with you."

"I don't know what else you want. I gave you space, thinking you'd be ready for a relationship by now."

"Eventually, I will be ready. Just not right now."

Stetson blows out a curt breath. "Sounds like it's time we both move on from our past and what might have been." He shakes his head as he stands. "I hope you don't regret this *again*."

It's *that* statement that tells me I won't.

SADIE

"WERE YOU SURPRISED by how Stetson reacted to your rejection?" Dr. Shinn asks at our next therapy session. I drive to Syracuse twice a month to meet with her. She helps me sort through the jumbled mess inside my brain.

"I didn't expect him to be so cold." I think back to Christmas Eve when I had an even tougher conversation. "I guess I expected Stetson to react more like Nash. To be patient and understanding. The fact that he wasn't gives me a glimpse of why I might've broken off our engagement in the first place."

"Do you still wonder about that? About the decisions you made three years ago?"

"Not as much as I used to."

Dr. Shinn tilts her head, narrowing her gaze. "Why do you think that is?"

"I guess the more time away from my accident, the easier

it is to see why I did what I did. I don't question those decisions anymore. I accept them."

"Does accepting your choices change how you feel about Nash?"

"I think it makes me appreciate him more."

"Where are you today with the whole Nash situation?"

My eyes drop to my hands as my fingers slide across the vacant spot on my ring finger. "I'm not sad anymore, but I think about him often. I regret how it ended, but I'm glad it happened. I don't miss him, but I miss the feeling he gave me." My lips lift as his smile crosses my mind. "Nash was more than just this one guy I married one time. He was the calm in the middle of my storm."

NASH

"NASH, YOU ARE about to be a wealthy man," my lawyer says as the elevator doors shut in front of us.

I lift my lips, wondering if I'm showing the appropriate level of excitement for someone who's about to sell his company to a private equity group for millions of dollars.

"What are your plans with the money?"

"I don't have any."

Laughter pours out of him. "You're the only millionaire I know with no plans for the future."

His words are innocent, but I still feel the sting of hurt.

It's been nine months. I should be coping with life better than I am.

Actually, I'm coping just fine. I'm just not moving on or moving forward.

I'm stagnant.

Sadie once told me that's how she felt about her life before she met me, and it's crazy to think that I'm the one who feels that way now.

No progression.

I'm the man who's going nowhere and doing nothing.

I rake a hand through my hair, turning to my lawyer. "I think I will travel for a bit. That's what I'm going to do with the money."

"Well, you'll certainly have the means to. After you sign these papers, you can circle the world a hundred times before you'll ever have to work again."

Maybe then I'll finally be able to move on with my life.

SADIE

"I'M LEAVING FOR the day." My dad pops his head into my office.

"It's not even lunch yet, and you're done for the day?"

"You don't need me here. You've got this place running more smoothly than I ever have."

I smile at my dad's kind words. "I don't *need* you. I'm just surprised. You never used to take off early, and now you're doing it all the time."

He steps into the room, sitting in one of the chairs across from my desk. "As far as I'm concerned, this is your business now. That is, if you want it."

"Yes!" My lips grow into a huge smile. "I want it."

I think I've always wanted it.

"Great. It's yours." He claps and stands like everything is all settled. "We'll announce my retirement, and you can throw me a big party after the holidays."

"Just like that?"

"I've taken this company as far as I can. You're the future now and more than capable of running it. What more is there to talk about? I'll get Stetson started on the official paperwork."

I scramble out of my chair and rush to him, throwing my arms around his neck.

"Thank you, Dad. For *everything*."

SADIE

"SADIE?" My mom knocks on my bedroom door. "Are you coming down for dinner?"

"No, go ahead and eat without me."

"What are you doing?" Her voice sounds concerned. "You've been in your room all day."

"I'm just cleaning out my closet. Going through some old things."

There's a pause before she speaks again. "Are you okay?"

"Yeah, I'm fine."

"Alright." She hesitates by my door for a second longer then leaves.

I turn back to the mess in my room. Pictures are scattered over the floor, and piles of notes, ticket stubs, and cards stack against the wall. The memorabilia makes up the fabric of the last three and a half years of my life.

Until now, I haven't been ready to go through the boxes Nash packed for me. But after talking to Dr. Shinn this week, I feel confident I can face what was lost and, instead of feeling sad about it, celebrate the life I had.

It's taken me a long time to get here. Almost a year to the

day from my accident. There's been a lot of mental growth. But I think the biggest has come in forgiving myself for things I can and can't control, trusting my inner voice, and loving myself where I'm at right now.

It's been a long time coming, but I'm ready to fill in the gaps.

∼

SADIE

IT'S THE FIRST snowfall of the year. My parents are out to dinner, and Annie is at her place, so I have the house to myself. There's only one logical thing to do on a Friday night in November, and that's watch Hallmark Christmas movies.

I curl into a ball on the couch, searching through the movie options on my streaming app, when one movie stops me in my tracks.

"A Swiss Christmas."

My body jolts up to a sitting position as I study the movie poster of a couple embracing in front of a Christmas market in Switzerland. There's an obvious pull to the movie, causing me to immediately push play on the remote. I sink back onto the couch as I tackle thoughts about how I was supposed to spend Christmas in Switzerland with Nash last year.

I'm not sad about it. I'm mostly grateful Nash was so willing to do something that was important to me. It's a rare man who can take a woman's dreams and actually fulfill them.

A year ago, even a few months ago, I wouldn't have been able to watch this movie or sit in these feelings, but I can now. I've come so far. I've healed and grown and forgiven and changed.

I would never want to repeat this last year, but I also wouldn't change the person I've become because of it.

It's been uncomfortable but beautiful.

For the first time since saying goodbye to Nash, I wonder what it would be like to see him again as the complete person I am today.

Would things be different?

Would my feelings for him finally have a chance to grow?

CHAPTER FORTY TWO

NASH

ICY WIND BURNS the tip of my nose as I walk to the gondola to take me up the mountain. I tuck my nose under my ski mask to escape the intense weather. Usually, a helmet and goggles are enough, but not in Switzerland. You need all the things to stay warm here, especially once the sun sets.

Lindy thought I was crazy when I told her I was redoing the trip Sadie and I were supposed to go on last year. I tried to explain that I had one year to use my reservations before they'd expire. She said I was rich enough to take the loss and that I should just spend Christmas with her.

I understand Lindy's worry. Traveling alone through Switzerland on a romantic trip isn't the dream. But this is my life now. Every trip from now on will be like this. I might as well get used to it.

I quickly arrange my skis and poles in the pockets on the door and then sit inside the small gondola, avoiding hitting the knees of the person on the bench opposite me. She has a helmet, goggles, and a ski mask on too, but her light-pink and gray ski clothes make it obvious she's a woman.

The gondola operator pops his head inside, walking with us as we slowly round the cable.

He says something to the woman in Swiss German.

"I'm sorry. I only speak English." Her words are muffled under her mask, but the operator understands enough.

"You riding again?" he asks in a thick accent.

"Yeah, if that's okay."

He nods and steps back from the doors, letting them close. The cart sways forward as a big push of momentum carries us up the mountain.

"You're American?" I say to the woman.

"Yes. And you?"

I nod. "Is this your first time in St. Moritz?"

"It's my first time in any part of Switzerland. What about you?"

"Yeah, first time in Switzerland. The skiing is great, don't you think?"

"Uh, I haven't been down a slope yet. I've just been enjoying the view of the mountains from the gondola."

My brows drop in confusion, but she can't see it through my gear. "Do you need some help?"

"No, I'm thinking about skiing…working myself up to it."

"But you know how, right?"

"Yes. I think so." Her gloved hand lifts, running over her helmet like a nervous reaction. The gesture reminds me so much of Sadie it scares me, as if her ghost will always haunt me.

"How many days are you here?" I ask, distracting myself from the unlikely similarities.

"I started in Lucerne and did some Christmas highlights there."

"What was your favorite?"

"Probably the Diorama Bethlehem where you see the

nativity with over four-hundred and fifty wood-carved figures."

"I saw it." I smile, my stubble getting caught on the fabric of my ski mask.

"So you know how incredible it was."

"Yeah. I did Lucerne and Lugano for about a week and then took the train to St. Moritz."

"Same. I have one more day here, and then I'll go to Zermatt."

"Same."

Her shoulders lift and even that small gesture has a familiar quality to it. "I guess we're doing the same trip."

"I guess so."

"It's a popular itinerary at Christmastime," she says.

"For sure."

I stare at her. She's the right size. Her ski clothes are different, but that's to be expected since the ones I remember were cut off after the accident. The voice, although muffled under a mask, sounds close.

What if...

My heart lifts with hope, picking up speed inside my chest. It's been a long time since I've felt it beat like this. The last time was six months ago when Sadie texted me out of the blue to say thank you for believing in her. That one innocent text sent me into a tailspin for weeks. I can't do that again.

I shake my head, reasoning with myself.

It's not possible. I'm delusional and lonely and trying to make something out of nothing.

The gondola skitters over the cable as it approaches the top of the hill.

"Are you going to get out?"

She shakes her head. "Not this time."

The doors open, and I stand to leave.

"I hope you have a great trip and a merry Christmas."

"Thanks. You too." I wave goodbye to the stranger.

Stranger is the keyword here.

She's not Sadie, no matter how much my heart and my mind want her to be.

CHAPTER FORTY THREE

SADIE

I FIGHT MY SUITCASE, trying to get enough leverage to lift it onto the luggage rack. Behind me, a man reaches down, grabbing the case from my hands.

"Let me help you."

"Thanks." I turn over my shoulder, smiling at the kind British man. "I was struggling."

"No problem."

I glance down at my ticket, checking my seat number on the train. I splurged and paid for a first-class ticket on the Glacier Express. Worth it when you consider I'll be spending eight hours on here today, traveling through the most scenic snow-capped mountains in the world. Every seat has a good view, but the first-class seats are individual—just two chairs facing each other—and since I'm a single, that seemed like a better option than being forced to sit in a group of four.

My assigned seat is in the middle of the cart, which feels like the perfect spot on this iconic train ride. I shove my bag under my chair and sit, already enjoying the snowy views out my window even though we haven't left the station yet.

Switzerland at Christmas is as magical as I imagined. It's

everything I hoped it would be. My eyes drift to the empty seat in front of me, but I don't allow them to stay. Going into this trip, I knew I'd be solo and was totally okay with that. My mom worries enough for both of us, so I don't have to. She wanted to turn my trip into a family vacation, mostly because she didn't like the idea of me traveling alone or skiing for the first time since my accident. Understandable. But she'll be happy to learn I haven't actually skied yet. Only got all dressed in my new pink ski outfit and rode the gondola up and down the mountain an embarrassing number of times. Baby steps. Maybe next time, I'll be able to ski down the hill.

A man passes by in the aisle, his cologne wafting down to me. Flashes of Nash bounce through my head—at the hospital, comforting me the night I slept at the brownstone, our first kiss on the pier by the Christmas tree, building a snowman in Clift Park. The smell of that cologne instantly brings him to the front of my mind.

I glance up, and my breath catches.

The build, the hair, the flannel jacket—it all fits.

My head cranes, and I even lift out of my seat to see if I can see his face better. Each millisecond that I don't know for certain pounds into my chest through every heartbeat. Hope grows, and I know if it's not him, I'll be so disappointed.

His feet stop, and his head turns to the side, checking the seat numbers above the chairs.

I see the stubble and the jawline, and my world stops. An overwhelming feeling I can only describe as complete joy washes over me.

He turns, walking back to my row, stopping to study the number above the chair across from me. Butterflies send my stomach into an absolute frenzy of happiness—something akin to love at first sight, which is crazy considering everything that's happened between us—everything I *didn't* feel a year ago.

And now we're here in Switzerland, at the same time, on the same train, sitting across from each other. My heart pounds with thoughts of fate and meant-to-be, fresh starts and second chances. The idea almost makes me burst into happy tears.

Then it hits me.

What if Nash isn't alone?

Disappointment seeps in as I quickly glance behind me. There isn't a beautiful woman anywhere to be found. It's just us.

I watch as he removes his flannel jacket and shoves it into his bag. Next, he pulls out some AirPods and a book. I move my head to read the title, *A Christmas Carol*, by Charles Dickens. I can't help my smile. He pushes his bag under his chair and then sits, looking at me for the first time.

Green eyes widen with wonder, like he's enchanted or maybe just in shock.

"I'm Sadie Bradley." I smile, extending my hand to him. "I just thought I should introduce myself since we'll ride this train together for the next eight hours."

He stares at my hand before bringing his gaze back to my face. The furrow between his brows says he's unsure if I'm real or a figment of his imagination, but he takes my hand anyway, surging warmth through my body.

His lips lift. "Nash Carter."

I love that he decided to play my game too. Our hands don't drop, just shake over and over between us.

"It's nice to meet you, Nash."

"Same to you, Sadie."

Reluctantly, we break apart, both still smiling at each other.

"I actually think we've already met," he says with some amusement.

"Is that so?"

"Yeah, on the gondola yesterday. You were riding back and forth."

"That was you?"

"It was."

How he put that together is beyond me. I bite my lip, trying to keep calm.

"Did you ever ski down the mountain?"

"No." A sudden rush of moisture pricks my eyes, but I blink it away. "You see, I was in a terrible skiing accident a little over a year ago and was trying to get back on the slopes and face my fears."

"I'm sorry about your accident."

"I am too." We sit in that feeling for a moment before I push a smile onto my lips. "But I'm doing much better now. I finally feel like myself again. That's why I'm here in Switzerland. I'm doing the things that I love for *me*, not for anyone else."

"So you're here alone?"

"I am." I watch how my answer immediately makes his smile glow. "And what about you? Are you alone?"

He nods, trying his hardest to suppress a smile.

"That's good." We both laugh a little, still trying to wrap our heads around this twist of fate.

Nash leans back, relaxing in his chair, and it's the best sight I've seen. I didn't know how much I missed this steady, confident man. "So tell me about yourself, Sadie."

"Well, I'm from Skaneateles, New York."

"Hmm." He nods in appreciation. "I love it there. Especially at Christmastime."

"I noticed your book. A real classic."

"My reading choice was inspired by your hometown and their charming Dickens Christmas. I have some amazing memories there."

"So do I."

We both puff out another laugh.

"And what do you do in Skaneateles?"

"I run a home health and hospice."

His brows lift in interest. "You *run* it?"

"I do." I beam with pride. "It was my father's company, but he's retired and left it to me."

"That's great."

I see in his eyes that he really does think it's great.

"What about you? Where are you from?"

"Originally from Chicago, but more recently, I've been traveling a lot."

"What about your job?"

"I had a one-stop shop healthcare staffing business, but this year, we went public, and I sold most of my shares to a private equity firm."

"You did?" It's my turn for shock. "Wasn't that hard to let something go that you loved so much?"

His head tilts, and his eyes stare straight into mine. "I've done it before with something I loved even more, so I knew I could handle it."

The meaning strikes my heart, and we're back to staring at each other with so many shared experiences floating between us.

An announcement in a different language comes over the speaker, causing us to glance up.

"I think we're leaving," I say.

"I think so."

"You're riding the train for the whole time, right? To Zermatt?" I don't want my words to sound too hopeful—or maybe I do. Maybe Nash and I are past games and pretenses.

"Yeah, I'm here for the duration."

The whistle blows outside, and the train begins to move.

Excitedly, I lean toward the window, watching as the station passes by.

I turn to Nash, but he's already staring at me.

He has the same look of complete acceptance in his eyes. After all this time, Nash is still the one person who I can be myself with—flaws and all—and he accepts me no matter what.

It's a gift I took for granted last year.

I won't make the same mistake again.

CHAPTER FORTY FOUR

NASH

HOW DO you get your hopes up without getting them up *too* high?

I don't know, but I'm probably past the point of no return, and we're only three hours into the train ride.

"Wait, you're telling me you go to the dentist *four* times a year for a cleaning?" Sadie's smile lights up her whole face like a Christmas market lights up a village. I couldn't look away from her if my life depended on it, which is tough when you're on a train ride specifically for the views.

"Why not go in for a cleaning four times a year?"

"I thought the limit was two."

"No, two is what insurance will pay for, but you can pay out of pocket for the other cleanings if you want them."

"That's weird and unnecessary."

"Or is it brilliant and next level?" I grin back at her. "Like right now, you're noticing how good my teeth look."

"I noticed your teeth, and they are pretty spectacular."

"It's the extra cleanings."

She laughs, and the way it fulfills me is crazy stupid.

A bell chimes, letting the passengers know to put their

headphones on to listen to a brief commentary about what we see out our window. Normally, I'd be all over something like that, but I hate when we have to stop talking, even if it's just for a few minutes.

Sadie glances out the window as she slides her headphones over her ears. I try to focus on the mountains and tunnels, but my eyes wander back to her. Her hair is a little bit longer, and she's returned to her pre-accident weight, rounding out her cheeks and curves. But the biggest difference from the last time I saw her is her countenance. Last December, Sadie's smiles were guarded, and her walls were up. But today, the carefreeness I fell in love with four years ago is back. I don't know how she did it, but she seems to have found herself again, and for that, I'm eternally grateful.

Her stare flicks to me. When I don't immediately glance away, pretending to care about the view outside, she scrunches her nose and points to the window. I roll my eyes, reluctantly switching my gaze to the snowy mountains.

THE SUN DIMS in the sky, signaling the train ride is almost over. I'd stay on and repeat the whole thing if it meant more time with Sadie.

"So you've just been traveling these last few months?" She shakes her head in disbelief, still trying to reconcile that piece of information inside her head.

"Mm-hmm."

"All by yourself? Like, you didn't take anyone on your trips with you?"

Is this her way of asking if I'm single?

It's hard because I want to believe in fate and hope for things with her, but I also know that if she thought there was any sliver of a chance she could love me again, she would've contacted me by now. And she hasn't.

"I was married once." My eyes turn soft as I gaze back at her. "She was the love of my life. After experiencing a love like that, you don't bother with anyone else because nothing will compare to what you already had."

Her lips press into a sad smile, taking in each word I said.

"What happened?"

"She forgot how to love me."

"I bet she wishes she could've remembered."

"I don't blame her for any of it." My shoulders lift. "It's just one of those things. Have you ever been married?"

"Yes." A solemn smile plays across her lips. "But I broke his heart because I needed space."

"I'm sure he understands and is trying to move on."

"I hope so, because he deserves to be happy."

"Life has a way of leveling relationships down to the bare bones, doesn't it?"

"It sure does." She shakes her head. "But I've learned to keep fighting and trying to find new footing."

"And have you found it?"

"I think so."

"With someone new?" I've been wondering all day about Stetson, but now I'm dreading her answer.

"After my accident, I just needed some time to myself. There wasn't enough room in my head for anyone old or new. So I've just been single, trying to figure it all out."

One year ago, I wasn't man enough to wish Sadie all the love she deserved, even if it wasn't with me. I'm in a better spot now. I could wish her happiness in love, but I'm glad I don't have to. A big part of me is relieved she didn't end up with Stetson after all.

The whistle blows, and our eyes meet, knowing our fated meet-up is ending.

An announcement starts overhead as the train rolls into the station. Passengers immediately stand, gathering their things. I help Sadie with her suitcase, carrying it onto the platform.

We turn to face each other, and a new heaviness fills my heart, a dread of losing her again despite not even having her. I should just be grateful for the time we spent together, for the reassurance that Sadie fought through the darkness and made it to the light again.

"Nash Carter." She reaches her hand out to me again. "I loved getting to know you today."

Her gesture feels like a pointed goodbye. She was happy to see me and catch up but has no intention of continuing anything else.

"I loved getting to know you too." I take her hand in mine, feeling that same spark that never died out for me.

Our hands drop, and it sucks. I'm back at her house on Christmas Eve, feeling her slipping out of my life like water in my hands.

"Where are you staying?" I glance behind me to the waiting shuttles. "Maybe we could share a ride or something."

"I'm at Hotel Escape."

"Oh." My shoulders drop. I guess it was too much to ask that the universe put us staying at the same place. "I'm at Zermatt Chalet Peak."

"Fancy! A chalet was actually my first choice, but I couldn't find one for the holiday season, especially on such short notice."

I laugh.

"What's so funny?"

"You're the reason I'm at a chalet." It's the first time we've broken out of our meeting-for-the-first-time game. I mean, it had to end sometime.

"Me?"

"You chose it last year, said the cottage style was your favorite because of the overhanging wood eaves and the rusticity mixed with breathtaking window views."

"Wow, I sound so smart." She smiles. "Are you sure I wasn't an architect in my lost years?"

"To my knowledge, you've never been an architect, but you did love the Zermatt chalets. Since we didn't take the trip and the room was non-refundable, they agreed to let me book something for this season."

"I'm glad you can use the room from last year. I'm sure it's amazing."

Now, I feel bad that I'm staying somewhere so nice when she's at a mid-grade hotel in the center of town.

"It's as much your hotel room as it is mine. Why don't we split it? It says it sleeps four."

What in the world did I just say?

"I mean," the backpedaling begins, "you don't have to. Since you picked it out, and technically, half of it is yours, I just thought you might want to stay there too—as acquaintances only," I sputter. "We just met, and you have your own trip agenda, and this is by no means a way to try and start something between us. It's just a friendly offer between acquaintances."

Her eyes narrow into a teasing stare. "A friendly offer between acquaintances?"

I scratch my head, realizing how dumb and desperate I sound. "Yeah, that's what I said." *Unfortunately.*

"I think we're a little more than acquaintances, Nash." She takes a step forward, flashing me one of her flirty smiles.

I wouldn't believe it if I didn't see it, and I wouldn't believe it if I didn't have three years of flirty smiles from our marriage to go off of. "We did just ride a train together for eight hours."

"And I told you how many times I get my teeth cleaned in one year."

"Intimate details." The flirty undercurrent behind her smile holds strong.

"So what do you say? Do you want to split"—that seems like a far better word than *share*—"the chalet with me?"

"Why not? I haven't paid for my hotel room at Escape yet. I think it was going to be a disappointment anyway. This is a way better option."

"I'm glad I bumped into you so you can experience the room of your dreams."

"Me too!" Her shoulders bounce up and down excitedly. "Alright. Which way? I'm assuming you have some kind of ride to the hotel."

"Uh, that way." I gesture to the curb.

She flips around, walking in the direction I pointed.

If the way my heart races is any indication, I'm in serious trouble here.

What a turn of events.

I allow myself one quick smile before following after her.

CHAPTER FORTY FIVE

SADIE

"Look at these floor-to-ceiling windows." I don't even give myself the chance to enjoy the incredible view. I continue my tour up the spiral staircase to another floor of the chalet. My head falls back, looking up. "A glass roof!" I tear my eyes from the master bedroom and walk to the bathroom. The most gorgeous Jacuzzi tub sits in the center with a glass shower on the side.

"There's not a lot of doors in this place, is there?" Nash follows behind, glancing around. "I'll just stay on the couch on the lower level and use that half-bath down there. You can have all of this."

"You don't have to stay on the couch. We're grown adults. We can lie beside each other on a bed and be fine. Besides, I'd never want to take this incredible view away from you."

"Yeah, that's not happening." The words come out with a distressed sigh, making me think he's a little more apprehensive about sharing this chalet than I am.

Should I be more like him, thinking cautiously about the arrangement instead of being won over by floor-to-ceiling windows?

There's a history here. I'm not naive to the fact that, one year ago, I pushed Nash out of my life, but I was lost back then, coping with a new reality that didn't make sense. My mind lived in constant fog and confusion. It took months of being patient with myself to get where I am today.

I've healed a lot this past year. And although I wasn't seeking or looking for love, I can't deny how my heart came alive when I saw Nash on the train. Like it truly beat for the first time since I woke up from my coma. It's the feeling I kept looking for last December. The confirmation that, although my head couldn't remember him, my heart could. And for the first time in a long time, I'm excited about what could be.

I didn't want to leave Nash at the train station and go our separate ways. I hoped he'd suggest we meet somewhere, but then he offered the chalet, which seemed like the perfect chance to spend more time with him.

I just have to find out if Nash is willing to see where things could lead.

Or maybe I'm too much of a risk.

He walks toward the stairs. "I'll let you unpack and do whatever you planned to do tonight."

"I was going to go get some dinner." I step forward, showing my eagerness. "Would you like to join me?"

"Uh..." He drags his fingers through his hair. "Sure, why not?" His arm drops dramatically. "I have to eat."

"So should we change and say leave in a half hour?"

"Sounds good." He nods a few times then heads down to the lower section.

～

NASH

KEEPING MY FEELINGS for Sadie in their proper lane is a mental gymnastics I did not train for. It's only been one hour of staying together, and I'm already exhausted.

I brought this on myself by inviting her here, but the chalet is incredible. I had to share it with her, especially when I know how excited the old Sadie was about this place.

But now we're going to dinner together.

It doesn't mean anything.

I know that.

But what if it does?

I pace back and forth in front of the windows, trying to get control over my thoughts. It's negative ten degrees outside, but I'm sweating like I'm in a sauna.

"How do I look?" Sadie says behind me.

I turn just as she steps down the last two stairs. My hand goes to my chest in self-preservation, as if I can somehow stop my heart from leaping out.

"You look great." I'm embarrassed by how rattled my voice sounds and by my chosen adjective.

Sadie looks more than *great*. Her black turtleneck dress fits her body snuggly, like a wool glove, wrapping each curve in a way that's hard not to notice. I'm a big fan of the healthy weight she's put back on. It does wonders for her body. The hem of the sweaterdress is short, showing off her thighs until knee-high black boots take over.

It's a deadly look for a man's heart—a man who is hopelessly in love with her.

"You look pretty impressive yourself." Her gaze scans me. "I like your button-up shirt."

My eyes drop to the blue fabric with a paisley pattern

inside the collar, lapels, and cuffs. "You bought this for my birthday last year. It's one of my favorites."

"I have excellent taste."

Momentarily, I get caught up in her charming smile before snapping out of it. The goal tonight is to keep things moving. Too much time in one place is dangerous.

"Should we go?" I gesture to the door. "I made a reservation at the hotel restaurant."

"That sounds amazing."

She walks in front of me, and I fist my fingers to keep myself from placing a hand on the small of her back to lead her out of the room and down the hall. It hurts that I can't do that—can't be with her how I want to.

Our table is ready when we arrive at the restaurant, and of course, it's something romantic with candles, a view, and a crackling fire.

We would've loved this last year. The old Sadie and Nash would've made the most of every romantic spot. Meanwhile, the new Sadie and Nash try to figure out how to be exes who are friends who don't touch each other. Or maybe I'm the only one trying to figure that out. She seems completely at ease and relaxed.

"I think I'm going to get the filet mignon." Her guilty grimace makes me smile.

"I'm glad to see you still like to order the most expensive thing on the menu."

"Oh my gosh, I do. When in Rome!" She laughs. "I can't believe you know and remember that about me."

I remember everything about her. Those memories make the days long and the nights even longer. But Sadie doesn't need to hear my tragic broken-heart story.

"Get whatever you want." I carefully place a cheerful expression on my face. "My treat."

"No!" She grabs my arm, and I tense my body in defense. "Let me pay. It's the least I can do for forgetting you and then divorcing you."

A surprised laugh escapes. "Yes, I think a two-hundred-dollar meal should cover all the emotional damage."

Her hand returns to her side of the table, making it easier to breathe again. "Well, order dessert. Let's make sure you're adequately covered."

"It's cheaper than therapy, so obviously I will."

"Nash, all joking aside, I'm sorry about how things ended between us."

I put on a brave face. "You don't have to apologize."

"But I want to. I shouldn't have gone to Stetson's house on Christmas Eve. It was stupid and insensitive of me."

"It's understandable. You still had feelings for him." Even saying it out loud hurts.

"It wasn't so much about having feelings for *him* as it was about familiarity and normalcy. I craved stability, and because I could remember him, Stetson felt stable. I confused my feelings with my need to feel secure in who I was." She shakes her head. "It probably doesn't make sense."

"It makes perfect sense. You did what you had to do to survive. I don't fault you for that."

"You were more understanding than anyone else last year. Thank you for that."

"Your happiness is all I've ever wanted."

"I wanted you to be happy too, even though I couldn't make it happen." Her earnest smile morphs into something lighter. "I kept thinking how awesome it would be if my memory randomly came back one day. I pictured myself showing up at Superior Health or our brownstone and leaping into your arms or doing some crazy grand gesture to make everything between us perfect again. I really wanted that for you. For *us*."

"Just promise me that if your memory ever does come back, I'll be the first person you call."

Sadie smiles. "I promise."

We say the words, but we both know the reality.

Her memory is never coming back.

But it's okay. Our relationship isn't the same, and it's been the worst, but she seems happy now, and I meant what I said. Her happiness is all I've ever wanted, even if it comes at the cost of mine.

SADIE

"So, besides traveling, what have you been up to this last year?" I reach for a warm roll from the basket in the center of the table.

Nash gestures to the waiter, calling him over.

"Can I help you, sir?"

"Yes, do you guys have ranch salad dressing?"

"We do."

"Can you bring a side for her to dip her roll into?"

"Yes, of course." The man smiles at me.

"Like, an obscene amount," Nash reiterates. "She really loves ranch dressing."

The waiter nods with a bow then rushes to the kitchen.

"Anyway, to answer your question"—Nash shrugs, unaware that he just rocked my world by remembering a small nuance of my personality—"I've mostly been working a ton. A lot of hours went into selling the company and putting that deal together."

"Are you glad you sold Superior Health?"

"Do you want me to be honest?"

"After everything we've been through, honesty is a given between us, isn't it?"

"It should be."

I smile. "Then let me have the truth."

"Selling the company was always the plan, I just did it sooner than I thought I would. So much about Superior Health was wrapped up in you. Once we got divorced, it was hard to go to work. Everything about the business reminded me of you. So selling it has been a good thing to help bring closure."

"At least closure came with several zeroes attached to it," I joke, hoping to show Nash I can handle his honesty and pain.

His brows lift in a teasing way. "I bet you regret taking our fifty-fifty split of Superior Health out of the divorce settlement."

"I don't need your money." I lift my chin with mock arrogance. "I have my own business now."

"Yes, you do."

The waiter returns with a bowl of ranch dressing.

"Here you go, miss."

"Thank you." I nod at him before diving into another question. "So you got over me by selling your business. What else?"

"I never said I was over you. But I am trying. I've been talking with a therapist, spilling all our secrets. Actually, I've spoken with her before. You encouraged me to talk about my parents' abandonment and Nolan's death. I hate going, but I see how it helps to talk things through."

I remember reading a text exchange between Nash and me where he talked about hating therapy. It was the first time after waking up from my coma that I saw Nash as a human being with wounds and pain, and I see it again today.

Not that I didn't think he had things to work through, but seeing his strength through hard times and how he's risen above all the bad in his life makes me respect him more.

"I've been seeing a therapist as well."

He tilts his head, smiling back at me. "Look at us, being so mature with our pain."

"Aren't we something?"

"How are you doing with Tate's death?"

"I still miss him. I don't think that will ever go away, but the pain isn't as sharp anymore. I can smile when I think about him and visit his grave without feeling the bitterness of grief. Did you feel like that with Nolan?"

"Yeah, the sting lessens as time goes by. That's what I keep telling myself about you. Losing you felt like losing my brother. I grieved the same way I did when Nolan died. But each day, it gets a little better. With time, the loss won't hurt so much."

My lips pull upward. "You almost got rid of me. Then I ruined your hard work by showing up on the same train as you in Switzerland."

"A happy surprise," he says, and I wonder if he means it.

"I wouldn't blame you if that isn't true—if you'd rather go your separate way and pretend I never existed."

"I don't regret a single moment between us. I'd do it all over again if it meant three more happy years with you."

Maybe we can do it all over again—minus the traumatic brain injury, memory loss, and divorce.

∾

"THAT MEAL WAS DELICIOUS," Nash says as we walk down the hall to our chalet. "I'm completely stuffed now."

"So am I." I hold my stomach where there's a food pooch. "But I'm glad we did it. I don't regret anything."

"Me neither." His green eyes glance down at me, sending my stomach swirling with butterflies.

This day with Nash feels like an amazing first date. Our connection is genuine and authentic. Maybe it's because of our history, or maybe that's how it always was between us. Love happens when you're brave enough to let someone see your pain, and we're past bravery—bearing our whole souls for the other to see.

So much about our past relationship accelerates how I feel right now. There's a friendship at the base of everything and a knowledge that we've been through dark times and come out the other side. Every difficult conversation makes me like Nash more. And on top of that, I remember all too well what it feels like to kiss him—the tender way he holds my face whenever his lips brush mine.

All of this combines, making me want him even more.

So I'm dying for Nash to kiss me—put a bow on our twist-of-fate day.

There's a very real possibility that I'm just a girl who wants to be kissed in Switzerland because it's Christmas and romantic. But something tells me my feelings are more than that.

I smile up at him, trying to flirt. I'm rusty to the point of questioning whether I've actually flirted with a man before. I'm doing everything short of batting my freaking eyelashes just to give him the hint that I'm interested, but it doesn't seem to work.

Nash flicks his gaze across my face then short-circuits for a second. That's the only way to describe his faraway eyes and intense thinking face. He turns from me and walks over to his suitcase against the wall, causing my chest to fall in disappointment.

I thought it would be easier than this, especially with everything he said at dinner about not being over me.

"I'll just sleep down here tonight." He kicks off his shoes, removes his watch, and untucks his shirt. "You'll enjoy the bed and stars more if I'm not there taking up space."

That's probably not true.

Another round of disappointment wedges between my ribs, which is stupid since I'd planned to just *sleep* beside him. Nothing else.

He starts unbuttoning his shirt, and I have two choices: stay and watch him undress or go to my room.

I have to choose my room.

"Okay, well, thanks for sharing your chalet and your glass ceiling."

"It's *our* chalet." He smiles, slowly working on those buttons.

Ugh, why is that so sexy?

"Right, *our* chalet." I point upstairs. "I guess I'll go get some sleep."

There's no opposition from him, so I climb the stairs one at a time, feeling defeated. Instead of heading to the closet to change out of my boots and dress, I throw myself onto the bed in a heap, glancing up at the stars.

Navigating my sudden feelings for Nash is more complicated than I expected. It's exciting, but at the same time, I'm not used to this distant version of him. He's always been the flirt, the pursuer, the driving force behind our relationship, but things are different now.

Our conversations were fine all day and night. But the second there's dead space when something physical can happen, his walls go up. Those interactions are guarded, making me think he doesn't trust me with his heart anymore. I understand why. I'm getting what I deserve. But just because I wasn't ready one year ago doesn't mean I couldn't be ready now.

I've finally felt the emotional spark between us. I can't just walk away from those feelings.

I have to try.

Fate brought Nash Carter back into my life, and now it's up to me to keep him there.

CHAPTER FORTY SIX

SADIE

DAY one of winning my husband—*who is now my ex-husband*—back, and we're off to a good start.

A knock at the door has me flying down the spiral staircase to answer it. Shades cover the windows from the morning sun, but there's enough light coming through the cracks that I can answer the door without breaking my ankle.

"Room service." The woman holds a tray up beside her.

"Yes, come in. You can put it on the table right there."

After setting the food down, she turns to me expectantly, and that's when I remember I forgot the tip.

I spin, crashing into Nash's very hard, very *bare* chest.

My gaze crawls from his pecs to his neck, to his Adam's apple, then his jaw, until they meet his green eyes. It's semi-dark but not so dark that I can't see exactly what I'm dealing with here. And what I'm dealing with is a very attractive man.

"I got it." He steps to the side, moving his chest away from my palms, and grabs his wallet to tip the woman.

The whole tipping scene unfolds before me as I check out Nash's sleep attire, which basically consists of briefs, and that's it. I've seen him dressed like this before when the barn door to the bathroom was cracked open. I said it then, and I'll say it again: he has a very nice male physique. I remember admiring him back then, but now I'm feelin' it more than ever.

The woman nods in appreciation over Nash's tip—maybe also his six-pack—and then leaves.

He turns around, and I'm awestruck by his mussed hair and lazy smile. How did I not feel this before? It's pretty intense.

"What's all this?" His eyes drop to the tray of food.

"Uh...breakfast." I start lifting lids. "I don't know—*er, remember*—what you like, so I ordered an assortment."

His lips lift. "I like it all."

"No, really. I want to know what you eat in the morning so I don't have to keep guessing every day."

"Pastries." He grabs a croissant filled with chocolate and somehow manages an adorable smile as he takes a huge bite.

"I don't believe that one bit. Someone who looks like this"—I wave my finger in front of his abs—"doesn't eat pastries every morning. Probably protein shakes and kale."

Laughter bursts out of him, shooting a piece of half-chewed pastry from his mouth into my hair. And now we're both laughing.

"Charming." I hold up the strand caked with his food and flick it away from me. "Real charming."

"That was an accident." He wipes at his mouth with his wrist, and even that action is so cute.

"So what are we doing today?" I pick up a square of cheese and pop it into my mouth.

"*We?*" His brows hike up.

"Yeah, did you think I would let you keep *our* Switzerland itinerary to yourself?"

336

He puffs out a laugh that's more nervous than humorous. "I don't know what I thought would happen today."

"What do you want to happen?" I infuse my words with a bit of flirtiness, just laying the foundation.

Nash lifts his arm, scratching the back of his head, and a Christmas chorus goes off in my mind, celebrating his triceps and lats. This man is just doing it for me right now on every level. Like, get a grip, Sadie.

He drops his arm, glancing at me. "Do you really think it's a good idea for us to spend so much time together? I mean, I want to," he sighs, "but we're not together anymore, and spending time just complicates things, you know?"

I want to scoop him in my arms and reassure him that my feelings are a sure thing he won't lose again, but even I don't know that for certain.

"Yes, hanging out complicates things. But when I saw you on that train yesterday, something came alive inside me. I can't explain it; I just know it's different from before. Different than last year."

"And what happens if you wake up tomorrow or the next day and decide you're not feeling it anymore? Do we just continue on our separate ways *again*?"

"Nash, I know that you've gotten the short end of the stick on all of this, and now I'm asking you to risk your heart again when I can't guarantee everything will work out. But what if it does?"

His lips lift into a solemn smile. "I thought the same thing yesterday. What if it does work out this time?"

"We'd regret it the rest of our lives if we didn't try."

He nods, really thinking it over.

"We can take things slow," I offer.

"Slow?"

"Yeah, just, like, date each other and see what happens."

"See what happens?"

I scrunch my nose at him. "Why are you repeating everything I say?"

"I'm just trying to wrap my head around all this."

"I don't know why you're so reluctant." I shoot him a charming smile. "Aside from the memory loss and the fact that I shattered your heart once before, I'm the whole package."

His head tilts, and his amused gaze travels over me. "I know you're the whole package. I've *always* known that."

"Then what's the problem?"

"The problem is, I've never stopped loving you. I can't just take things slow, casually see where things lead."

He steps to me, fingers combing through my hair as his hand grabs the side of my face.

Oh, the hand grab. I've missed that so much.

There's a desperation behind the action that equally melts me while driving me mad with desire. My breathing halts—there's nothing left in my chest besides my pounding heart. His green eyes tunnel through me to my soul.

"Sadie, you're *it* for me. If you open this door, I'm all in. There's no way I can't be."

I place my hands on his hips, feeling the warmth of his smooth skin. He shudders under my touch, just as affected as me.

My chin lifts. "Then be all in."

"And if you're not?"

"Give me a chance, Nash. Let my heart and my feelings catch up to yours."

The gap might not be as broad as he thinks.

His eyes slowly drift across my face, stopping on my lips. I hold his waist tighter, thinking he might kiss me, hoping for it.

"Fine, we'll take things slow." He steps back, dropping his hand from my cheek.

"Slow it is." I nod.

"I mean, *slow*," he reiterates.

"Got it."

"I guess we better get dressed, then. I have a full day planned for us."

I salute him. "Yes, sir."

But as I run upstairs to change, I can't help but feel excited.

Nash is putting his heart on the line for me one last time.

CHAPTER FORTY SEVEN

NASH

"WHAT WAS your favorite thing we did today?" I ask Sadie as we sit in a lit-up pub in Zermatt village, sipping warm spiced wine.

"I mean, how can I not say the Gornergrat Cog Railway? The ascent to the viewing platform and the view of the Matterhorn were incredible, not to mention the unparalleled views of the Swiss and Italian Alps." She glances out the window. "But then you have the postcard-perfect, snow-covered village and this delicious gooey cheese fondue. Right now has to be an honorable mention, doesn't it?"

"So what you're saying is you liked it all?"

"Yes!" She uses her stick to pick up another piece of chicken and dunks it into the cheese before bringing it to her mouth. "Mmmm. Thatsh good." Her words are muffled by the food.

I smile as I watch her, amused by everything she does. I still don't understand how I ended up in the middle of Zermatt, Switzerland, with Sadie by my side. I was hesitant this morning when she said she wanted to give us a try. Not because I'm not interested but because I didn't know if I dared put my heart through the loss again.

She's the love of my life. How could I not risk it all?

If we take things slow, and she decides I'm not the one, maybe it won't hurt as bad as the first time.

So, slow it is.

But I can already see a shift in her by the sparkling way her eyes look back at me. How she reached for my hand as we walked along the cobblestone streets today. She smiles like there's no other person she'd rather be with.

All of that was missing last year.

And though I've never stopped loving her, I've also never felt this way before. An excitement of something new and magical lingers between us, intensifying feelings to another level. And if this works out, I think we'll end up stronger than we were before.

"What was your favorite part today?" she asks when she's done chewing.

"I don't know. Ask me tonight when it's all done."

Her brows lift in a teasing way. "What plans do you have for tonight?"

"I'm thinking we stay in, maybe try out the Jacuzzi with a bottle of wine, then lie on the bed under the glass ceiling and look at the stars."

"I thought you wanted to take things slow."

"I never said anything about touching. We're just two people hanging out."

"Dating," she corrects with a smile. "We're two people *dating*. And I love your plan for our date tonight. I think we should start immediately."

"Don't you want to finish your fondue?"

"Check, please!" she jokes as a signal she's ready to leave the pub.

I scoot my chair back and stand, reaching my hand out to her. She slips her fingers into mine, letting me pull her to her feet. I hold her coat while she stuffs her arms through, then I tug her beanie down so it covers her head more fully.

"You're all set."

She dives into me, looping her arm through mine and resting her head on my shoulder. "Now I'm all set."

My head tilts, leaning against hers. I close my eyes and relish in the feel of Sadie cuddled up against me.

For an entire year, this is all I've wanted.

"OUCH!" I immediately pull my foot back from the steaming hot tub water.

"Did you get it too hot?" Sadie calls from the closet, where she changes into her swimsuit.

"No," I lie, turning on the cold water to cool it down.

"I told you the windows were getting steamy in here."

"No, that's just from us. Not the water."

"You wish the steam was coming from us."

"You're telling me," I say under my breath.

But I've already given myself the gentleman's talk. First- and second-date rules apply to this evening's activities. Touching is only permitted in safe zones.

No. Matter. What.

That's not the kind of relationship I'm here to build with Sadie. Physical chemistry has never been our problem. Even last December, when she barely knew me, we didn't struggle with that. It's a proven connection on both sides. It's the emotional connection I'm interested in. I need to see if she loves me or *can* love me, and I don't want anything confusing her or getting in the way of real, deep, and lasting emotions.

I test the water again and decide the temperature is cool enough to turn off the faucet. Slowly, I step into the tub, letting my body get used to it.

"How does it feel?" Sadie comes around the corner in her black bikini, and I shamelessly check her out.

So much for my gentleman's talk.

My gaze slowly travels down every curve and exposed inch of her body, like a starved man.

"I think you like my swimsuit," she teases as she steps into the tub beside me.

"No, I like *you* in that swimsuit." I glance down at the black ruffles lining her cleavage. "You bought that suit last year, specifically for this trip, but I never got the chance to see you wear it."

She wraps her arms around my neck, smiling up at me. "I hope it doesn't disappoint."

"It's better than I imagined." My hands go to her waist, deciding it's part of the safe zone.

Molten fire flows through my body.

There's nothing I want more than to pull Sadie to me. I don't think she'd stop me, but I'm not an idiot. My future happiness is on the line, and I'm not going to screw it up by making things more intimate than they need to be right now.

So, I'm back to my motto of keeping things moving so I don't get in trouble.

"We should sit."

Her lips curl in amusement. "Okay."

I hold her hand as she lowers to her butt, scooting over to make room for me. The Jacuzzi is bigger than a standard bathtub, but it's still tight for two people. I sit on the opposite end of her, with my legs out straight.

She leans back against the rim, looking up at the glass ceiling. "This is incredible."

It's dim enough, just the glow of the Christmas tree by the bed and the moon outside, that you can see the outline of the Matterhorn and a few stars.

"Have I ever been anywhere this magical before?"

I grab her foot and begin massaging it because I know she loves it, and my hands need something to do, or I'll go mad. Feet aren't sexy—they're in the safe zone.

"We've been to a lot of cool places and done a lot of memorable things—"

"Not *too memorable* since I forgot them." Her eyes glimmer.

"Yeah, poor word choice by me." I smile. "But despite all the amazing things we've done, I have a feeling Switzerland at Christmas can't be topped."

"Then I'm glad it's a new memory I can remember."

"Me too."

∾

SADIE

AFTER THE MOST ROMANTIC bath known to man, Nash and I meet in our sweats in the middle of the bed. We lie down, facing one another instead of the windows above us. I guess the view of each other is more important than the Swiss Alps.

"You look cute." He wiggles the messy bun on top of my head. "I've always loved you like this. Natural and makeup-less so your freckles stand out."

I can't help my goofy smile. "You like my freckles?"

"There are probably dissertations on how much I like your freckles."

"I didn't know that."

"I think I told you all about my love of your freckles the first day we met at the Cubs game."

My head falls back as I laugh. "You did not!"

"I'm embarrassed to say I did." His fingers trace my lips, stealing my breath. "But I also love your smile and expressive brown eyes—especially when they look at me like I'm your everything. I've missed that since your accident."

"Are you seeing it again?"

"I'm starting to."

"Good." My lips grow into a small smile. "Do you want to know what I like about you? I mean, you probably already know, but—"

"No, no, no." He shakes his head as much as he can while lying down. "Don't just assume I know. I want the whole rundown."

"I'm sure you do." I laugh. "The first thing I noticed about you in the hospital was your smile."

"Here I thought you were going to say my butt."

"I mean, I did see a lot of your butt, but I'm sticking with your smile. Final answer."

"You told me my smile was the first thing you noticed about me at the Cubs game too. I guess those four dental cleanings a year are paying off."

"Must be." I laugh again. "But after your smile, I noticed how kind and thoughtful you were. You took care of me without hesitation and let me be myself. You didn't push too hard or pull away. You just loved me even though I wasn't at my best."

His lips lift. "I promised I would."

That's the kind of loyalty and dedication every woman dreams about.

I reach out, softly caressing his cheek. His eyes close as my fingers drift over his stubble.

Nash leans in, pressing his forehead against mine. "Is this real?" His words come out on a breath between us.

"Yes."

I inch my body closer to his, wanting his arms around me. My fingers run through his hair as his hand goes to my back, drawing me to him. Our mouths hover close to each other but never touch. Instead, he presses small kisses to the corner of my mouth. My cheek. My crow's feet. My want grows with each gentle kiss, making our deal of taking things slow the worst idea I've ever had.

"Nash?" My eyes open, meeting his half-open gaze. "Tell me a memory about us. Something happy."

"A memory?" He lifts his chin to the glass ceiling, thinking. "Right after we got married and moved into our brownstone, you accidentally locked our bedroom door, and we couldn't find the key to unlock it. It was late, and I wanted to go to bed, so I said I'd just drill through the doorknob, but you were adamant we needed to call a locksmith because the doorknob was brand new and expensive. I was irritated, but you got your way."

"Wait." I stop him. "I said to tell me a *happy* memory."

His head flops to me. "It is happy, I promise. So anyway, we wait one hour for the locksmith to arrive, and by this time, it's twelve-thirty in the morning, and we're both grumpy and tired. The punk kid—"

"Why was he a punk kid?"

"I don't know. He looked like Nick Jonas with black skinny jeans that barely covered his butt, so we saw his greasy boxers when he leaned over. The kid tries all of his tools, but nothing seems to work, and the whole time he's blatantly flirting with you."

"He was not." I laugh.

"He totally was, right in front of me too. He kept turning

over his shoulder to make bedroom eyes with you, as if I couldn't see it. Then he decides to drill the doorknob like I wanted to do in the first place. Shrapnel gets everywhere, and he doesn't even try to clean it up. But the final blow was when he handed me his receipt pad with the total cost. We had to pay double because it was after hours, and he drove across town. It was, like, four hundred dollars. I was furious. I took his stupid receipt pad and chucked it across the apartment."

"No, you didn't!"

"It literally spun through the air in slow motion. You picked it up and paid the guy, and when he left, you were so mad at me. We got in our very first fight."

"Out of all the memories you could've chosen, why did you pick our first fight?"

"Because after you chewed me out for being mean to Nick Jonas"—Nash rolls to his side, draping his arm over my body —"we started uncontrollably laughing, and then one thing led to another, and we ended up spending the next hour making up."

I smile. "I like that story. It feels real."

His fingers skim my face as he whispers, "It was very real to me."

The delicate way Nash touches me makes me feel wholly loved and adored. I don't think I'd ever get sick of being treated this way.

"I need to let you go to bed."

"No," I whine as I snuggle into his body. "Don't leave me."

"I have to. You need to save your energy for skiing tomorrow."

My head rears back, feeling like he just killed the mood. "Skiing?"

"Yeah, let's get you on the slopes tomorrow." His fingers trace the scar on my forehead. "Only if you want to."

"What if I can't do it? Or what if I get hurt again?"

"I won't let that happen. We can do a small hill together."

"I don't know."

"Sadie, I know you, and I know you'll regret it your entire life if you don't at least attempt to ski in Zermatt."

"It's not even about skiing or the accident. I don't remember any of that. It's the waking up from the coma and feeling so helpless and not recognizing myself or my life. I hated that feeling and don't want to do anything to make it happen again. It's irrational, I know."

"It's not irrational, but I'll stay with you and make sure nothing bad happens."

"You'll stay with me?"

He hugs me closer. "The entire time. I promise."

One thing I know about Nash is that when he promises something, he never goes back on that promise. He promised to love me forever, no matter what, and he's already kept that.

"Okay, my time is up." He presses a kiss on my forehead.

"No!" It's pathetic how much I want him to stay. "Can't you sleep up here with me tonight?"

"Slow, remember?" His smile widens to something big and amused. "But I do like this vixen side of you—probably a little too much."

"Vixen." My brows drop as I think. "Isn't that one of Santa's reindeer?"

"I believe it is."

Nash rolls his body across mine, and I grab his shirt to keep him with me. He pauses when he's on top. I feel the weight of his chest, the wild beats of his heart, and the comfort of having him close.

"Stay," I beg as I run my fingers through his hair. "We'll just sleep."

"We will just sleep. Just in separate beds." He bends down, kisses my cheek, then rolls off me to his feet.

He pulls the blankets up over my body, tucking me in.

"You're giving me hospital-room vibes. I think you tucked me in there too."

"Trust me, this is *way* better than the hospital." One more kiss presses against my forehead. His head stays close, showcasing his lovable smile. "Probably because you like me a lot more in Switzerland."

"I do like you a lot more."

"I want you to keep liking me." He straightens and walks to the stairs. "That's why I'm leaving."

I never thought a man physically leaving my side could hurt so much, but my heart is in pain.

Sleep needs to come fast. I'm already counting down the minutes until I can be with Nash again.

CHAPTER FORTY EIGHT

NASH

"YOU'RE DOING GREAT." I stay by Sadie's side as we slowly ski down the intermediate hill for the second time. "How do you feel?"

"Um…"—her skis wobble in front of her—"good, I think. Does it look like I'm in control?"

"Yeah, you're killing it."

"I just don't want to *kill* me."

"We're almost to the bottom. Just keep this pace."

She goes silent, concentrating on bending her knees and leaning her body for the last few turns until we're safely at the bottom.

"I did it!" she huffs, pulling her ski goggles onto her helmet so I can see her eyes. "I'm a skier again."

"You're a skier again."

She glances up at the mountain. "I mean, I don't want to keep doing it, at least not today, but I skied in Zermatt."

"You sure did."

I know what a big deal this is for her, and I couldn't be prouder.

I click out of my skies. "In a way, we both got over our fears today."

"Oh, yeah?" She follows my lead, clicking out of her skies too. "What were you scared of."

"Keeping you safe. I was behind you when you got cut off and hit the tree. I saw the whole thing."

"I bet that was awful."

"It wasn't great," I joke to offset the emotion taking over my eyes.

"Like you said, we both got over a fear today." Sadie reaches for me with her free hand. I can't feel it through all the layers, but it still means a lot.

This new version of our relationship swings back and forth between serious and fun. Both are equally important for us to move forward, but I've had enough serious for now.

I bend my knees and wrap my arms around her stomach like an offensive lineman.

"Nash!" she yelps as her poles and skis drop into the snow.

I pick her up, throwing her over my shoulder with no real plan of what to do with her—it's all just part of flirting and dating. A giant snowbank with pure powder seems like the perfect place to drop her. I carry her to the pile of snow, flinging her body into it. She screams even though the landing is like cotton balls. I bodyslam her like they do in WWE and then spend the next twenty seconds trying to defend myself from the snow she shoves into my face. It takes me a second, but I pin her arms above her head, stopping the fight.

"Now, you're in trouble," I say, leaning over her.

Her pretty lips pull into a smile. "Or was this my plan all along?"

"You *planned* to lose our snow fight?"

"No, I planned to get you close." The flirtation behind her stare has my head swimming with all sorts of ideas.

"Why do you need me close?"

"Do you realize we haven't kissed?"

The corner of my mouth lifts. "Yes, I'm *very aware* we haven't kissed."

"So what are you going to do about it?" Her voice has a challenge, a dare I'd love to take her up on, but in my mind, we're still taking things slow.

I playfully scrunch my nose. "I'm probably not going to do anything about it."

"Nash, why won't you kiss me?"

I lean in, lowering my voice to a whisper. "Because if I kiss you, I won't be able to stop."

"Please tell me at some point you'll change your mind."

"At some point, I'll change my mind."

"Then I'll wait."

"You know, while you wait for our big kiss on the lips, I could remind you of other things you liked," I say as I drag my body off hers.

"Like what?"

"I believe you also loved it when I kissed your neck."

Sadie smiles mischievously. "Hmm, I don't remember that. You'll have to show me."

I sling my arm around her shoulder. "Deal."

SADIE

"HI, MOM!" I answer my cell phone.

"Hi, sweetie. I'm glad we caught you. What are you doing right now? It's late there, isn't it?"

"I'm on my chalet balcony." My eyes drift to Nash. He wags his brows up and down, giving me the feeling he can hear my mom through the phone.

"Just sitting there in the cold?"

"No, I'm by a fire." Technically, I'm sitting on Nash's lap, but since I haven't told my family that I ran into him in Switzerland, it would be hard to explain the lap-sitting.

It's not that I'm hiding Nash from my family. I just don't need the added pressure of someone knowing we're spending time together and asking questions about how it's going. Focusing on my feelings for him is all I want to do. We're in our little Switzerland bubble, and that's how I want it to stay for a bit.

"A fire on the balcony," my mom gushes. "That's sounds cozy. I just wish you weren't alone."

Nash squeezes my body, hugging me close. "Trust me, I don't feel alone."

"Oh, that's good. What did you do today?"

"Well"—I sit up a little taller—"you'll be proud to hear that I went skiing."

My dad cheers in the background, listening in on the call.

"Are you serious?"

I beam at Nash, and he smiles back. "I am serious. I started on the beginner hill and worked my way up to the intermediate."

"I hope you were careful."

"I was."

"And did you wear your helmet?" my dad chimes in.

"Yes, of course."

"How did you work up the nerve?"

"I had a charming ski instructor. I had to put my best foot forward for him."

I give Nash a sideways smile, and in return, his hand

squeezes the tender part above my knee, which is so ticklish all I can do is jerk my leg out straight to get away. A squeal comes out with my leg jerk, and I quickly cover my mouth with my hand.

"What was that?"

"I thought a bat was flying toward me, but we're all good."

Nash's smile turns wicked, making me think he's not done interrupting my phone call.

"So where do you go tomorrow?" my dad asks. "You were only two days in Zermatt, right?"

"Tomorrow, I go to Montreux," I say as Nash kisses my neck. The touch of his warm lips against my skin sends an explosion of chills down my body.

"Is that the one with the Christmas markets and the flying Santa?"

"Mm-hmm."

I tilt my head, letting Nash's lips have free rein over the side of my throat. His soft kisses drive me insane with desire. He's right—I'm a big fan of this.

My, oh my, is it nice.

"Sadie?" The impatience behind my mom's voice is my first clue that I wasn't paying attention to her.

"Sorry. What did you ask?"

"How are you getting to Montreux?"

"Train." I close my eyes as Nash nibbles on the bottom of my ear. His hot breath tickles my skin, and I feel like I just died and went to heaven, or cloud nine, or wherever the best place to be is. That's where I'm at.

"What are you doing once you get there?"

His lips burn a trail of passion from my earlobe down my jaw and back to my neck. That's when I decide I'm not a good multitasker.

"Mom, my phone is cutting out. I'll have to call you tomorrow. Love you guys!"

I end the call and look directly into Nash's blazing eyes.

"You little liar."

I could kiss that mischievous smile right off his lips.

"Did you really expect me to be able to concentrate with you kissing my neck like that?"

"Nope." His grin gets more prominent. "You're at a huge disadvantage. I know just where and how to kiss you."

Playfully, I punch his shoulder, which causes him to tickle me. I squirm in his lap until I eventually settle, curled up in a ball with my head on his chest and his arms around me.

"I canceled my room in Montreux," I say.

"Really?"

"Yep."

"Where are you going to stay, then?"

My lips drift upward. "I got a note that said, 'Nash and Sadie. We hope you're enjoying your time in Switzerland. Should you choose to forego your individual rooms, please use this key to stay as a couple in the fantasy suite.' I decided to forego my individual room."

Nash's chest lifts up and down as he laughs. "You can't remember me or anything about our three-year marriage, but you can remember—verbatim—*The Bachelor* fantasy suite note?"

"Some things just stick with you."

He hugs me closer, pressing a kiss to my head. "I guess I'll let you stay with me in my fantasy suite."

"Was it always like this?"

"What do you mean?"

"You and me. Did our marriage always feel like this?"

"For me, it did."

"Did we ever fight? I mean, besides the Nick Jonas night."

"We were just like any regular couple. We had disagreements."

"What did we fight about?"

"Stupid little things."

"No big things?"

"I mean, the biggest thing was probably your family."

"Why, 'cause you didn't like them?"

"No, not that. You'd get annoyed at me whenever I tried to get you to call your parents or pressed you to make up with them."

I shift my head, looking at him. "I should've listened to you instead of getting irritated. You were right to push me toward forgiveness."

"I could've tried harder. Done more. That's one of my biggest regrets."

I rest my head on his chest. "Restoring my relationship with my family was the only good thing that came from my accident."

"It's not the *only* good thing."

"What else?"

"You get to fall in love with me all over again."

I smile because it's true.

Not everyone gets to fall in love with their favorite person twice.

But I do.

CHAPTER FORTY NINE

NASH

AFTER A THREE-HOUR TRAIN ride to Montreux, we checked into the hotel and then made our way into the town village for the Christmas Eve festivities. Noël Montreux is absolutely stunning with its twinkling lights, holiday music, enticing aromas, and wooden shops all along Geneva Lake.

The best part is watching Sadie go from shop to shop, looking at the handmade crafts and home-baked treats as she sips her mulled wine.

I glance down at my watch. "Hey, we better find a spot to watch Santa fly across the sky. It's almost time."

Sadie plants her feet, but her body falls into me like a tree tipping over. Her chest lands against my chest as her arms wrap around my neck. She presses a quick peck to my cheek then turns to go. She flashes me the cutest smile over her shoulder, extending her arm like she's waiting for me to grab her hand.

Boy, I love this woman.

More today than I did last year or even three years ago.

It's the type of love that grows with time, deepens with experience, and changes with life.

Through all the ups and downs, my feelings are still all-encompassing and overwhelming. I'm not over the butterflies or the excitement. I don't think I'll ever get used to those things.

I reach for her hand, letting her guide me through the rows of shops and people.

"How about here to watch Santa?" she asks when we get to the main area.

"It's perfect. And then after this, I'm taking you for a ride in that." I point to the giant Ferris wheel that towers over the market square.

"You better." She backs into me. I gather her in my arms, pulling her against my chest and hugging her from behind.

The crowd cheers as the music and countdown begin. Over the lake, a sleigh and reindeer light up the sky as they slowly drift across a cable. Halfway through, fireworks shoot out the back of Santa's sleigh, sparking Christmas magic.

Sadie turns her head, looking up at me. "Promise me that someday when we have kids, we'll bring them back here to see this."

I peer down at her brown eyes. "Nothing would make me happier."

Under the twinkling lights, she's never looked more beautiful and lovely. But it's not how Sadie looks. It's what she said. It's the promise of a future, the planning of more, that hits me.

For the first time since her accident, I truly feel like our love will conquer all the setbacks and loss.

It's finally time to move on.

∾

SADIE

THE VIEW FROM the top of the Ferris wheel is unmatched. And it's there, above the glittering lights, with my head on Nash's shoulder and my hand in his, that I know with one thousand percent certainty that I don't want anything else. Nash is the endgame—the lifetime love everyone searches for. It's as right today as it was four years ago. I should've known it sooner, but at least I know it now.

"I love you," I say through the silence.

I feel his head shift to me, and I straighten to look at him. Moisture fills his eyes, making me smile.

"I love you, Nash." I want him to hear it again, to feel it in his heart.

A tear hangs on the rim of his eye. I climb into his lap, wiping the wetness with my thumb.

"I want to marry you, have your children, and live my life by your side. I want it *all* with you." I smile as another tear drips down. I wipe that tear too, kissing the edge of his eye. "I love you."

He laughs through his tears. "That's all I've ever wanted too."

"I don't want to lose you again. Come back to Skaneateles with me." My fingers glide down the sandpaper stubble on his face. "We can run the home health and hospice together, build a house on the lake, raise children, and grow old together."

"Promise?"

"I promise." I gaze into his eyes, his face in my hands.

We both feel the shift in our relationship, the deeper connection built on a foundation that can't be broken. Even the darkest fog in my brain couldn't erase Nash from my heart.

He's meant to be mine, and I'm meant to be his.

Forever.

Slowly, we both lean in, savoring the delicious build-up. Our lips brush together, and my whole system comes alive. The kiss is measured—like a deliberate game we're both committed to even though it's killing us. Soft skims and gentle glides over and over again. Both crave more but are willing to take our time, knowing the significance of the promises our kiss seals upon us.

The tip of my tongue swipes across Nash's bottom lip, and a soft groan comes out with his breath, quiet enough to be a whisper. His hands grab my waist tighter, shifting my body so I'm sitting on him more fully. There's so much satisfaction in knowing he wants me as much as I want him. My fingers slide from his face into his hair, clutching the curls at the nape of his neck. His hands splay across my back, holding me close.

The slow sensual kiss was nice, but I'm ready for more. I've *wanted* more since our first night in Switzerland. I press my body into him and take control, deepening my passion. His reaction is instant, returning my kiss with an urgency that drives me crazy with desire.

The Ferris wheel cart rocks back and forth as we rotate around the sky. We're a frenzy of want, need, and hot fire burning us inside out. Passing the minutes with desperate affection. Showing each other just how deep our love goes but never truly able to convey the depth.

The rush of attraction is addicting and heated, fun and exciting. This is what love is supposed to feel like—an emotion so intense you've lost your mind and your heart to it. The feelings between us transcend time and memory. My mind may have forgotten Nash, but my body and soul haven't.

"The ride is almost over," I mumble against his mouth.

His lips travel to my neck, spreading a fiery sensation over my throat. "We're riding again."

I throw my head back, laughing. "I thought you'd want to head straight to the fantasy suite."

"We have forever for that. Let's enjoy this moment." He takes my face in his hands, forcing me to meet his gorgeous green eyes. "Running into you on the train was the best gift this life has ever given me."

A smile stretches across my face. "Merry Christmas, Nash."

His mouth covers mine, kissing me again and again under the Swiss stars.

EPILOGUE

One Year Later

SADIE

"THERE'S one more present under the tree!" Nash stands, shaking a box in the air.

"Oh, where did that come from?" My mom feigns surprise, but she's not fooling anyone. Whatever that present is, she definitely knows about it.

Nash makes a show out of reading the tag. "It looks like it's for Sadie." He turns to me, his entire face lit up with an excited smile.

"Who's it from?"

"A secret admirer," he whispers in my ear, kissing my lobe before pulling back.

I take his present, noticing how my family watches in anticipation. The Christmas tree wrapping paper doesn't stand a chance. I tear through it in one sweep, slowly open the box, and peek inside.

It's a square book with a picture of us on the front—a picture I don't recognize from the lost years. Carved into the cover is *The Story of Us*.

I shoot my gaze to Nash. "What's this?"

"Open it."

My smile grows as I flip the book open. There's a picture of the note Nash wrote Tate at the Cubs game and then written words to the side. My eyes scan, reading the paragraph.

The first thing I noticed about you was your smile and how your brown eyes lit up with happiness. Even from four rows back, I knew you were the one. I leaned over and told Reggie, 'I'm going to marry that girl.' He laughed and said that, first, I'd have to get rid of your boyfriend sitting next to you. The boyfriend seemed like a formidable opponent, but I didn't care. I was hooked, drunk on your smile and how the sun kissed your freckles. For seven innings, I watched you and waited. I hoped you'd get up from your seat, and when you did, I was ready.

I was so nervous to talk to you I thought I might throw up. I followed you to the concessions line and told myself to just go for it. I think I went for it a little too much, because my hello made you jump.

Then you came with your first witty comeback—something about how me watching you all game was stalkerish, and I knew I'd never be okay again without you in my life.

I glance up with tears in my eyes and a smile.

"It's every memory of us you lost from those three years."

"You wrote them down?"

He shrugs as if it's not a big deal, as if it's not the most thoughtful thing anyone has ever done for me.

I throw my arms around his neck. "Thank you."

"I think she likes it," he says into my hair, hugging me back.

"Nash spent an entire year on that book," my dad adds.

"Nothing could be more perfect." I release him, gingerly touching the pages of the book. "But I may be able to one-up your present."

A furrow forms between his brows. "What do you mean?"

I walk to the fireplace and retrieve a small, long present. "This is for you." I smile at my family. "For everyone, really." Nash pulls at the gold wrapping paper, tossing it aside as he lifts the box open. Inside is a positive pregnancy test.

His head whips up to me, and my favorite smile he's ever given me splashes across his face. "Are you serious?"

I nod with misty eyes.

"What is it?" my mom asks.

"I'm going to be a dad." Emotion rounds out his words as he holds the pregnancy test up.

The room explodes with excitement, but I'm only focused on the absolute look of happiness in Nash's eyes.

He takes me in his arms. "We're having a baby!"

"We're having a baby."

Our road to happily ever after came with a lot of twists and turns and bumps in the road that felt more like mountains. But we made it through.

We survived an internship.

A *kind of* boyfriend turned fiancé.

One elopement.

A successful business.

Three years of marital bliss.

A tragic skiing accident.

Amnesia.

Divorce.

A year of loneliness.

Finding each other again in Switzerland.

A giant second wedding.

Another successful business.

Building a house on Skaneateles Lake.

And now a baby.

It's the happy ending we always hoped for.

Now, we just have forever to look forward to.

THE END

Thank you for reading! Need more of Nash and Sadie? Head to my website at www.kortneykeisel.com for BONUS SCENES that show what happened after they came home from Switzerland.

Still in the mood for holiday reads? Be sure to check out my other Christmas books. Later On We'll Conspire and The Holiday Stand-In

Everyone loves a Christmas surprise—
just not a spy in disguise.

It's everything I've ever wanted. It's just
with the wrong brother.

ALSO BY KORTNEY KEISEL

Romantic Comedy Books

Summer Ever After

Why Trey Let Me Get Away

How Jenna Became My Dilemma

Commit

Compared

Complex

Complete

Later On We'll Conspire

The Holiday Stand-In

The Desolation Series (Dystopian Royal Romance)

The Rejected King

The Promised Prince

The Stolen Princess

The Forgotten Queen

The Desolate World

PLEASE REVIEW

Did you know reviews help other readers find my books? If you loved One Foggy Christmas, please consider leaving me a review. I think it's so fun to hear what readers liked about my books.

Thanks for reading and reviewing!

ACKNOWLEDGMENTS

I can't believe my fifteenth book is behind me! One Foggy Christmas was such a fun one because I allowed myself to write the story I wanted.

Huge thanks to everyone who helped me with this book! Stacy, thank you for reading early and helping me see a pathway forward. To Madi, Chelsea, Meredith, Kaylen, and Michelle for beta reading. I loved all of your thoughts and insights.

Big thanks to Melody for such a gorgeous cover. Thank you to my editor, Jenn, for always working with my crazy deadlines and schedules. Thank you to the bookstagrammers who agreed to be on my launch team at the last minute. Thank you to my author friends for giving advice and commiserating with me. Thanks to my readers for being excited about tropes and stories that aren't as popular and for trusting me with your leisure time. You're the best!

Thanks to Kurt for inspiration, ideas, and help around the house so I could get the book done. Thank you to my children: Mason, Sadie (yes, I named the FMC after her), Kenley, Nixon, and Tyce for being patient with me while I busted this book out.

Thank you to my Heavenly Father and Jesus Christ for EVERYTHING.

ABOUT THE AUTHOR

Kortney loves all things romance. Her devotion to romance was first apparent at three years old when her family caught her kissing the walls (she attributes this embarrassing part of her life to her mother's affinity for watching soap operas like Days of Our Lives). Luckily, Kortney has outgrown that phase and now only kisses her husband. Most days, Kortney is your typical stay-at-home mom. She has five kids that keep her busy cleaning, carpooling, and cooking.

Writing books was never part of Kortney's plan. She graduated from the University of Utah with an English degree and spent a few years before motherhood teaching 7th and 8th graders how to write a book report, among other things. But after a reading slump, where no plots seemed to satisfy, Kortney pulled out her laptop and started writing the "perfect" love story...or at least she tried.

Kortney loves warm chocolate chip cookies, clever song lyrics, the perfect romance movie, analyzing and talking about the perfect romance movie, playing card games, traveling with her family, and laughing with her husband.

If you'd like to learn about future books and get bonus chapters, sign up for my newsletter at www.kortneykeisel.com.

Made in the USA
Las Vegas, NV
17 November 2024

11978439R10225